JONATHAN VALIN IS "A MAJOR TALENT."
—Kirkus Reviews

"Jonathan Valin is one of the masters of the regional detective novel."
—Cincinnati Post

"He's a smooth storyteller and . . . has plenty of talent."
—The New York Times Book Review

"He's the best of all the writers who have appeared in the past decade. . . . He goes on nerve and his genuine feeling for both people and language—and that puts him in the very small class of people who transcend the noble ghosts of Chandler and Hammett." —Peter Straub

"Valin's prose is spare and at times chilling, the plot is complex yet coherent, and Cincinnati emerges as a city with a vibrant and distinct personality."
—Publishers Weekly

By the same author

The Lime Pit
Final Notice
Dead Letter
Day of Wrath
Natural Causes
Life's Work
Extenuating Circumstances

FIRE LAKE

JONATHAN VALIN

A DELL BOOK

Published by
Dell Publishing
a division of
The Bantam Doubleday Dell Publishing Group, Inc.
666 Fifth Avenue
New York, New York 10103

ISBN: 0-440-20145-4

Reprinted by arrangement with Delacorte Press

Printed in the United States of America
Published simultaneously in Canada

February 1989

10 9 8 7 6 5 4 3 2 1

KRI

To Katherine, as always, and to Jim

I

I got the phone call around one-thirty on a rainy December morning, half an hour after I'd gone to bed. The man on the line sounded edgy and tired, as if he, too, had been awakened by a late-night call. I laid the phone on the pillow beside my ear, glanced at the clock, and shook a cigarette from a pack lying on the nightstand. The man's voice, thin, reedy, and countrified, wasn't familiar; so if it was trouble, and it certainly seemed to be, given the hour, I figured it was the impersonal kind, the professional kind. I couldn't have been more wrong.

"Is this Harry Stoner's house?" the man asked doubtfully, as if he was afraid he'd dialed the wrong number.

"I'm Stoner," I replied.

There was a pause, and when the man spoke again he sounded confused. "You're Stoner's father?"

"I'm Stoner's son, Harry," I said. "What's the trouble?"

"Hold on, now," the man on the phone said warily, "are you saying *you're* Harry Stoner?"

I plucked the receiver off the pillow and stared at it. "Maybe you better tell me who *you* are," I said, lighting the cigarette.

"My name is Jenkins. Claude Jenkins. I'm the night manager at the Encantada Motel, out here on Wooster Pike. We got us . . . some trouble, Mr. Stoner."

"What kind of trouble?" I said.

Jenkins put his hand over the phone, and I heard someone else firing questions at him in an excited voice. Jenkins came back on the line and asked, "You're not a junior, are you, Mr. Stoner? I mean there ain't no other Harry Stoners in your family, are there?"

"For chrissake!" I said, losing my temper. "*I'm* Harry Stoner. Got it?"

"Just trying to make sure I'm talking to the right party, that's all," Claude Jenkins said defensively.

Fully awake now and irritated because of it, I kicked the blankets off my legs and straightened up against the headboard. "Look, Jenkins, why don't you tell me what the problem is, then maybe we can decide if I'm the right party."

"Guess I better," Claude said, after thinking it over for another second. "You see we got this guest at the motel tonight, and . . . well, he must have some trouble or other 'cause he damn near killed himself. Took a whole shitload of pills. Puked all over his room and wandered out into the lot. Gladys, our girl, just happened to find him, lying beside his door with the pill bottle in his hand. We've been pouring coffee into him here in the office, but he's still pretty doped up."

I waited for an explanation, and when it didn't come I said, "That's damn interesting, Claude, but why call me?"

"He registered under the name of Harry Stoner," Jenkins said.

"Who did?" I asked—not getting it.

"The guy who tried to kill himself."

I felt a shudder run up my spine, as if I'd seen my own obit in the newspaper. "You're kidding," I said, aghast.

"I hear you, mister," Claude said sympathetically. "But that's the long and short of it. He registered under your name and gave your phone number, too. That's why I called. That's why I had to be sure."

I understood his confusion.

" 'Course, now I don't know what to think," Claude went on. "If you say you're Harry Stoner, then I guess this one can't be who he said he was . . . can he?"

There was just enough hope in Claude's voice to make

me smile. Only it wasn't particularly funny. The suicide could have picked Harry Stoner out of the phone book, I told myself. But deep down I knew that when the message in the bottle has your name on it, it isn't by chance.

"You figure he's a friend of yours, maybe?" Jenkins said, dropping it squarely in my lap. "I mean him using your name and all."

I glanced at the clock and sighed. "I don't know. It's possible." A friend or an enemy. "What's he look like?"

"Kind of scruffy-looking," Jenkins said. "Scraggly beard. Shaggy black hair. Bad teeth. About five ten, one-sixty. Maybe forty, forty-five years old. Walked bent over. Had an attitude. That ring any bells?"

"Yeah," I said. "But most of those guys are in prison."

"Maybe he's fresh out," Jenkins volunteered. "He's dressed like it. Work shirt, work shoes, and dungarees."

Great, I said to myself. "What's his condition now?"

"He ain't fully conscious yet, if that's what you mean," Jenkins said. "He keeps slipping in and out. Babbling a lot. Puking and moaning. I don't think he's going to croak, but he's a far cry from walking out of here under his own power."

"If he's really in bad shape, you better call an ambulance," I said.

"Ambulances cost money," Jenkins said uneasily. "And it ain't just the money. You call an ambulance in a situation like this one and you're all over cops. We run a little bar and restaurant alongside the motel, and this boy here did a good deal of drinking at the bar before he decided to end it all. We just don't want to call the cops if we don't have to. It's for his good, too," Jenkins added.

But I could tell he was thinking about his liquor license, and maybe the poker table in the back room or the video game that paid off in cash. It looked like Claude Jenkins was intent on making his suicidal guest my business. And for all I knew, his instinct was right. It would bother the hell out of me if I *didn't* find out who the scruffy son of a bitch was.

"All right, Claude," I said. "You keep pouring coffee into Mr. Stoner. I'll be out there in about an hour. If I know him, I'll take him off your hands. And if I don't, we'll call the cops. Deal?"

"Thanks a hell of a lot, Mr. Stoner," Jenkins said gratefully. "Honest to Christ, I got no idea what to do with him —whoever the hell he is."

"Neither do I," I said, but he'd already hung up.

II

It was almost three-thirty when I pulled into the Encantada Motel parking lot. Drowsiness and the cold December rain had slowed me down getting started. And then it had been a pretty good jaunt out Columbia Parkway, through Mariemont to that tag-end stretch of Wooster Pike known as Miamiville. I sat in the car for a moment, with the motor running and the wipers clearing the sleet from the windshield, and stared at the little flock of white-faced stucco cottages huddling beneath the ice-shagged red-and-yellow neon motel sign. There wasn't a single light on in any of the cottages; in fact, several of them were tacked over with plyboards, as if they'd been condemned. To the west of the cottages, a slightly larger shack, with an Office sign on the door, glowed dimly in the darkness—a frail yellow light that leaked through the blinded front window and puddled up on the rain-soaked asphalt of the lot. The bar that Jenkins had mentioned was behind the office and to its right—a dark Quonset hut with a Miller sign flashing in one tiny window. A beat-up Jeep Cherokee with icy wheel wells was parked in front of the hut. Aside from my Pinto, it was the only car in the motel lot.

I gazed through the rain at the office window and knew that I didn't really want to go inside. I wanted to go home —back to sleep. But curiosity and an obscure, ludicrous sense of obligation kept me sitting there, albeit with the motor running. Be real, I told myself. This is a dead-end place, and whomever you find inside that office, whoever borrowed your name for an epitaph, is going to be a dead-end case. Nobody you want to know, much less look after. The truth was, I didn't have any friends who'd end up in the Encantada Motel. I didn't have that many friends, period.

I cracked the car window open and let a little icy rain spatter my face. As I sat there trying to make up my mind about whether to go in or not, the office door opened. A sharp-faced man with paper-white skin and a shock of red hair stuck his head out and hollered at me. I couldn't hear him over the wind, but I could see him plainly enough. And he could see me. He waved his arm in an unmistakable gesture of welcome.

God damn it! I said to myself. I should have thrown the car in reverse and sped out of the lot. Instead, I turned off the engine, bundled my pea coat at the collar, and stepped into the rain.

The man waited for me in the doorway, a smile of relief on his face.

"Howdy, howdy!" he said cheerfully.

I grunted at him. "You Jenkins?"

He nodded. "I'm Claude Jenkins. Come on in out of the rain."

I walked into the office—a square, paneled room, furnished with a couple of egg-shaped orange plastic chairs and lit by two lava lamps bolted to pine end tables. An L-shaped counter with an empty plastic brochure-holder sitting on it divided the office in two. There was a beaten wooden desk behind the counter and a door marked Private behind the desk. Jenkins ushered me over to the orange chairs.

"Nasty night," he said, sitting down.

I shook some ice from my sleeve and sat down next to him. Up close Jenkins looked like his motel—stale, seedy, and corrupt. If he'd been blond, he would have been an albino: his skin was that white and his eyes were that pallid blue. But the red hair and eyebrows just made him look wan and poverty-stricken—the kind of guy who spends his life hiding from the sun in the darkness of a one-room apartment in Riverview or a motel office in Miamiville. He had a thin, surly, chewed-over mouth trained, like a spit curl, to hold a constant, insincere smile. He wore a wrinkled white dress shirt with a pack of Luckies in the breast pocket.

"Guess you'll be wanting to see your friend," he said anxiously. "He's in the back office there, sleeping it off." He started to get up—to show me to the door marked Private. But I put a hand on his sleeve to stop him. He sat back down slowly, brushing his sleeve where I'd touched it, as if I'd left a mark.

"What happened here tonight, Claude?" I asked.

"Already told you," he said. "Your pal got drunk, took some pills, and tried to kill himself."

"That's it?" I said.

"That's it."

"Did he talk to anybody while he was in the bar?" I asked. "Meet with anybody?"

"Wouldn't know. I don't work the bar."

"Who does?"

"Clem does," Jenkins said. His mouth was beginning to droop into a scowl, as if someone had taken a steamer to that spit-curl grin. "Look, why all the questions? Clem's gone home. So has Gladys, our girl. I'm the only one left here. And I'm just trying to do the right thing. Now why don't you take care of your friend and let me get back to doing my job."

"We had a deal, remember?" I reminded him. "If I don't know him, we're going to call the cops."

"No cops," he said firmly.

"Why? What would they find?"

"Nothing," Jenkins said, trying to look innocent and not doing a good job of it.

He was obviously lying, but I was too tired to push it. For all I knew, the guy in the back room was a stranger, and whatever he'd been up to at the Encantada Motel was none of my business.

"All right, Claude," I said, getting to my feet.

I followed Jenkins across the office to the door marked Private. He put his hand on the knob then glanced back at me, with a warning look. "He's not in the best of shape. Got some nicks and bruises. From bumping around in the parking lot, I guess."

"There aren't any other cars in the lot, Claude," I said.

"There were earlier," Jenkins said, "when the bar was still open. We had a pretty good crowd tonight, actually."

I thought about the ice storm I'd driven through. The rain and sleet had been falling since sunset—hardly the kind of night for a "good crowd" at a dive like this one. But I let the lie pass, again, and followed Claude through the door into the inner office.

It was a dark room—a little bigger than a utility closet—with a cot on one wall and a stubby plastic table with a TV on it, set across from the cot. The TV was the only light in the room. The floor was littered with styrofoam coffee cups, and I could hear a coffee machine burbling somewhere in the dark. The room smelled strongly of coffee and faintly, but noticeably, of vomit.

A man was lying on the cot—his face toward the wall. He didn't turn toward us as we walked up to him. He was wearing blue jeans and a government surplus flight jacket with an American flag stitched on one sleeve and a serial number stenciled on the back. His long black hair curled wildly over the collar of the coat.

"There he is," Claude said with disgust. "I'd watch your step in here. I been cleaning up his puke since midnight. But I might have missed some."

I walked carefully to the cot—the styrofoam cups crunching underfoot—and touched the man on the arm. When he didn't respond, I shook him. He turned over on his back.

"Son of a bitch," I said, staring at his ravaged face. I

hadn't seen that face in eighteen years. But I recognized him, all right. Lonnie Jack.

"You know him, then?" Claude said hopefully.

"I know him," I said.

I shook Lonnie's arm again and he opened one blood-shot eye. "How you doing, Lonnie?" I said. "How you doing, man?"

Lonnie smiled at me, then fell into a stupor.

"His name is Lonnie?" Jenkins asked.

"Yeah. Lonnie Jackowski. Lonnie Jack, to his friends." I turned to Jenkins and said, "Help me get him to his feet."

Jenkins sighed heavily, then walked over to the cot. Together we managed to loop our arms under Lonnie's arms and hoist him to his feet. Lonnie opened his eyes, smiled goofily, and puked on himself.

"Christ," Jenkins said, letting go of Lonnie's right arm and backing away.

I managed to catch Lonnie around the middle, before he fell. Giving Jenkins an ugly look, I worked Lonnie's left arm over my shoulder and guided him to the door.

"Open the door," I said to Jenkins.

"Don't take him out there," he said. "He'll just puke all over everything. Take him out the back." He nodded toward a fire door beside the cot.

"Open the fucking door, Claude," I said, giving him another look.

"Shit," Jenkins said under his breath, and opened the door to the office.

I guided Lonnie into the office and over to one of the orange plastic chairs. I hadn't been able to see him clearly in the gloom of the utility room, but in the lamplight I could see that his face was a mess. And it wasn't the sort of mess that came from bumping into cars.

"How'd he get the black eye and the split lip?" I said to Claude after I'd deposited Lonnie in the chair.

"Like I said, he must have knocked into some cars in the lot."

I grabbed Claude by the shirt collar and jerked him to me, butting him hard in the forehead with my forehead—like the West Indians do when they want to make a point.

"Jesus!" Claude cried, grabbing his forehead with both hands. His knees buckled and he started to wobble. I held him up by the front of his shirt, until he got his legs back, then pinned him against the counter with my body.

"Who beat him up?" I said, glaring at him.

"Christ, you hurt me," he moaned, kneading his forehead with his fingers.

I balled a fist and he winced and turned away, throwing up his right hand weakly to ward off the blow.

"Okay, okay," he said. "Why the hell are you getting so physical all of a sudden?"

"Because he *is* a friend," I said.

Jenkins rubbed the red spot on his forehead again. "There was a fight. At least, that's what I heard."

"Before or after he took the pills?"

Jenkins sighed. "Before. Some bikers. They hang out at the bar on Thursday nights. I guess he rubbed one of them the wrong way."

"You can do better than that, Claude," I said menacingly.

Jenkins flinched again. "I wasn't there. But some of those bike guys . . . they sell shit."

"What kind of shit?"

"Whatever," Claude said. "I don't bother them. They're regular paying customers, and around here we can't afford to be choosy."

"Sure," I said. Six, ten, and even, Claude got a cut of the action. It was a hell of a good reason not to want the police nosing around. "Let's see the bottle you said you found in Lonnie's hand."

"It's in the desk," Claude said.

I let him go, and he walked behind the counter. I watched him closely as he opened the desk drawer.

"If you come up with anything but a pill bottle in your

hand, Claude," I said, "I'll break your fucking wrist off. I swear to God, I will."

"Take it easy, mister," Jenkins said, looking frightened. He plucked a pill bottle from the drawer and brought it over to me. "Here."

It was a druggist's pill bottle—the kind they dole out prescriptions from. The printed label was heavily stained with mud, but I could still read some of it. *Valium, 10 mg. 100 Tablets.* I tilted the bottle up and looked inside. It was empty.

I stuck the bottle in my pocket and walked over to where Lonnie was slumped in the chair. "C'mon, buddy," I said to him, "we're going to get you some help."

I worked my right arm around his middle and lifted Lonnie to his feet. He opened both eyes for an instant and stared at me. "Harry," he said, with a silly smile. His eyes rolled back and his head slumped down again.

"C'mon, Lonnie," I said, giving him a shake. "You gotta help."

He moved his legs as if he were treading water. Slowly, I worked him over to the front door.

"You ain't going to the police, are you?" Jenkins called out.

I glanced back at him. "If I don't, it's because of him. Not because of you. And if I find out you were fucking with him, I'll be back."

Lonnie laughed stupidly. "That's tellin' him," he said.

I turned to Lonnie. "You asshole, you haven't changed much, have you?"

He laughed again, then teetered as if he was going to fall.

I caught him and put him back on his feet. "Save your strength, buddy," I said, steering him through the door. "You've got a long night ahead."

III

Somewhere around Tusculum, Lonnie got sick again. I pulled the car off the parkway into a gas station lot and sat there as he retched out the open window.

"You want to go to a hospital, Lonnie?" I said to him when he'd stopped gagging.

At first, I wasn't sure that he'd understood me. But after a moment, he shook his head decisively and fell back against the car seat. "No hospital. No cops," he said heavily, as if the one meant the other. He groaned like a sick animal. "No luck. No luck at all."

He began to sob. I sat there, helplessly, watching him cry. After a time his head lolled to the left, and he was out cold again. I started up the car and eased back onto the parkway.

The rain kept falling, harder now, then turning to wind-whipped flurries of snow, then back to icy rain. He'd picked a good day for it, I thought. But then he'd had a flair for the dramatic. At least, he'd had when I'd known him in college—an age ago.

Eighteen years. I could feel it like another passenger, like a teenage kid sitting between us. His kid, my kid. A separate lifetime. I didn't know a thing about the man. Hadn't seen him since we'd stopped talking to each other, one fall day in 1968. And like that he'd dropped out of sight. I'd heard he'd gone to L.A. Then to New York. And then I'd stopped hearing.

And now, on a miserable December morning, he was back—beaten, burned out. A suicide.

I glanced at him from time to time in the rearview mirror. He'd changed terribly. Face grown coarse, heavy-jowled. His eyes scorched to the sockets. His flesh yellowed. His mouth, fat and red from the beating he'd taken. He looked fifteen years older than he really was and ready for death.

When I'd first met him, he'd been a handsome, twenty-year-old kid. Sad-eyed, thin-lipped. Like a short, black-haired Peter Fonda. In fact, when *Wild Angels* came out in '67, Lonnie'd taken to wearing a motorcycle jacket and posturing in front of Harleys. He'd never gotten a cycle of his own—he was scared to death of getting killed on one. But he'd liked the way he looked standing in front of them. So had the coeds at the University of Cincinnati. Lonnie's ladies. He'd had a gift with them.

After we'd stopped rooming together and he'd gone off to L.A. to make his fortune as a guitarist, I'd asked one of his women—a pretty sociology major named Joyce—what it was that Lonnie'd had, why it was that so many coeds had been so taken by him. She'd smiled and said, "Remember the scene in *Wild Angels,* when the girl says to Peter Fonda, 'You're so cool, Blue'? That's what he has. Lonnie's cool." I didn't remember what I'd said to her, although I did remember being ticked off by the Peter Fonda comparison, since Lonnie had cultivated it so carefully. But if *cool* had been the currency in 1967 and 1968, Lonnie'd had it all.

We'd become good friends during the summer of '67, right after I'd come home from the war. After a couple of weeks of living with my family, I'd enrolled at UC and, in my off-hours, started hanging out on Calhoun Street where the hippies lived. At that time, I felt more comfortable with the street people, with their foxhole mentality, than I did with my folks or with other college kids. Plus, the hippies liked to talk, to rap, as they said back then. And I had this insatiable urge to talk—to justify what I'd done in 'Nam, to explain it out loud, as if it were the plot of a movie I'd seen.

For several months, I was ruled by that need—to work off the bad karma, the war karma. And I scared a lot of people away. My folks, my friends, my professors, my classmates. I didn't scare Lonnie. He'd lost an older brother to the war, and he was eager to hear what it had been like. Eager to serve as a sounding board for my rambling, nervous, nonstop monologues. He sat with me for hours, in Love's, where I first met him, or at the Black Dome, where he sometimes played guitar with a local band —listening to that movie scenario I was recounting. And then one day in September, I realized that I wanted to talk about other things. With Lonnie's help, I got over that first hurdle. And started getting over the war. In a way, he never did.

His older brother, Steve, haunted him. They had been close as kids, and Lonnie had been badly hurt by his death. So had his parents. They were lower-middle-class, patriotic folks who thought that their son had died for the best of all causes. They also thought that Lonnie was a sluggard and a coward for not following his big brother into the grave.

In his blackest mood, Lonnie agreed with them. He saw himself as a coward too—an underground man who'd climb back into the society he'd rejected as soon as the war was over and it was safe to come up again for air. The things he believed in—the love and peace all his songs celebrated—were excuses to ball, to smoke, to have fun, to turn a dollar. If he didn't have love and peace, he'd have found other reasons to drop out. Unlike his brother, unlike me, he wasn't taking real chances. And until he was willing to risk it all, like I had done, like Steve had done, he wasn't a man.

There was nothing to say to him when he was in that mood, except that he was wrong. And, to be honest, I wasn't really sure that he *was* wrong. Although I lied to

him about it, I think he knew that my heart wasn't in my
words. Even then, I had the feeling he just wanted to hear
another voice—a strong voice, a sympathetic voice, a
brother's voice. Later on, I wondered if a part of him
hadn't wanted to hear the lie in the voice too.

We'd rap for hours—about 'Nam, about Steve, about his
folks, about risk-taking and manhood and all the other
crap that twenty-year-old men talk about. Then Lonnie'd
hole up in his room. Smoke weed, listen to his own tapes.
And in a day or two, he'd resurface—himself again. Bright,
funny, with a new girl or two on his arm. His black mood
forgotten. That was the pattern for the first year that we
roomed together. It started to change in the summer of
1968.

When I thought about it later, I realized that I'd seen it
coming for a long time. From the first time I'd heard him
talk about his brother, really, and then watched him go
into his room, put on the stereo, take out his lid of grass
and shut the door. It didn't stay grass for very long. Acid
hit the street in late 1967. Then came Blue Meanies.
Soapers. PCP. STP. MDA.

We talked about it a lot, Lonnie and I—the drugs. I
thought they were bad. He thought they were good. That
was what it came down to. And since I was a minority of
one and since experimenting with drugs was in the air, like
the music and the sex, both of which I *did* enjoy, I felt too
much like my own father, harping on it for very long. I just
let it be, like one of those family disputes that sits on the
table every night along with the silverware.

I thought later that I had been wrong not to look after
him more carefully. But in those days, I didn't believe men
were supposed to look after one another, except on the
battlefield. I think I thought that's what it meant to be a
man—to look after yourself and not to ask jack shit from
anyone else. I was forgetting, of course, the charity Lonnie
had shown me, when I first met him. And just not seeing
or not accepting the communal spirit that was alive all

around me. But when you're trying to get stronger, your vision narrows. You overlook certain things. Maybe you have to overlook them to *get* stronger.

In the early fall of 1968, expense money started to dry up. Money we kept in a kitty, for meals and beer and grass. Lonnie's rent money. I fronted him some, and after a time it got to be a pretty large tab. I don't know what I told myself—that he was buying equipment for his band, maybe. I had some explanation that I half believed in or wanted to believe in.

Then one night in August, Lonnie brought some friends home with him, and I couldn't tell myself those lies anymore. They were from Miami, his friends. And they weren't kids, although they were dressed like kids. They were grown men. On their way to Cleveland, looking for a place to crash. They never stopped talking, these men. When the second one interrupted the first one, the first one's jaws kept working, like a ventriloquist's dummy. They crashed with Lonnie that night. And that night, for the first time since I'd come back from 'Nam, I unwrapped the government-issue Colt I kept in my closet, loaded it, and slept with it in my hand.

They left at first light—Lonnie driving them to the bus station in his old Ford van. When they were gone, I turned over Lonnie's room and found works and crystal meth under the mattress. I thought about leaving them out in the open, where he could see that I'd seen them. But after a while, I put them back and put the room right. When he came home again that night, I told him that I knew what he was doing and that if our friendship meant anything to him, he'd stop, because I wasn't going to sit around and watch him turn into a speed freak.

I thought of that moment again as I drove through the December sleet toward home. It was one of those scenes that you know at the time is a turning point. I looked at him in the rearview mirror, slumped unconscious on the backseat, and thought of how he'd looked then—when I'd told him I was going to move out if he didn't quit shooting up. He'd cried. Not in front of me, but in his room, with the door shut. Then he'd shouted, cursed. Then he'd shot himself up and gone out, leaving the works where I could see them on his bed.

We kept rooming together until the end of September, because that's when the lease was up. We didn't talk much, except for polite talk about how I was doing with my summer courses and how his gigs were going. I think we both wanted to reconcile, to forget the whole thing. But we'd said too much, gone too far in our posturing—me as the big brother he was mourning, Lonnie as the true child of the sixties I could never become. Neither one of us had enough sense to back down and start over.

The last time I saw him was on the last day of September, 1968. He'd played at the Black Dome that night. I'd gone to hear him, for old times' sake. He brought a woman back to the apartment with him. I had a girl of my own by then—a beautiful black-haired English major named Linda. The four of us shared a bottle of wine in my room, listened to some Jimi Hendrix, and talked about old times. There were no hard feelings that night—I think that was the point we were both trying to make. We shook hands warmly, told each other we'd stay in touch, and went to bed.

We saw each other on the street a few times after that, and I went to hear him play at the Dome again. Then the fall term started for me, and I lost touch with him. I heard he went to L.A. and New York. Several years after that, someone told me they'd heard him play at the Winterland in San Francisco.

And now, eighteen years later, he was back. Still trying to kill himself. I stared in the rearview mirror and wondered what I was going to do with him—this time. Wondered if I could help—this time. Or if anyone could.

IV

It was almost five A.M. when I got Lonnie to the Delores. I half carried him to the apartment—through the parking lot and up the back stairs. Once I got him inside, I stripped off his filthy clothes and threw him into the tub. I left him soaking in a couple of inches of tepid water while I called Ron Fegley—a doctor friend.

"Jesus Christ," Ron said when I told him how many pills Lonnie had apparently swallowed, "he must have a hell of a tolerance for drugs."

"I think he's had his share," I said.

"He probably vomited up most of them earlier tonight. And it has been better than eight hours since he swallowed them. But if I were you, I'd take him to the emergency room—pronto. That's my advice."

"I don't think I can do that," I said. "Attempted suicide means psychiatric confinement and, possibly, a police report. I don't know what kind of criminal record Lonnie might have, but I don't want to put him in jail or in Longview. Besides, he said he didn't want to go to the hospital."

"He's in great condition to decide for himself," Ron said acidly. "Did it occur to you that he might be better off in jail or in some detox center."

"I'm not going to make that choice for him. At least, not while he's in this kind of shape."

"Then keep him warm and keep an eye on him. If he starts looking shocky or goes into convulsions—call an ambulance. And I mean quick. You know you're going to have a lot of explaining to do if he dies on you."

I thought it over and said, "I'll just have to take that chance."

"It's your life," Ron said. "And his."

After hanging up on Ron, I pulled Lonnie out of the tub and dried him off. With the dirt and blood washed off him, he looked a lot better than he had in the Encantada Motel—like a haggard, graying version of the kid I remembered. His face was bruised; but the split lip wasn't serious, and although the black eye was mousing up, it wasn't a bad injury either. I took a look at his arms, expecting to find needle tracks. To my surprise he didn't show any. What he did have was an oval twelve-inch scar on his right side that pinched the flesh between his hip and his rib cage, exactly as if some animal had taken a bite out of him. It looked like a gunshot wound, although it was awfully large for that. I noticed that his fingertips were heavily callused, which meant he hadn't lost touch with his music —whatever else he might have lost.

Hoisting him up over my shoulder, I carried Lonnie into the bedroom and lowered him onto the bed. He groaned as I covered him with blankets.

"Where am I?" he said groggily.

"You're at my place."

He nodded and smiled, as if that were good news. Then he fell back to sleep.

After putting Lonnie to bed, I took some fresh bedclothes out of the hall closet and made the living room sofa up for myself. It wasn't until I actually sat down on the couch that I realized how cold, wet, and tired I was. I stripped off my clothes, curled up on the cushions, and listened to the December storm tapping its nails against the living room window. In the bedroom I could hear Lonnie snoring evenly. I closed my eyes, telling myself that I'd just doze off for a few moments, and immediately fell asleep.

* * *

I woke up around one o'clock that Friday afternoon, and the first things I heard were the measured sound of Lonnie's snoring and the patter of the icy rain on the living room window. I walked down the hall and took a look at him in the gray afternoon light. The color had returned to his face and he seemed to be sleeping soundly. I thought about trying to wake him, then thought better of it. The fact that he hadn't died on me in the night was a relief. But I knew that Lonnie wouldn't see it that way. Junkies have a saying: "Dying is easy." I let him sleep.

After fixing some coffee in the kitchenette, I gathered Lonnie's clothes together and went through them, looking for some clues to his recent past. I found a slip of paper in his shirt pocket with a local phone number penciled on it. When I dialed it, it turned out to be the office of the Encantada Motel. Claude Jenkins answered in a cranky voice. I hung up before he'd finished saying hello.

In Lonnie's pants pockets I found a dog-eared social security card, an expired Missouri driver's license, and a snapshot of a brown-haired woman and two smiling children, posing in front of a Christmas tree. The photograph had a date printed on its back—December 25, 1984. The woman was very beautiful; so were the children. It didn't seem possible that it was a picture of Lonnie's own family. And yet I couldn't think of a better reason for him to have kept the photo on him. There was an address on the expired license—Klotter Road, University City, Missouri.

In his parka, I found a crumpled pack of Camels, a ticket stub from the Bijou—a theater here in town—and a round-trip Greyhound bus ticket, to Cincinnati from St. Louis and back. I also found a page that had been ripped out of a Cincinnati phone book and folded into a square. I unfolded it, knowing already that it was the page with my name and number on it. I was right. My name had been circled in pen and a little note was scribbled beside the listing. *Sorry, Harry.*

I stared at the note for a second and wondered if he'd written it before or after he'd taken the pills. Either way, it was the closest thing to a suicide note he'd left. *Sorry, Harry.*

I folded the note back up and stuck it in my desk drawer. I piled the rest of his belongings on the coffee table. The parka could be cleaned; the rest of the stuff was hopeless. Bundling up his clothes, I threw them in a plastic trash bag. I figured he could wear some of my things until he could buy some new ones. Or until *I* could buy new ones for him.

I'd have to do the buying, because I hadn't found one dollar in his clothes. Not even a few pennies of change. He was flat broke. Except for the return bus ticket, he'd had nothing on him of value. He must have spent his last few dollars on the Bijou ticket, the motel room, and the drinks he'd had at the Encantada's bar. Maybe he'd spent all his money deliberately—squandering his cash before killing himself. But if that was the case, I didn't understand why he'd kept the bus ticket, instead of turning it in at the terminal. Which suggested another possibility—that he'd been robbed. By the bikers he'd had the fight with. Or by someone at the motel. Judging from Claude Jenkins, I figured that the Encantada's staff wasn't above fleecing one of their guests—especially if he was out cold because of a drug overdose.

Speculating about Lonnie's attempted suicide on the basis of a few shreds of circumstantial evidence made me feel too much like a detective and too little like a friend. And Lonnie apparently still regarded me as a friend. There was no other way to explain why he'd picked me out of the phone book. Even after eighteen years, there must have been a dozen other names he could have chosen—musicians, ex-girlfriends, other roommates. But he'd picked me. And before he tried to kill himself, he'd left me that little apology. *Sorry, Harry.* It was an unsettling thought—to imagine that I'd been on his mind before he'd swallowed the pills—because the truth was that up until about three that morning, I hadn't thought of him in better than sixteen years.

That fact bore the truth in on me forcefully. And the truth was that, old friend or not, Lonnie was a stranger. And until I could talk to him or to someone who knew him, I wasn't doing him any favors by reading a lifetime into his last few acts. What I should have been doing was trying to locate someone who could tell me who Lonnie Jackowski was *now*.

I glanced at the driver's license again, picked up the phone, dialed the operator, and asked for University City, Missouri, information.

University City information didn't have a listing for Lonnie Jackowski. But there was a listing for a Karen Jackowski at the address on the expired license. I wrote the number down on a piece of scrap and hung up. I stared at the number for a long time, before dialing it. It wasn't just a question of breaking the news, if, indeed, there was someone to break the news to. Lonnie hadn't come all this way without a reason. If he'd left someone behind, he'd left them for a reason too.

I made the call anyway. A child answered the phone—a little girl.

"Yes?" she said in a tiny, tentative voice.

"Honey, is your mom home?" I asked.

"I dunno," she said flatly.

"Could you look and see?"

"Uh-huh," she said. She dropped the phone with a thud. I could hear her shouting, "Mommy, Mommy."

While she was off the line, I picked up the snapshot I'd found in Lonnie's pants and stared at it curiously. It just hadn't seemed possible that a guy like Lonnie—a guy so obviously at the end of his rope—could have had a pretty wife and two beautiful kids. I studied the room with the Christmas tree in it. There was a white sofa along one wall. A fleecy off-white rug. A mahogany coffee table with fluted legs. Plenty of gifts beneath the tree, including a new bike. It looked like a typical middle-class household at Christmastime. Certainly nothing to be ashamed of or disappointed in. Nothing to run away from—to a run-down afternoon-delight motel in Miamiville. As I was thinking about the picture, someone picked the phone up again.

"Yes?" a woman said warily. "Who is this?" She spoke with a husky lisp. Like Lizabeth Scott.

"Mrs. Jackowski?" I said.

"Yes," the woman said. "I'm Karen Jackowski."

"My name is Stoner, Mrs. Jackowski. Harry Stoner. I'm calling you from Cincinnati."

"Oh, yes," she said, with sudden warmth. "I remember your name. Lonnie's mentioned you many times, Harry. You two used to room together in college, right?"

I took a breath. "Mrs. Jackowski—"

"Call me Karen, please," she said.

"Karen. It's about Lonnie," I said.

"What's wrong?" she said sharply.

I sighed into the phone. "He tried to kill himself last night, Mrs. Jackowski," I said, getting it over with.

Karen Jackowski didn't say anything for a moment. When she finally spoke, her voice sounded measured and cold. "Did he succeed?"

"No," I said, trying to disguise the shock I felt over the way she'd taken the news. "He's all right. At least, he's not dead."

"And what do you want *me* to do about it?" Karen Jackowski said with that same measured coldness.

"You're his wife, aren't you?" I said with some coldness of my own. "Don't you care?"

"Harry, Lonnie and I have been separated for better than two years. Besides, there's nothing new about Lonnie's trying to kill himself. He's been killing himself for as long as I've known him. It's what he does, Harry. Kill himself and everyone else who cares for him." Her voice broke.

I started to feel very bad. I shouldn't have made the call. I should have handled it on my own. "I'm sorry," I said to the woman. "I was trying to help. I didn't know you two were . . . separated."

"It's all right," she said, but her voice still sounded broken.

"Is there anyone else I should contact?" I said.

"No," she said in a whisper. "His folks are dead. I'm the only one left." She took a deep breath. "I guess I'd better come there."

"No," I said firmly, "I can take care of him."

"Want to bet?" Karen Jackowski said bitterly. "You don't know him, Harry. You really don't."

What could I say? I *didn't* know him.

"I'll have to find somebody to look after the kids," Karen Jackowski said. "Thank God it's a weekend. At least I won't have to explain it at work."

"Look," I said, "you don't have to do this."

"Yes, I do," she said, as if she felt an obligation. "He's still my husband. It's not fair to saddle you or anyone else with Lonnie Jack."

I hadn't heard anyone say that name in so long that I smiled, then felt foolish for having done so.

"Could you pick me up at the airport?" Karen Jackowski said.

"Sure," I said. I gave her my phone number and told her to call me collect when she knew her flight number and arrival time.

V

Karen Jackowski called back around four-thirty to let me know that she'd be coming in at eleven. I tried again to talk her out of making the trip, but she was adamant. I arranged to meet her at the airport when she arrived.

After talking to her, I fell asleep on the couch. When I woke up it was fully dark outside. The living room was quiet, except for the sound of the rain on the windows. I walked through the dark over to the desk, clicked on a lamp, then went back to the couch. As I sat down again, I realized that Lonnie was sitting there too—in my easy chair.

"Christ!" I said, startled. "Are you okay?"

He nodded, his lean, battered face coming into the light. "I didn't know where I was," he said. "It was dark. I thought maybe I'd died."

He was sitting Indian style in the chair. Jay naked. A blanket wrapped around his shoulders. In the dim yellow lamplight, he looked like the kid I'd known in 1967. So much like him that I felt a chill run up my back.

"I guess I fucked up," he said with a forced smile.

"Do you remember last night at all?"

Lonnie shook his head and winced. "God, my head hurts." He coughed—a deep, hacking cough. "I caught a cold, too. My throat hurts like a son of a bitch."

"You threw up a lot," I said. "It's probably pretty raw."

He smiled at me. "You brought me here?"

"Had to do something with you, man," I said, smiling back at him.

"You couldn't just let me die, huh?" He said it like a joke, but it didn't come out funny.

I had the feeling he was going to make a lot of jokes that didn't come out funny. I decided, on the spot, just to ignore them, until he was ready to talk seriously about the suicide attempt. "You want some coffee?" I asked.

He nodded. "Something warm would be nice." He coughed again. "Is this where you live, man?"

"This is it," I said, getting up from the couch and walking into the kitchenette.

"It's like Lyon Street," he said.

"Not much better."

"You remember Lyon Street, Harry?" he called out hoarsely from the living room.

I doled some coffee into the machine. "Yeah. I remember it."

"I stopped there yesterday. At least, I think I did. It hadn't changed much."

"The rest of Clifton has," I said.

"Yeah, I could tell. All Styrofoam now. No more Black Dome. No more peace and love."

The coffee machine started burbling. I poured two cups of coffee and brought them into the living room. Lonnie looked like he'd fallen asleep again—head back out of the light. When I walked over to him, I saw that his eyes were wide open, staring at the ceiling. I handed him the cup of coffee and he glanced at me.

"I'm sorry, Harry," he said with real feeling in his voice.

"Forget it," I said. "Drink your coffee."

He took a sip of coffee, choked on it, but managed to gulp it down. "Tastes good." He took another sip. "Remember the Toddle House restaurant on Clifton Avenue?"

I laughed. "Yeah. We drank a lot of coffee there."

"And killed a lot of time." He grinned. "Picked up a lot of chicks at *chez* Toddle."

"You picked up a lot of chicks everywhere."

"You did all right too," he said, charitably. "What happened to that one—that Linda."

"I don't know," I said. "We lost touch."

"*Ou sont les* Lindas of yesteryear, huh, Harry? I think about that a lot."

"About what?"

"About how people go different ways. They spread out so far . . . you can't call them back." Lonnie dropped his eyes to the floor. "This talking over old times isn't doing me much good," he said heavily. He put the coffee cup on an end table and covered his face with his hands. "Oh, God. What the fuck have I done?"

He started to weep. Hoarsely. Uncontrollably. His hands and shoulders shaking as if *he* were being shaken. Pulling the blanket tightly around him, so it shielded his face, he cried to himself.

I got up from the couch and walked down the hall to the bedroom. Caught a glimpse of myself in the wall mirror and didn't have the guts to look into my own eyes. I dug an old plaid lumberjack shirt and a pair of jeans out of a drawer, sat down on the bed, and waited until I could hear Lonnie's sobbing die down. Then I walked back up the hall.

"Here," I said, tossing him the clothes.

They fell at his feet. He wiped his red eyes with the corner of the blanket, reached down, and picked up the jeans.

"They're going to be a little long," he said hoarsely.

"Roll the legs," I said.

He picked the shirt, then glanced down at himself. "I could use a shower, I think."

"Down the hall on your right."

He rubbed his jaw. "You got a razor I could use, maybe?" I must have given him a startled look, because he said, "Don't worry, Harry. I wouldn't do that to you twice."

"There's shaving stuff in the medicine cabinet," I said, trying to look unconcerned.

He folded up the shirt and pants, got up, and walked down the hall. When he got to the john door, he looked back at me. "You haven't asked me," he said.

"What?"

"Why I used your name."

"Why did you?" I said.

" 'Cause if I croaked, I knew you'd look after me. And if I didn't . . ." He waved his right arm. "Here I am." Lonnie dropped his arm and said, "Nobody else I know would have come through for me like that."

"How did you know that I would?"

"I knew," he said softly as he stepped into the john.

VI

When Lonnie came out of the shower, he was singing, in a mellow baritone that brought back memories of Calhoun Street.

It was a Bob Seger song full of motorcycles, leather jackets, and beautiful women. Lonnie toweled off his wet hair. "You like Bob Seger?" he said, as he walked into the living room. He'd rolled the jeans up at the ankles, although they were still a size too large at the waist.

"Yeah, I like Seger," I said.

"I used to do a lot of his stuff with my last band."

"What was that?" I asked.

"The Hawks," he said, dropping into the easy chair and crooking a leg over one of the arms. "We called ourselves the Hawks. Like the Band, when they backed Ronnie Hawkins. Christ, did you read about Richard Manuel?"

I nodded.

"That's some sad shit there, buddy," he said, wiping off his ears. "That's a *real* loss. Not like some nobody who never was nothing, swallowing pills in a fleabag motel."

I grunted and he smiled.

"It's okay, Harry," he said. "It's gotta be talked about. No way to avoid it. Everything's connected, after all."

"How are you feeling?" I said.

"Don't know yet," he said. He started to cough again and pounded his chest, theatrically, with his fist. "Who knows? This cold might kill me."

I leaned forward on the couch. "I need to talk to you about something. You feel up to it?"

Lonnie gave me a tentative smile. "Depends on what *it* is."

I glanced at my watch. "It's ten o'clock. I'm going to have to leave here for a while. I've got to pick someone up at the airport."

"I could come along, maybe," he said, as if he really didn't want to be left alone.

"Sure," I said. "You're welcome to come."

"Who you picking up?"

"That's what we've got to talk about," I said.

"This is making me a little nervous," Lonnie said with a sick grin. "You aren't going to spring any doctors or shit on me, are you, Harry? You haven't been making a lot of calls, have you?"

I said, "No."

"Good," Lonnie said, looking relieved, " 'cause I've had my fill of doctors. And I'd just as soon nobody else heard about . . . last night."

I could see a problem coming up. But there was no way around it, except to lie to him. And that would only create more problems. I decided to give it to him straight. "I did make one call, Lonnie. Earlier today I called University City, trying to track down someone who knew you. You know it has been eighteen years, old buddy."

"Aw, fuck," Lonnie said, with a bloodless, horrified look. "You called my old lady, didn't you?"

"Yeah, I did."

"Aw, fuck!" he said again, loudly. He jumped up from the chair and began to pace the room. "God damn it, man! I wish you hadn't done that."

"I didn't know, Lonnie," I said, feeling bad for him.

"God damn it!" he said. "Is she the one you're going to pick up at the airport?"

I nodded reluctantly.

"I don't want to see her, man," Lonnie almost shouted. "I don't want her to see me."

"She wanted to come," I said, even though it wasn't true.

"Sure," he said contemptuously. "So she can see what a fuck-up I am." He stopped pacing and glared at me angrily. "Just keep her away from me, man. I'm asking you. She took my kids, man. She broke my fucking heart."

"All right," I said. "I'll keep her away."

"Send her back home."

"I'll try," I said.

He sat back down heavily on the easy chair. "That bitch, Karen. She's the whole reason why I'm here."

I looked him over carefully, wondering if he was going to lose it again. "Are you going to be all right while I'm gone?" I asked.

"Yes," he said angrily. "Sure. I'm not a kid, you know."

"You're not going to do anything stupid, right?"

"For chrissake, Harry," Lonnie said. "I told you I wouldn't do that to you twice. I'll be all right. I'll catch some z's. Okay?"

I said okay. But I wasn't sure.

VII

All the way out to the airport, I worried about leaving Lonnie alone. I even thought of turning back a couple of times, but managed to talk myself out of it. After all, I told myself, he was a grown man. And there was a limit to what anyone can do for anyone else. I couldn't play big brother to him for the rest of his life, like it was 1968 again. Still, I worried.

By the time I made it through the snow and rain to Cincinnati International, it was well past eleven. I parked in the short-term lot and bulled my way through the wind to the Delta terminal, one of three huge hangar-shaped buildings flanking the runways.

The ground floor of the terminal had the eerie, untenanted look of a building under construction. The ticket counters, rent-a-car booths, and luggage carousels were unmanned and dimly lit. The only signs of life were the ubiquitous TV monitors, flashing their endless stream of flight information. I checked one of the screens, hoping that Karen Jackowski's flight had been late. *I* was late; her plane had arrived on schedule.

I took the elevator up to the arrival and departure gates on the second floor. It was deserted too, except for a few groggy attendants behind the counters. I checked the coffee shop on my way to the arrival gates—in case Karen had gotten tired of waiting. Aside from a rent-a-cop hunched over a racing form and one lorn waitress sitting on a stool, the place was deserted.

I headed down the broad, fluorescent walkway that led

to the gates. About halfway down the hall, I spotted Karen
Jackowski, sitting alone in one of the arrival bays, a canvas
duck travel bag at her feet. She spotted me, too, and
waved a hand. It wasn't until that moment that I asked
myself what I was going to do with her. I knew what I
wanted to do—put her and Lonnie together again and see
if they couldn't lend each other some support. But I didn't
think Lonnie would sit for that. And from the way she had
sounded on the phone, I figured that Karen Jackowski
wouldn't either.

"Are you Harry Stoner?" she called out.

"I'm Harry," I said, walking up to her. "Sorry I'm late.
The weather slowed me down."

She smiled at me. "I figured."

I smiled back at her. She had the kind of good looks that
would have made me smile at her, even if she'd been a
stranger. Her hair was light brown, almost blond, cut in
bangs in front and piled in a bun on top. A few loose hairs
curled at her cheeks, giving her a casual, earthy look. She
had a full, square face, sunburned and lined attractively
around the eyes and mouth. Her eyes were wide and a
pale, cornflower blue. Her top lip flared up, with the sug-
gestion of a pout, although there was nothing snotty about
her smile. She was wearing jeans and a pale yellow fur
jacket that had gone tatty at the cuffs and the collar.

I must have been staring at her a little too openly, because she started to look embarrassed.

"I guess I sounded like a monster on the phone," she
said, as if she thought that was why I'd been ogling her.
"Was that what you were expecting?"

"I didn't know what to expect," I said, sitting down
across the aisle from her.

"You look like I expected," she said with genuine
warmth. "You know, Lonnie used to talk about you a lot.
His famous roommate who became a private eye." She said
the private eye part with a touch of irony. But it was good-
natured irony. After the way she'd sounded on the phone,

the lightness of her manner came as a surprise. "He kept saying he'd put us in touch some day. But . . ."

She looked down at the floor, as if talking about Lonnie embarrassed her.

"How is he?" she said, without looking at me.

"We're going to have to talk about that," I said.

"How so?"

"He has a problem about seeing you right now."

Karen Jackowski smiled knowingly. "It isn't something I haven't already seen."

"He's tried this sort of thing before?"

"All his life," she said, and for a moment her voice filled with the same bitterness with which she'd spoken over the phone. Then she made a face, as if she'd heard that bitterness herself and didn't like what it did to her. "He's never intentionally taken an overdose of pills before, but God knows he's overdosed enough."

"On what?"

"Ludes, soapers, smack. You name it."

"Lonnie is a junkie, then?" I said, without much surprise.

Karen nodded. "He's been in a federal drug rehabilitation program for the last two years, Harry."

"When did he get out?"

"As far as I know," she said, "the week before last."

We walked back up the long hall to the check-in counters. Karen was taller than I'd expected—taller than Lonnie. And she moved quickly, with long deliberate strides— the way runners walk. As we approached the X-ray machines, Karen glanced at one of the TV monitors flashing flight information and began to laugh.

"The last time I was at this airport in '72," she said, "Lonnie and I got stoned on acid before we boarded the plane back to St. Louis. I remember standing in front of one of those monitors and staring at it as if it were a soap opera. A flight attendant came over and asked me if he could help. He was coming on to me, but I was so stoned, I didn't realize it. I thought he really wanted to give me a hand, so I asked him if he could change the channel on the TV." She laughed again. "You should have seen the look on his face. Lonnie got hysterical and said he couldn't take me anywhere. We were goofing so openly, it was a miracle we didn't get busted."

"I did acid once," I said.

"Once?"

I nodded.

"Under a doctor's supervision?"

I grunted and she laughed.

"You're kind of square, aren't you, Harry?" Karen Jackowski said, in her husky, amused voice.

"My whole life," I admitted.

"Well, I did acid more than once. And everything else that Lonnie did." She gave me a frank smile and said, "I was a junkie too."

Whether she'd intended to or not, she'd surprised the hell out of me. I tried to cover my shock by acting as casually about it as she had. "When did you quit using?" I asked.

"When Lonnie got busted in '76," Karen said, as if she'd answered the question many times before. "Lonnie was so sick in those days that he needed that first one or two bags just to get well. One morning, he shot himself up in both arms and OD'd on the bathroom floor. I had to call the life squad to our apartment, and they brought the cops with them. The paramedics brought Lonnie back to life and the cops busted him on the spot. Do you know what he said when he regained consciousness?"

I shook my head.

"He said it was the best high he'd ever had," she said. "He wanted to do it all over again."

"And that's when you quit?" I said.

She nodded. "That was it for me."

"What happened to Lonnie?"

"They sent him to a halfway house for six months. Then put him back in a methadone clinic. We were both going to stay clean, after that." She laughed bitterly. "Yep, that was the plan, all right. Get married. Have kids. Go back to school. A new life."

"It didn't work?"

She eyed me balefully. "No, it didn't work. He stayed in the clinic for a while—six months, maybe. And then he started getting stoned again. He'd lip the methadone pills and sell them on the street for junk. He lied about it, at first. But towards the end he didn't even bother to lie. We were living apart when he got busted the last time. I filed the divorce papers the day he went off to Lexington."

We'd come to the end of the hallway. I stopped for a moment and stared at Karen. She'd spoken so freely about her sensational past that she'd almost taken my breath away. And then it was always sobering to hear about the lives other people have led. It gave you a healthy sense of your own inconsequence, like having your picture taken in front of the Grand Canyon.

As we started down the escalators to the ground floor, I asked her, "Why did you come after him today?"

She thought about it for a second, then said, "I didn't think I had a choice."

"You still love him?"

She shook her head decisively. "No. But I still want to, if you can understand that. I still have the need. Lonnie's a lot like junk—you never really kick him. All it takes is a taste and you're hooked again." She turned to me with a resolute look. "I don't want to get hooked, Harry. I can't afford to anymore. I've made my own life now, and I don't want to go backward."

"How do you expect to help him?" I said.

"*I* can't help him. I don't have the strength or the desire. All I can do is fly him back to St. Louis and take him to someone who can get him straight. After that, it's up to him."

We stepped off the escalator into the dim, deserted ground-floor waiting room. There was a phone booth beside the escalator. I thought about calling Lonnie—to check up on him. Then decided against it. I also decided to take Karen back with me to the apartment, whether Lonnie approved of her or not. It was clear, now, that I was way out of my depth when it came to dealing with him.

I guided Karen to the exit. She took one look out the plate-glass doors—at the blowing snow and rain—and shivered.

"Welcome to Cincinnati," she said lugubriously.

VIII

As we were walking through the lot to the car, Karen slipped on the icy tarmac. I caught her before she fell and lifted her to her feet. In lifting her up, I inadvertently cupped my hand around one of her breasts. I pulled my hand away immediately and gave her a quick, embarrassed look. She looked amused.

"That was a cheap way to cop a feel," she said.

"Hey!" I protested. "It was an accident."

"There are no accidents, Harry," she said with a laugh. "But we should know each other a little better, I think, before you go any further. Especially in an airport parking lot."

As she got into the car, I thought that I'd very much like to know her better.

"You have somebody back in St. Louis?" I said curiously as I got into the car beside her. "Somebody you . . . know a little better?"

"I've known a lot of men better," she said in her husky, ironic voice. "Better and worse."

"Seriously," I said. "Have you hooked up with someone else, after Lonnie?"

"Seriously?" she said in a vaguely mocking voice. "Seriously, no. At least, no one for very long. I guess Lonnie spoiled me for other men."

"He's that good?" I said, feeling a twinge of ancient jealousy in spite of myself.

"Oh, he's very good in bed," Karen said indifferently. "But that's not what I meant. What I meant, I think, is

that I haven't wanted to get involved with another man
since I separated from Lonnie. There were a few one-
night stands, especially right after we broke up. But nothing lately. I've got my kids and my job at U-City Elemen-
tary. I don't need anything else." She laughed dryly. "I
sound pretty arrogant, don't I?"

"No."

"Well, I do to myself. You'd just have to have lived with
Lonnie for close to fifteen years to understand it."

"You want to tell me about it?"

"About the woes of my marriage, you mean?"

"Sure," I said.

She shrugged. "Why not?" She turned toward me on
the car seat. "Lonnie and I met at a concert at Washington
University in 1969. His band was the opening act for
Quicksilver Messenger Service. And I was a sophomore
coed, majoring in protest. From that first night until he
went off to prison two years ago, I didn't have a life outside of his life. I didn't have a thing of my own. It was like
I'd caught a fast train back there in St. Louis, and I
couldn't get off. We just kept rolling—all over the country.
From one gig to the next. Up and down. Two years in
Hollywood, when Lonnie was hot. Two years in the Big
Apple, when he cooled down. Then four years in an East
St. Louis tenement, when nobody would touch him. And
all the time, there was the dope and the games. Kinkiness,
ugliness. Servicing Lonnie's supplier for a dime bag. Copping fifteen bags with the rent money. Pushing seven on
the street to keep the other eight. Every day worrying
about how to get well—how to get the bread to cop. It
was, as they used to say, a trip."

She tapped her leg nervously with her fingertips. "So
you'll just have to forgive me, Harry, if I don't meet your
expectations when it comes to men," Karen said in a voice
that was meant to be lighthearted but that was cracking
under the strain of the past. "When it comes to men, I've

had it. All I want now is my own life. No more train rides,
thank you. No more commitments."

I glanced at her. She'd turned her head away, toward
the side window.

I cleared my throat and said, "Are you okay?"

"Fine," she said abruptly, without turning around.
"Strolling down Memory Lane always has this effect on
me. Put on the radio, will you? I don't want to be the main
attraction anymore."

I flipped on the radio and concentrated on the road.

As we rounded the final cut bank above the river, the
city came into view, white and shimmering in the snow,
like a city of marble.

"He always liked this place," Karen said. "He made a lot
of friends here."

"Do you think that's why he came back, yesterday?" I
said. It was a question that had been bothering me since
Claude Jenkins had phoned the previous night.

Karen didn't answer me—just stared at the beautiful
skyline.

"What I said before," she said after a time. "It wasn't
always like that."

"We don't have to talk about him anymore," I told her.

"No," she said stoutly, "let me say it."

"All right."

"He was never really a bad man," Karen said. "He was
just too naive about things. The sixties did that to him—to
all of us. Primed us for disappointment. Raised our hopes
too high. The old J-curve. When expectations outrun your
ability to meet them." She laughed. "I sound like a graduate student, but who could have guessed what the last
fifteen years were going to be like? Who could have
guessed what a falling-off there was going to be? God,
what an awful decade this is. So selfish and inhospitable.
So cocksure of itself. So unimaginative. You know what I
mean?"

I nodded. "It's different," I said.

"The last ten years practically killed Lonnie," she said bitterly. "He just couldn't stop living the sixties dream. Me neither, I guess. The accommodations I've made . . . I've had to make. But inside . . ." She touched her breast, over her heart. "I'm still for peace and love. I still make the marches, when they're marching. I still want to believe in all that stuff. Like I still want to love Lonnie, I guess. The two of them are hard to separate out in my head—Lonnie and the past." She lowered her voice to a whisper. "He never really meant to hurt anybody. Christ, he really believed in peace, love, sharing. He just didn't want to be hurt himself. And he'd been hurt so many times. His parents, his brother, the band, agents. Me. You. Did you know that you hurt him, Harry?"

"Yes," I said, "I think I do know that."

"All he ever really wanted was to be loved uncritically— the way he thought he loved other people. It's what we all wanted, wasn't it? He'd open himself up to strangers, time and time again. Really show them his heart and soul. And every time they'd disappoint him or use him or hurt him. It got so that he expected it. And then it got so that he couldn't handle it without a fix. He just didn't have it inside. It was like he was born without the right stuff. He used to joke about it, feebly. He said he was missing a bone —the heart."

"We all have to live with disappointments, Karen," I said.

She stiffened up on the car seat. "I'm not excusing him," she said coolly. "I'm the last person on earth who would excuse Lonnie Jackowski. I'm just saying that he did what he did out of weakness and despair—not out of any deliberate desire to hurt."

I crossed the river on the Brent Spence and took I-71 north to the Reading Road exit. We didn't say another word, until I pulled into the Delores's parking lot on Burnett.

"We're here," I said, flipping off the engine.

Karen looked up at the red-brick apartment and shivered.

"If you don't feel like this," I said gently, "we could get you a hotel room."

She shook her head. "I came to help him."

"There could be a scene," I said in a warning voice.

"I can handle Lonnie," Karen said, with just a touch of contempt in her voice. "Let's go."

I guided her around to the front, up the stairs leading to the narrow court. The slush in the courtyard was dimpled with footprints, filling up with new snow. The limbs of the dogwoods were encased in ice, dripping down in sharp, conical icicles. Karen brushed against one of the dogwoods and the icicles tinkled like wind chimes.

As we stepped into the lobby, Karen stared ominously up the stairs.

"All set?" I said.

She took a deep breath and nodded.

We walked up two flights to my floor. When we got to the top floor, I put my hand across her chest, brushing her breasts again.

She laughed and said, "Are you trying to tell me something?"

When I didn't laugh, she stared at me curiously and asked, "What's wrong, Harry?"

I pulled her back to the landing. "My apartment's at the end of the hall on the left."

"And?" she said.

"The door is open."

"Maybe he opened the door," she said, "to air the place out?"

I shook my head. "I don't think so."

"Well, we don't have to make a melodrama out of it," she said, peeking around the corner of the landing, "let's just go see."

"*I'll* go," I said.

She gave me a disappointed look. "You're not going to be like that, are you, Harry? A male chauvinist prick? Lonnie would have told me to go ahead. In fact, he would have pushed me in front of him."

"I'm not Lonnie," I said.

I put my hand on her shoulders, backed her gently against the landing wall, and stared into her eyes. "Humor me and stay here, Karen. Okay?"

"For chrissake," she said with disgust. "All right. Go already."

I stepped back into the corridor and walked slowly down the hall. As I got closer to the door, I could see that the apartment had been ransacked. I unbuttoned my topcoat and pulled the Gold Cup out of the shoulder holster. It was cocked and locked. I flipped off the safety and stepped into my living room.

All the drawers of my desk had been emptied on the floor. The cushions on the couch were slashed; and the stuffing had been pulled out and scattered around the room. A big wad of it was hanging from a lamp by the door. I swiped it off with the gun barrel.

"Lonnie?" I called out.

Nobody answered.

I walked into the bedroom and flipped on the light. The bureau drawers had been emptied and the mattress had been ripped open.

I walked back into the living room. Karen Jackowski was standing in the doorway, surveying the damage with an aghast look on her face.

"Did Lonnie do this?" she said with horror.

"I don't know. He's not here now."

"He must be completely out of his mind," she said, giving me a helpless look. "God, what are we going to do?"

I put the safety on and stuck the gun back in my holster. "Find him," I said.

IX

I searched the apartment to see if Lonnie had left anything behind that might tell us where he was headed. But the closer I looked, the less certain I was that Lonnie had done the damage. There was something unmistakably methodical about the way the place had been tossed—bureau drawers emptied, mattress slashed, the shoe boxes and clothes bags in the closets opened and rifled. Very little had been broken; and that seemed strange too. No broken mirrors, no broken dishes, no broken lamps or glasses. It seemed to me that a man in a frenzy, a man enraged enough to tear open the mattress and the cushions on the couch, should have been a little less careful about what he broke or didn't break. It almost looked as if the apartment had been tossed by professionals. Of course, the fact that I didn't want to believe that Lonnie had wrecked my apartment colored my judgment. And thirty bucks *was* missing from a glass tray on the bedroom bureau, along with Lonnie's Missouri license, the photograph, and the return bus ticket to St. Louis. Still, the rest of the mess made me dubious and more than a little worried about what might have happened to Lonnie. Although it was hard to believe that he could have involved himself in drug trouble so soon after he'd been released from Lexington, that was what the evidence suggested. Karen herself saw that.

As I came back into the living room, she looked up from where she was kneeling on the floor and said, "It looks like a bust."

I nodded grimly. "Yes, it does."

Stuffing a handful of loose wadding back into the sofa, she asked, "Why would he do this?"

"I don't know," I said. "If this was somebody else's apartment, I'd say that it had been searched by pros."

"Pros?" she said, dropping the wadding she was holding. "Looking for what?"

I shrugged. "For whatever you might conceal in a cushion, a mattress, a desk drawer, or a shoe box."

"Drugs?" Karen said, with a frown.

"That would be my first guess."

Karen shook her head. "I don't understand any of this. Did Lonnie have drugs on him when you found him last night?"

"No."

"Then what . . . ?"

"I don't know, Karen. I don't know what he's been up to since he got out of jail. I don't know why he came back to Cincinnati yesterday. I don't know what he was doing at that godforsaken motel. Or why he did this."

"Maybe he didn't do this," she said with a tremor in her voice. "That's what you're implying, isn't it?"

"I don't know," I said, trying not to sound overly concerned. "It's possible."

She gave me a nervous look. "Then what happened to Lonnie, while these . . . people were searching for drugs?"

"I don't know that, either."

I walked over to the desk and started to pick up the phone.

"Who are you calling?" Karen said.

"The police. I think we can use their help tracking Lonnie down."

"No!" she said sharply. "Don't do that!"

I turned back to her. "Look," I said, "be reasonable, Karen. Either Lonnie did this, which means that he's gone over the edge and may try to kill himself again. Or somebody else came looking for him and did this, which means that he's in deep shit with the worst kind of people."

"People who did what? Ransacked your apartment and kidnapped Lonnie?" she said it facetiously, as if she were trying to make herself believe the possibility was preposterous. "You just don't know him, Harry. You don't know what he's like when he's mad or stoned. He probably tore your bed up because of me. It's a symbol. Get it? That's how his mind works."

"And the couch and the bureau and the desk?"

She shrugged. "He was looking for money. He was looking for . . . I don't know what. For some way to strike back at the world."

"There aren't any signs of a struggle," I admitted.

"Signs of a struggle?" she said blankly. The certainty drained out of Karen's pretty face. "You mean Lonnie might have been hurt, right? Somebody might have come here and . . . hurt him?"

"I don't know, Karen," I said. I was beginning to scare her and I didn't want to. But it was a scary situation, any way you looked at it. And the fact that there weren't any bloodstains on the floor didn't mean that all the violence had been directed against the furniture.

"How did these kidnappers know Lonnie was here?" Karen said, as if she was trying to confound me with common sense.

It was a good question. And the only answer I could come up with was the Encantada Motel. Lonnie had used my name and address when he'd registered. Someone might have noted it, and then followed us to the Delores. That was, if Lonnie hadn't trashed the apartment himself, as Karen had said.

The Encantada seemed like a good place to start looking for Lonnie anyway. Something was wrong at that motel. I'd known it the night before. The beating Lonnie had taken, the fact that his money was missing, Claude Jenkins's intransigence about the police—there was something wrong with all of it. It would have helped to know why Lonnie'd gone to the Encantada in the first place. But the fact that Jenkins had said there were bikers there—bikers who dealt dope—was a fairly disturbing piece of information.

I explained to Karen about the Encantada, the bikers, and the fact that Lonnie had registered under my name. "I realize it's a long shot, but I'd better try to find out what was going on at that motel. And whether Lonnie did this or not, I also think we should call the cops."

"But we can't throw him to the police," she said in a shaken voice. "He just got out of prison, for chrissake. He'll kill himself for sure if he gets busted again." She put a hand to her mouth. "I don't think I could stand that—if I put him back in jail."

"Karen . . ." I said.

"Please, Harry."

I gave Karen a sharp look.

"I know, I know," she said helplessly. She had begun to blush. She wiped her cheeks with her palms, as if she could rub away the embarrassment she felt over still caring for Lonnie. "I'm acting like an idiot. I shouldn't give a damn what happens to him anymore. Neither should you. He ruined your apartment, for chrissake. Aren't you mad?"

"I'm worried," I said pointedly.

She stared at me for a moment, blank-faced. "I guess I never stopped thinking of the police as the enemy. It's a throwback to another era of my life." She took a deep breath. "Go ahead. Call them."

"You're doing the right thing—for Lonnie," I said with conviction.

She nodded slowly, but she didn't look convinced.

I called Al Foster at Central Station and told him that I was looking for a missing person. I made up a story about being hired by Karen, then gave Al a description of Lonnie. I also told him that Lonnie was unbalanced—a possible suicide. I didn't mention anything about Lonnie's record or about what we'd found in my apartment.

"If you do turn him up, Al," I said, "I'd appreciate a call. The wife is very upset."

"Okay, Harry," he said. "I'll see this goes in the morning report."

I thanked him and hung up. Karen was staring at me nervously, from where she was standing by the sofa.

"That didn't hurt, did it?" I said.

"It didn't hurt me," she said balefully.

I walked over to her and put my arm around her shoulder. "C'mon," I said. "Let's get out of here."

"Where?" she said, staring up at me with an uncertain look.

"We've got to find you someplace to stay."

"I've got enough money for a couple of nights in a motel," she said as we walked to the door.

"I'll cover your expenses," I said.

She shook her head. "I'll pay for my own mistakes. It's better that way."

She started down the hall. I took one last look through the door at the wreckage, and sighed. "God damn it, Lonnie," I said to myself.

I pulled the door shut, locked it, and followed Karen down to the lobby.

X

I got Karen a room at the Clarion, downtown. She wanted something less expensive, but I managed to talk her into letting me split the bill with her.

"After all," I said as we rode the elevator up to her room, "he's half my responsibility now."

She eyed me sleepily. "I'm too tired to talk about it. Tomorrow, we find someplace cheaper."

The room was neat and banal. A couple of double beds, nightstands with brassy lamps on them, a bureau with a framed mirror, a painting of a meadow hung over a color TV. As Karen unpacked her duffel I sat down on one of the double beds. It smelled of dust and laundry soap—that peculiar young-old smell of hotel rooms, like new shirts that have been hung in old closets. There was a phone on the nightstand by the bed. I picked it up and dialed the Greyhound bus terminal, on Gilbert. Lonnie had left so many possibilities in his wake that I had trouble keeping them straight. But I didn't want to let something as obvious as that return bus ticket go by, without checking it out.

The clerk at the terminal told me that the next bus to St. Louis left at three that afternoon. When I asked him if it was possible to find out whether someone had cashed in a return ticket or not, he said it could be done, but that it would take some time. I gave him Lonnie's name and my home number, and told him there would be some cash in it for him if he could get the information to me promptly. The mention of money shook the sleep from his voice. He said he'd get right on it, and I believed him.

As I hung up the phone Karen glanced at me, from where she was kneeling by the bureau. "Where are *you* going to sleep?"

"My place, I guess."

"Aren't you forgetting that you don't have a mattress?" She gestured to the other double bed. "Might as well get our money's worth."

"I don't think so," I said, getting to my feet.

Karen stared at me for a long moment. A lock of hair had fallen across her eyes, and she brushed it back with her hand.

"You know I wasn't inviting you to sleep with *me,* Harry," she said with a touch of asperity. "I don't make a habit of balling my husband's friends. I'm sixties, but not that sixties, if you get my drift."

I smiled at her. "I appreciate the offer of the bed. But I think I'm going to take a ride out to the Encantada."

"At this time of night?" She pointed at an alarm clock bolted to the bureau. It was close to two.

"If Lonnie is in some trouble," I said, "the sooner I get going on this, the better. There's a chance I can make things right, if I know who to talk to or who to pay off."

"You'd do that for him?"

"He's still my friend," I said, although I didn't feel particularly friendly toward him at that moment.

Karen shook her head wearily. "He doesn't deserve you, Harry."

"What about you? You came when he needed you."

Karen glanced around the hotel room and shuddered. "What the hell *am* I doing here? I should be home with my kids. I've got papers to grade." She slapped her right thigh, as if she were disciplining a child.

"You know you could go home," I said. "This is turning into a search for a missing person, and that's my business. Not yours."

Karen edged over to the corner of the bed and cribbed her hands in her lap. "I don't think so," she said after a time. "I mean I don't believe that Lonnie's been kidnapped. I think he just blew his stack. He's done it plenty of times before." She stared at her left hand, at the ring finger. I hadn't noticed it before, but there was a light band of flesh around the bottom joint where she'd once worn a wedding band. She rubbed the faded imprint idly, as if the ring were still there. "Still, if something were . . . wrong. I'd better stay. Through the weekend, at least."

"It's up to you."

I started for the door.

"Will I see you tomorrow?" Karen asked.

I said, "I'll treat you to breakfast."

"If you find anything out at that motel, give me a call."

"It could be very late, Karen," I said.

She said, "Call anyway. I'm not going to get much sleep."

I left her sitting on the bed, staring at her invisible ring.

It took me about forty minutes to drive out to Miamiville. I tried not to think about Lonnie on the way. But it was hopeless. And the question that kept running through my mind was the same one that Karen had posed in the hotel room: Why the hell are you doing this for him? It was past two in the morning, on a treacherous winter night. My apartment was in ruins. A smart, attractive woman—more attractive to me than I'd wanted to admit to myself or to her—was probably tossing sleeplessly on a rented bed, worrying over a man who had almost destroyed her life and was still trying to destroy his own. And the man himself, the man I was looking for, was either crazy or criminally stupid or both. Why the hell was I doing it? Why wasn't I back in that hotel room, with Karen? Or at my own apartment, trying to repair the damage?

I couldn't think of an answer to my own questions. Worse, I knew that the chances were good that I was on a wild-goose chase. Karen hadn't thought that Lonnie's

friends had broken into my apartment. She'd thought that
Lonnie himself had torn it up, in a fit of rage. If I hadn't
wanted to believe that Lonnie wouldn't do that sort of
thing to me—to his old pal, Harry—I might have come
around to her way of thinking. She knew the man; I didn't.
I was just going on an old cop's habit of mind and some
fairly dangerous sentiment.

Yet, in spite of the logic and the unanswerable questions, I kept on driving. For old times' sake. For that dangerous sentiment's sake. For the odd chance to make
things right again. For my peace of mind. So I could tell
myself I'd done the right thing—this time.

At a quarter to three, I pulled into the Encantada lot
and parked beneath the huge yellow-and-red neon motel
sign. The view through the icy windshield hadn't changed
from the previous night—right down to the lone Jeep
parked in front of the Quonset hut with the Miller sign in
its window. The sign was off and the hut was completely
dark. At least I wouldn't have to check the bar, I told
myself. I hauled my butt out of the car seat and walked
through the blowing snow to the cottage with the Office
sign above the door. The lights were dimmed inside the
office, and, this time, Claude Jenkins didn't come out to
greet me.

I rapped on the office door. When nobody answered, I
tried the knob. The ice made the door stick. I yanked it
open and stepped inside.

Claude wasn't sitting at the desk behind the counter,
but the TV was on in the little storeroom where I'd found
Lonnie. Someone had turned the volume up—so loud that
I could hear it blaring, even though the storeroom door
was shut.

There was no point in calling out. The TV was too loud
to talk over. I walked behind the counter and jerked on the
storeroom doorknob.

Claude was sitting inside the storeroom, his back to the

door. A small black-and-white TV was propped on a stool
in front of him. The whole room flickered with the light
from the television, as if it were a green campfire burning
in a box. The back of Claude's white shirt looked green.
Even his red hair looked green. I couldn't see his face from
the doorway.

"Jenkins?" I called to him, over the blare of the TV.

He didn't answer me. I wasn't sure he'd heard me, so I
took a step into the room and froze.

I looked down at the floor. It was too dark to make
anything out clearly, but I'd stepped into something slick
and sticky. The TV flickered dimly. When it went bright
again I saw the light reflect off the floor, running like a lit
fuse from the pool I was standing in over to Jenkins's
chair, where another dark puddle had formed by his feet.

"Jesus," I said softly, knowing already what it was.
Knowing but not believing it.

Then I began to smell it, over the burned-coffee smell,
the stale urinous smell of old cardboard boxes, the ozone
smell of the blazing TV. I covered my mouth with one
hand, and with the other, I pulled the Gold Cup out of its
holster.

Glancing quickly behind me, to make sure I was alone, I
walked over to Jenkins's chair. The front of his white dress
shirt was open, his black pants were unbuckled and unzipped. The rest of him was all red, from neck to thigh. A
sock had been stuffed in his mouth. When I looked down
at his feet, I realized it was his own sock. One of his feet
was naked. It was red, too, from where the blood had
dripped down his legs. The fact that the blood had
stopped dripping registered somewhere in the back of my
mind, although if you'd asked me, at that moment, what it
meant, I wouldn't have been able to tell you. I wouldn't
have been able to make a sentence.

I didn't look at Claude's face for very long. Rigor had
begun to set in and his mouth was beginning to stretch
into a gruesome, yawning smile. It was a particularly horri-

fying sight with that sock still wedged between his teeth. I could see from the rope burns on his wrists that he had been tied to the chair. I turned off the TV, stuck the gun in its holster, and walked back into the office. My shoes left bloody imprints on the linoleum. I sat down behind the wooden desk and stared blankly at the telephone on the desktop.

I'd just picked up the phone—to call the cops—when I saw Lonnie's driver's license sitting on the desk. I stared at the dried blood spots on its frayed plastic surface and felt my heart sink. Putting the phone back down, I picked the license up and slipped it into my coat pocket.

Outside, on the highway, a semi passed by with a rumble that made me jump. Its headlights flashed through the blinded windows, making barred shadows fly up the office walls and across the ceiling.

Unnerved, I got up and walked quickly across the room. I knew I was leaving a trail of bloody shoeprints behind me. But nobody could connect them up with me. Nobody could connect the murder up with Lonnie, either, I thought grimly. Not as long as I had his license in my pocket. Only that wasn't true. Nothing short of a thorough search of the office and storeroom could guarantee that there was no other evidence linking Lonnie to the crime. And I just didn't have the heart to make that search.

I stepped outside and walked across the lot, dragging my shoes through the dirty snow to wash off the blood. I glanced at the motel cottages when I got to the car. They looked as deserted as they had the night before.

Getting in the Pinto, I sped out of the lot.

XI

I stopped at the Frisch's Mainliner in Fairfax and phoned Station X from an icy phone booth outside the restaurant. I told them to check the office storeroom at the Encantada Motel in Miamiville. I didn't tell them what they'd find. After hanging up on the desk sergeant, I dug another quarter from my pants and called the Clarion. It was almost four A.M., but what I'd found at the Encantada wouldn't wait.

Karen answered the phone on the sixth ring. Her voice was shot full of anxiety.

"It's me," I said. "Harry."

"Christ, what time is it?" she said.

"Late. Karen . . ."

I suddenly realized that I didn't know what to say to her. That I didn't know what any of it meant. I only knew that Lonnie was in deep, deep trouble.

"Harry?" Karen said with concern. "What is it? What's wrong?"

"A man's been killed," I said. "The clerk at the motel."

I heard her suck in her breath. "And Lonnie?" she said, still holding her breath.

"I don't know," I said. "I found his license on the clerk's desk."

"Oh, my God," she said with horror. "You're not saying that Lonnie murdered him, are you?"

"I'm saying that I found his license there and took it with me." My voice sounded out of control. I could hear it

myself. I drummed my fingers on the icy glass of the
phone booth and told myself to calm down.

"I don't know if he killed him, Karen," I said after a
time. "Maybe it was meant to look that way. Maybe whoever broke into my apartment planted the license to incriminate Lonnie. I just don't know."

"What the hell has he gotten us into?" Karen said in a
stricken voice.

"I don't know," I said again. "But it's pretty goddamn
awful."

I told Karen I was going home—to get some sleep. She
asked me if I thought that was a good idea. And I didn't
know what to say. If my place *had* been searched for
drugs, if Jenkins *had* been murdered because of the same
drugs, then going back to the Delores probably wasn't safe.
The trouble was that I didn't know if anyplace was safe
anymore. The only person who could tell me that was
Lonnie. And he was either completely out of his mind, or
on the run, or dead too. Carved up like Jenkins had been
and dumped in the river.

One thing was certain. Someone had been very pissed
off at Claude. Unless you were crazy, you didn't make the
kind of example that was made of Jenkins because of a
grudge. You did it to set a mark, to scare other people into
toeing the line, to make sure that mistakes didn't happen
again. Unless you were crazy.

I let Karen talk me into spending what was left of the
night in her hotel room. It was less risky than going home.
And I figured I was going to need some sleep before facing
whatever was in store on Saturday. Besides, part of me
wanted to spend the night with her, even if it was in
separate beds.

It took me another thirty minutes to drive from Fairfax
to the Clarion. I parked in a garage across from the hotel.
Maybe it was paranoia, but I was damn careful about walking over to the Clarion lobby. To be doubly safe, I took the

lobby elevator to the floor above Karen's, then walked down the stairwell to her room.

She'd apparently remained awake after my call, because she answered my knock immediately. She was wearing a terry robe, and she smelled, beneath it, of night sweat and nerves. Her pretty face was leaden with fatigue. Her long brown hair, undone for the night, fell to her shoulders in an uncombed tangle.

"Excuse the way I look," she said nervously.

She ushered me through the door. Her robe parted slightly as she waved me in, and I caught a glimpse of the tops of her breasts, white as snow where a bathing suit had shielded them from the sun. She smiled ruefully when she realized I was staring at her, and closed her robe gently with one hand. "It's a funny time to be thinking about *that*."

I nodded. "*Funny* is not the right word."

I walked over to the far bed and sat down heavily on the mattress.

"You look wrung out," Karen said, sitting down across from me on her bed.

"I am wrung out. This has been a very bad night."

"Poor Harry," she said with genuine sympathy. "You don't deserve this."

I agreed with her.

Karen dropped her eyes to the floor. "What are we going to do?" she said with a hopeless look. "I mean, about Lonnie?"

"We're going to find out what happened to him," I said confidently, although I didn't feel much confidence.

"How?" Karen said.

"He must have some other friends here, in town. Old hippies. Ladies. Dope friends. Somebody. Tomorrow, we'll go looking for them."

"I think I remember a few people," she said. "But they might not be around anymore. It's been fourteen years." She folded her legs, Indian style, and tucked the robe in tightly beneath her. "Maybe we ought to get in touch with some of Lonnie's old friends in St. Louis. He might have made some contact there, before coming here."

"He did have that bus ticket," I agreed. "We'll check it out."

I took off my coat and started to unbutton my shirt, as if I were at home, alone. I stopped and glanced at Karen. She was staring at me. It wasn't exactly an inviting look, but it wasn't uninterested, either.

"I haven't watched a man . . . undress in quite a while," she said, almost as if she were reading my mind. She ran a hand through her hair again. "I guess we need some ground rules."

"Turn your back?" I said. "Hang a blanket between the beds?"

She laughed. "This isn't 1934. And I'm not Claudette Colbert."

"Then what?"

"I used to know how to handle this kind of scene," she said with a touching look of perplexity, "but it's not 1969 anymore."

"What would you have done in '69?"

She smiled at me wickedly. "You don't want to know."

Rolling on her side, she reached up to the lamp and flicked it off. The room went dark.

"That's one solution," I said.

I heard her laugh softly and then I heard the bedclothes rustle as she settled herself in bed.

I finished stripping down in the dark. I pulled the Gold Cup out of its holster and tucked it beneath my pillow. It felt like a little stone under my head. I lay there with my eyes open for a few minutes, then pulled the blankets up over my shoulders.

"Harry, Lonnie didn't kill that clerk," Karen said, in a voice so full of certainty that it startled me as much as if she'd turned the lights back on. "He'd never do something like that. He just isn't that kind of man."

"He may have changed in two years, Karen," I said.

"No," she said firmly. "That's Lonnie's whole problem. He doesn't know how to change."

It was an ironic thing to wish for, but I hoped she was right.

XII

I dreamed of Lonnie—a curiously placid dream at the start, right out of our Lyon Street days. We were painting the apartment. That was the first thing you did back then —paint. Lonnie wanted to paint the walls electric blue. I wanted them white. We split the difference. As we were painting, Karen walked in. In the dream, she looked young and fresh and sexy. She smiled at me and went into Lonnie's room. I was intensely jealous of the fact that she'd chosen to go into Lonnie's room rather than mine. I went over to his door and opened it. Karen and Lonnie were lying on Lonnie's bed. For some reason, I didn't realize they were making love and I kept walking over to the bed. Karen looked up at me from the bed and smiled. When I caught my mistake, I backed out of the room and closed the door behind me. As I was going to my room I heard someone cry out from Lonnie's room. I turned around and went back to the door, but I couldn't open it anymore. It was coated with ice. I tried peeking through the window, but the blinds were closed. Then someone inside Lonnie's room started screaming horribly. I pulled at the door and slammed it with my fist. But it wouldn't budge. Claude Jenkins came up behind me, his shirt red with blood, and told me that it was too late—that they were dead. "That's the price you pay," he said with a terrible grin. And I woke up.

It took me a few seconds to remember where I was. I glanced over at Karen's bed. It was empty—the blanket scattered and the sheets a swirl of white, like drifted snow.

I felt my heart race. For a moment I thought she was dead,
like in the dream. Then I heard the shower going and the
dream faded quickly, leaving me feeling a vague mingling
of want and dread.

I glanced at the clock on the nightstand—it was half
past eight. I thought about catching a couple more hours
of sleep. But the room was hot and it smelled, like the
blankets, of creosote and dust. And I didn't want to have
any more dreams.

As I lay there, letting the sleep clear from my head,
Karen stepped out of the john. She was naked, except for
a towel that she'd wrapped, turban-like, around her head.
She walked over to the bureau and opened a drawer. Then
she glanced up in the bureau mirror and saw me staring at
her. She made a startled face and put one hand over her
breasts and the other over her hips. She stared at me for a
long moment—in the mirror—then slowly dropped her
hands and turned around to face me. She pulled the towel
from her head, shook her wet hair, and gave me a long,
contemplative look. At that moment, I didn't think I'd ever
wanted a woman more.

After a time, Karen started walking slowly toward my
bed. I watched her with pleasure—her breasts, her legs,
her pretty, pouty face. She was a beautiful woman. Without a word, she came up beside me, so close I could smell
the soap she'd used on her skin. I reached out for her
hand. She stared at my hand for a second, curiously, uncertainly. And stared into my face with the same look. She
looked down at herself—at her naked body. Then glanced
at me again. She started to say something—to talk us out
of it, I thought. I didn't give her that chance.

I threw the bedclothes back and grabbed her hand, pulling her down on top of me. She was still wet from the
shower. I could feel that wetness on my flesh. She felt cool
and clean. I ran a hand through her damp hair, and she
nuzzled her face against my chest, tentatively. She looked
up at me suddenly—looked me straight in the eyes—and

her own eyes lost their tentative look and grew hazy, hot and certain. I kissed her passionately. And then we were on each other, and I made love to her with a fierceness that I hadn't felt since I was a kid.

I simply couldn't get enough of her. Or she of me. We did everything we could think of. And a few things you only think of. When we were through, my whole body smelled of her—salty-sweet—and the cool shower drops on her flesh had boiled away and turned to sweat.

We'd literally worn each other out. For a while we just lay there, staring at the ceiling, catching our breath. After a time she rolled on top of me, working her hips gently against mine and smiling at me with her whole face— mouth, eyes.

"That was pretty nice," she said, running a finger along my upper lip.

"It was better than that," I said, smiling back at her.

She pressed into me with her hips.

"Again?" I said, putting my hands on her buttocks and pulling her to me.

She laid her head on my chest. "Tonight," she said. "As much as you want."

"Forgot what you were missing, huh?" I said.

"Oh, I didn't forget," she said softly. "Like I told you, I just don't want to get involved again."

"Then why do this?"

"I can't speak for you," she said with a laugh. "As for me, I'm scared and lonesome and, when it comes down to it, I guess I still am pretty goddamn sixties when it comes to men. Besides, I felt like we knew each other, even though we'd just met."

It was strange, but I'd had the same feeling of connection, of relatedness. The fact that we were more or less of the sixties generation was part of it. But I couldn't help thinking that the fact that we were both connected to Lonnie was a bigger part of it—that it was the guilty burden of Lonnie himself that made us feel as if we'd spent time together.

Thinking about Lonnie stirred my conscience enough to make me blush and duck my head. "You feel bad about . . . this?" I looked down at the rumpled sheets covering our legs.

"A little," she said. She glanced at me furtively. "Do you?"

I nodded. "Technically, you're still his wife. He still needs your help. And mine."

"I'm sick of giving him help," Karen said bitterly.

"We can't just let him go," I said, even though my heart wasn't in it—just my conscience and that old tug of the past.

"I guess we can't," Karen said with a sigh. She glanced up at me. "But what the hell are we going to do?"

That *was* the question, all right.

I climbed out of bed. "I'm going to take a shower. While I'm in there, I want you to think of some names. Some people Lonnie might have run to, if he was desperate."

She nodded. "Then what?"

"Then," I said, staring at her, "I'm going to ask you to do me a favor."

She grinned at me knowingly. "What's that?"

"I want you to go back to St. Louis for a while," I said to her. "Look after your kids."

Her smile faded. "You don't want to be with me again?"

"I don't want you to get hurt," I said gently. "As soon as I've found Lonnie, it'll be different."

Karen eyed me uncertainly. "What makes you say I'll get hurt?"

I sat down on the bed again and put my arm around her shoulder. "If we assume that Lonnie didn't kill Jenkins—"

"He didn't," Karen said with utter certainty.

"Then whoever did, whoever left Lonnie's license at the motel and searched my apartment last night, may think that I'm in it with Lonnie—whatever it is. And they may make the same assumption about you. I don't want to scare you too much, but believe me, if you saw what they did to Jenkins, you'd know why that worries me."

Karen shivered. "What could Lonnie have done to make someone so vicious?"

I'd been thinking about that ever since I'd discovered the systematic wreckage in my apartment. A botched drug deal was the obvious answer. Since Lonnie had only been out of Lexington for a couple of weeks, the drugs couldn't have been his own. Which meant that he'd been acting as a middleman for someone else.

"Has Lonnie ever acted as a mule in a drug deal?" I asked Karen.

Her face reddened. "We both have," she said with embarrassment. "In '73 and '74, when Lonnie was down on his luck, we use to go to New York regularly to cop for a druggist in Forest Park. It was a way to pay the tab for our habits."

"Did he ever screw up when he was carrying?" I asked her.

She shook her head. "It was the one thing he was absolutely reliable about."

"What would have happened if he *had* screwed up?" I asked.

She stared at me for a long moment. "I see where you're heading, Harry. But I don't know how to answer you. Back then, heroin was a communal thing, the way coke is now. All the dopers more or less knew all the other dopers on the block. No one ever tried to take anyone else off." She turned her face away from me. "I don't like talking about this in front of you. I think it makes you hate me. It makes me hate myself."

"It's old business," I said, touching her on the cheek.

She didn't say anything.

I pulled her face around and kissed her on the mouth. She resisted the kiss for a moment, then opened her mouth and kissed me passionately. When we broke off, she smiled at me, as if the kiss had made her feel better.

"Look," Karen said, "I'll go back to St. Louis tomorrow, if you think I should. I'll do anything you want. But first I want one night with you. One whole night. Okay?"

I smiled and said, "Okay."

XIII

When I came back out of the shower, Karen was sitting on the bed, talking on the phone. She waved her hand at me, as if to say that she'd only be another moment. She was partly dressed, in a white cotton blouse and bikini underpants. I got an erection staring at her. She noticed and laughed into the phone.

"No, sweetheart," she said, still smiling at me. "I'm not laughing at you. Mommy's got to go now. Take good care of your sister. And I'll see you tomorrow."

She hung up. "You need a hand?" she said to me.

"If we get started again, we'll never stop."

"Yes," she said, looking a little perplexed. "It's weird, isn't it. Like 1969 again."

"Worrying about Lonnie has made us regress," I said.

"You think?"

"A little. But there's something else going on here." I glanced down at myself and Karen laughed.

"Face it, Harry," she said. "You've got the hots for me."

"Is that all right?"

"I think it's great," she said with a smile.

Karen kept smiling at me as I walked over to my bed. The only clothes I had were the ones I'd worn the night before. I picked up the trousers and stared at the bloody cuffs. Karen's smile died immediately.

"God," she said, "is that blood?"

I nodded. Reaching into my pants pocket, I pulled out Lonnie's bloodstained driver's license. Karen turned her face away.

"Why did they kill that man?" she said in a shaken voice.

"I don't know, for sure," I said. "But if Lonnie *was* acting as a mule, and he got clipped at the Encantada by Claude for the buy money or the drugs themselves, it could explain a lot of things. What we really need to know is, who Lonnie was supposed to be copping for."

"Maybe it was somebody in St. Louis," Karen said.

"Why don't you call some friends," I said. "In the meantime, I'll go down to the lobby and make a few calls of my own."

I slipped the pants on and Karen shuddered. "I'll stop at the apartment later on," I said apologetically. "And get some fresh clothes."

As I put on my shirt Karen said, "I've thought of a few people here in town we could check with, too. Some of Lonnie's old crowd."

"Fine," I said. "We'll get right on it."

I took the same precaution I'd taken early that morning, walking up one flight before I took the elevator down to the lobby. I was probably being paranoid, but until we had a few solid facts I figured my paranoia was excusable.

Karen's room had been heavily curtained. And the daylight pouring through the lobby doors made me wince. The storm had blown over sometime during the morning, and it had turned into one of those cold blue winter days, with a high sky full of blazing, cheerless sun. I bought an *Enquirer* at the hotel newsstand and sat down in a lobby chair to read it. I didn't have to look very hard to find what I wanted—it was all over the front page. CLERK MURDERED IN MOTEL ROBBERY. I skimmed the article, looking for some mention of a possible drug tie-in; but the newspaper was playing up the robbery angle.

I folded up the paper, stuck it under my arm, and walked over to a phone stand opposite the reception desk. The clerk smiled at me pleasantly, although his smile wilted a bit when he took a closer look at my trousers. *That* was going to be a problem. I decided to drive over to the Delores when I was done on the phone. There was no point in taking Karen with me.

I called Al Foster at Central Station and asked him if there'd been any news about Lonnie.

"It just went out an hour ago, Harry," he said irritably. "Give us a chance."

"You must have had a busy night," I said.

"Meaning?"

"Meaning that motel thing," I said with as much casualness as I could muster.

"It was pretty ugly, all right," Al said. "Somebody must have really had it in for that guy."

"The newspapers said it was a robbery."

"That's what we told them," he said.

"What are you telling me?"

"You got a reason to ask?" he said.

"Just plain old curiosity."

"Take it someplace else," Al said, and hung up.

I slipped another quarter in the phone and called George DeVries at the D.A.'s office. Al was a cop with principles; George wasn't. DeVries regarded police work as the choicest flower of the free-market system.

"Can't talk right now, Harry," George said after we'd exchanged hellos. "Got a million things on my desk."

"How'd you like to make it a million, one hundred?" I asked.

"Sounds interesting," he said. "Whad'ya have in mind?"

"The motel murder—tell me about it."

"Don't have much yet, Harry," George said sadly, as if he could see that one hundred dollars flying south for the winter.

"Was it a robbery, like the papers said?"

"There was money missing from the till. But, Christ almighty, nobody carves somebody up like that for a few dollars. We figure it was personal. Revenge, maybe."

"Revenge for what?"

"This guy Jenkins was a two-time loser. Real unsavory character. Statutory rape, indecent exposure, petty larceny. Dope."

"What kind of dope?" I said with interest.

"Small potatoes. Grass. Ludes. Probably a little coke. He was in tight with a bunch of bikers out in Clermont County. We're thinking maybe he screwed one of them, somehow. The way he was taken out—it looks like bikers. Or some other kind of psychopath."

"Thanks, George," I said. "The check will be in the mail."

" 'Preciate it, Harry," he said. "Always good talking to you."

I hung up and stared dully at the chrome facing on the phone box. "Personal" didn't get me very far. Personal could be bikers *or* Lonnie. Or someone else altogether. At least I'd learned a little more about Claude, whose criminal past hadn't surprised me. The man was as venal as they come—I'd known that on Thursday night. It was still possible that his murder had had nothing to do with Lonnie Jack. But I didn't believe that. There was a connection. It was just going to take a lot of dangerous work to piece it together. I hoped that it was worth the effort, that it got me closer to Lonnie, because if it didn't, I knew that I could end up dead too—for "personal" reasons.

XIV

After finishing with George, I located a house phone, sitting on a console beneath a gilded mirror across from the newsstand. I picked it up and rang Karen's room.

"It's me," I said. "Any luck with your friends in St. Louis?"

"Not really," Karen said. "You've got to remember, Harry, that I haven't lived the life in almost ten years. Most of the old crowd knows that."

I sighed. "So nobody's talking?"

"Lonnie was in St. Louis, late last week. Down-and-out. That's about all I've been able to discover."

"I'm surprised that he didn't contact you."

"Well, I'm not," Karen said with a grim laugh. "The last time we talked, right before his trial two years ago, I made it very clear that he and I were history. I think he finally understood that I was serious. It takes a while with Lonnie. He'll just keep sticking his finger in the socket, unless someone turns off the juice."

"How did you turn it off?" I asked.

"At the trial, I told him that if he showed up at my house or tried to see the kids, I'd call the cops again."

"Again?"

"I called the cops on him the last time he was at my house," Karen said without apology. "He'd come over to see the kids—stoned out of his mind, as usual. We got into an argument over his life-style, if that's the right word, and he began raving about how he was going to take the children away with him, so far away that I'd never see them again. Then he started to break things—little things, stuff my mother had given me and I had given the kids. He was completely out of his head. I didn't want to see him get busted—you know how I feel about cops. But I didn't think I had a choice."

"The cops busted him?"

"It didn't come to that, thank God. Lonnie left before they showed up, and I didn't press charges. A couple of weeks later, he got caught for possession in an East St. Louis shooting gallery."

"And that's when they sent him to Lexington?"

She said yes. "I worked hard to get my house, Harry," Karen said with sudden defensiveness, as if I'd accused her of selling Lonnie out. "I worked hard to build a life for me and my children. He had no right—"

"I understand, Karen," I said in a soothing tone of voice. "You did the right thing."

But she didn't sound convinced. "What's the 'right thing' to do with a man like Lonnie?" she said despairingly. "Sometimes I think if I'd had a little more patience with him, if I'd given him one more chance . . . And then I ask myself, 'Who are you kidding? You, of all people!' That day at my house, he claimed he was going to get straight— that he had a big deal cooking with some booking agents that was going to make him healthy again. But when you've heard a thing a hundred times, maybe two hundred times, and it never happens . . . well, it gets old. I told him he was full of shit, and that's what started the argument that ended with my calling the fuzz."

She sighed wearily. "During those last few years, from about '80 on, it seemed as if Lonnie always had a 'big deal' cooking. It was like his bow to the spirit of the age. You know, fuck the sixties. Fuck sharing and peace and love. He was going to become a capitalist, like the rest of the country. Lonnie, a capitalist! Well, as he said, who knew more about the consumer mentality than he did? If he couldn't figure out what would make people buy it all, who could? His whole life had come down to engineering a big score. To a magical fix. Something that would even it all up—all those years of sticking a needle in his arm. He really believed in his own fantasy—that the clouds were going to part one day and a savior was going to descend and carry him off to Fire Lake."

"Fire Lake?" I said.

"It's a private joke," Karen said. "A song Lonnie liked. He thought it summed up his life. Going off to Fire Lake meant taking a gamble, having the guts to tell society to go fuck itself, and daring to live your dream. It was also his buzzword for shooting up. Going off to Fire Lake."

"Maybe this time he got there," I said grimly.

I told Karen that I was going back to the Delores to get some fresh clothes and that I'd pick her up at her room around two-thirty. Then we'd go look up some of Lonnie's old friends.

"I don't want to sound like an alarmist," I said, "but do me a favor and stay in your room until I come back. Okay?"

She laughed nervously. "Okay."

I hung up the phone and walked out of the lobby into the cold, brilliant December afternoon. It was Saturday, which meant the streets were crowded. Since it had been raining for better than three days, they were especially crowded. And that made it next to impossible for me to pick up anyone who was on my tail.

I walked down Fifth, past a couple of black street vendors who had set up stands on the curbside. One of them was selling T-shirts and sunglasses from a folding table. The other was hawking paste jewelry, decals, and knives from a wheeled cart.

"For your lady," the one with the jewelry said, holding out a pair of blue glass earrings.

I shook my head and he shrugged good-naturedly, dropping the earrings back into his cart. He was a middle-aged black with processed hair, a pencil mustache, and a thin, pockmarked face, glazed like marzipan.

I glanced back at the vendors when I reached Plum Street. The one hawking the jewelry was wheeling his cart east on Fifth, toward the square. For a second, I felt like following him. It was paranoia, and I knew it. But just to be sure, I watched him until he'd walked past the Clarion lobby and was well on his way toward Walnut.

When the vendor had drifted out of sight, I walked straight down Plum to the garage where I'd left the car. The pedestrian traffic thinned out as I neared Fourth Street, and by the time I reached the garage, there were only a couple of other people on the sidewalk—a smart-looking woman in a fur coat and a teenage kid in a parka and a Cougars cap. I figured I was safe.

It was twenty degrees colder in the shade of the garage than it had been in the brilliant sunlight. I pulled my top-coat tightly around me and started down an oil-stained ramp to the basement floor. There was a chilled-looking attendant, bundled in sweaters and coats, sitting in a booth beside the ramp. He had a tiny TV set up on the counter in front of him and a glowing space heater hung on the wall behind; but he still didn't look at home. I waved at him, as I started down the ramp. He nodded in an un-friendly way, as if he didn't like being disturbed; but I'd just wanted him to notice me.

The Pinto was still covered with ice on the hood and back windows. I should have cleaned them off, but all I wanted to do was get inside the car and get out of the garage. Claude Jenkins's murder had unnerved me a lot more than I'd let on to Karen. Drug dealers scared me. It wasn't 1970 anymore, when every doper had known every other doper on the block, like Karen had said. Drugs were a multibillion-dollar business—the biggest business in the country. And although every business had its rules, this one was less predictable than most. There were always strange little eddies, little pockets of weirdness, in the mainstream. Even in my sedate town, people ended up nastily dead because of smack or coke or both. It happened every day. I just didn't run into it every day, like I had with Claude.

After a couple of misfires, I managed to start up the Pinto and nurse it, coughing and sputtering, up the exit ramp, past the surly attendant, and out onto Third Street. Once inside the car and on the move, I felt safe again.

I felt fine all the way out Gilbert to Reading. But when I got to the shadows of the McMillan overpass—about a block from the Delores—I started to get antsy again. I pulled into the Delores's parking lot and stared nervously at the tall red-brick walls of the apartment house.

"For chrissake," I said to myself. "It's your home."

I was acting like a wimp and I knew it. Slapping myself on the thigh, I got out of the car and walked quickly up the stairs. The courtyard was still frozen in ice. Rivulets of it ran from the eaves down the sides of the building, like glass ivy. I knocked an icicle off a dogwood branch and walked briskly into the lobby. I went up the stairs and down the hallway to my apartment.

No problem, I told myself. No problem at all.

I'd just put my keys in the lock when someone opened my apartment door and said, "Come on in."

XV

No problem at all, I said acidly, and stared through the half-open door.

There was a young black man, no more than twenty years old, sitting on the easy chair and smiling at me with every tooth in his mouth. My first impulse was to reach for my gun in its holster. But the door was angled in front of me, and I couldn't see all the way into the room. Whoever had opened the door was still standing behind it, in the kitchen. And for all I knew there were several others in the bedroom. Under the circumstances, pulling my gun was likely to get me killed.

I glanced quickly down the hall, toward the landing. Another black man—tall and heavyset—had come down the stairs from the floor above me and stationed himself at the end of the hall. He had one hand buried in his long-skirted overcoat. It looked like he was concealing a sawed-off shotgun under the coat.

This is crazy, I said to myself. But that didn't make the man with the shotgun disappear.

"Ain'chu gonna come in, homes?" the black kid sitting in the easy chair called out again, in a scatty, high-pitched voice.

"Do I have a choice?" I said to him.

He grinned. "We all got choices, bro'."

I pushed the door fully open and walked into the room. Another black man stepped out from the kitchen. He was a huge kid, with a drooping lip and a nose like a wad of bubblegum stuck under a desk. He was wearing a stocking

cap on his bullet head and a stained cord sweater that
hung in tiers, like layers of fat, above greasy, pinstripe
gaberdine pants.

I looked at the one sitting on the pieced-together easy
chair. He was small, thin, and brindled brown. He was
wearing a camel's-hair overcoat and a white plantation hat,
crooked rakishly above his forehead. I couldn't see all of
his face, because of the hat and because of the wrap-
around sunglasses he had on his nose. He wore his hair in
oiled ringlets, with a milk mustache and a cute little spit
curl right in the center of his forehead—like Prince. He
even spoke with a touch of a lisp, just like Prince. He had
big yellow teeth and red, receding gums that made his
smile a lot less sexy than he thought. It wasn't until I got
close to him that I realized there was a gold Star of David,
with a little diamond in its center, embossed on one of his
incisors. The kid stank of sweat and of something else—
something like decay.

"Where's your partner, huh?" he said in his cheerful,
lisping voice. "Where you got him stashed?"

"I don't know what you're talking about," I said.

"Chill, man," he said merrily. "That's cool. We don't
care about him. We just want our goods back, dig?"

"What goods?" I said.

The kid rattled with laughter, like a shaken gourd.
"Hear what the dude say, Maurice?" he said to his Fat
Albert friend.

"Bet," Maurice grunted.

Maurice stared at me in what I assumed was supposed
to be a menacing way. I knew I was in trouble, but I had a
problem dealing with this eighties version of Cosby's kids.
They just didn't look old enough or tough enough to be as
dangerous as they pretended to be. Prince and Fat Albert.

"We want the lady back, jack," the kid in the chair said,
and then smiled again, as if he'd been amused by his own
rhyme.

"Cocaine?" I said.

"Bet," the kid said lazily. "Your partner be fucking with the man. Don't nobody fuck the man."

"My partner?" I said, starting to understand. "You mean Lonnie?"

"Who the fuck you think we're talking 'bout, homes?" the kid said drily.

"Look," I said, "I don't know where Lonnie is and I don't know anything about cocaine. You've already searched the apartment, so you know it's not here."

"Yeah, but we ain't searched you, yet, bro'," the kid said with a grin. He glanced at Maurice, who took a step toward me.

All of a sudden it didn't seem like a Saturday morning serial anymore. I reached inside my coat for the Gold Cup. But before I could pull it out, I felt someone press something cold and hard against the back of my head. It was the guy from the stairway. The guy with the shotgun. I left the automatic in its holster and pulled my hand out of my coat slowly, raising it, palm-up, to show them that I was clean.

The kid tut-tutted me with his lips and waved a warning finger. "Don't be uncool," he said. He snapped up out of the chair, as if he was hinged at his middle like a knife. Reaching into his pocket, he pulled out an ivory-handled razor.

Sweet Christ, I said to myself.

"You gonna do some cuttin', Bo?" Maurice said, with a booming laugh that made him cough. The man with the shotgun laughed too. Maurice cleared his throat and spat phlegm on the floor.

I thought of the sock in Claude Jenkins's smiling face.

Bo took off his sunglasses and came right up to me, moving his head in jerky little turns, like a parrot, as he stared furiously into my face. He had a mad, drugged-out look in his bloodshot eyes. He kept hefting the razor in his hand, as if it were a bag of shot.

"Yeah," he said, still staring at me. "I might do me some

cuttin'." He glanced at Maurice. "Take him on back to the shitter. We'll do him in the tub."

"Gonna clean up his act," Maurice said with another booming laugh.

Maurice pulled a bandanna out of his back pocket, twirled it around to make a gag, and started toward me, snapping the handkerchief between his hands. Bo backed away to give Maurice room. I knew that as soon as Maurice gagged and tied me, it was all over. It was probably all over anyway. But I'd be damned if I was going to end up like Claude Jenkins, with my own flesh hanging around my waist like a tattered shirt.

I didn't really have time to think about it. The shotgun was propped against the back of my skull, like the headrest of a barber's chair. If the guy behind me pulled the trigger, I'd lose my head. But, at that moment, it seemed like a better way to go than watching myself being cut to ribbons by a coked-out kid.

I let out a scream—as loud as I've ever screamed in my life. At the same time, I dropped into a crouch and threw myself backward into the man with the shotgun, driving him through the open apartment door into the hall and slamming him against the corridor wall. The shotgun went off above my head, deafening me with its enormous blast and tearing a gaping hole in the hall ceiling.

The guy with the shotgun and I danced against the wall for a split second, then our feet got tangled and he fell backward to the floor. I fell backward, too, landing on top of him.

He groaned and shouted, "Get off me, motherfucker!" I could feel him trying to work the shotgun loose underneath me.

Pinning the guy with my body and jabbing him with my left elbow, I clawed for my pistol with my right hand. By then, doors had begun to open up and down the hall.

In a flash, Bo and Maurice came barreling out into the hall. Grabbing the front of my shirt in one huge hand,

Maurice pulled me off his partner and tossed me against the opposite wall. The Gold Cup skittered out of my grasp. Bo kicked it down the hall and swung his right arm at me. I could see the razor blade glittering in his palm. I threw my right arm up to block him. Our wrists hit hard, and the razor went flying out of his hand. It stuck in the plaster wall with a twang, like a thrown knife. Giving me a ferocious look, Bo kicked me in the leg with his pointed boots. I groaned and he kicked me again.

"C'mon, Bo," Maurice said with a wild look, and started running up the hall. The guy with the shotgun had already disappeared.

I could hear police sirens in the distance.

Bo pointed a finger at me and shrieked, "You mine, motherfucker! You all mine!"

Glancing up the hall at where Maurice was already bobbing down the stairwell, he took off like a bird dog. His hat flew off his head, skittering around on the tiled landing and finally rolling to a stop against the stair post.

I stared down the hall at his hat. A large chunk of plaster fell from the ceiling with a thump, landing just beyond my outstretched legs and covering me with dust. It was a good thing it had missed me, because I didn't think I could have moved if a truck had been bearing down on me. I'd used up every bit of energy in my body. I sat there, pouring sweat, my chest heaving, my lungs on fire, the plaster dust swirling around me like a mist. One of my neighbors opened his door and stepped out into the hall.

"You asshole," he said, staring at me. "Either you're going to move or we are. I'm sick of this shit."

I laughed dully. He went back in his apartment, slamming the door behind him. The sound echoed down the hall. I stared at the gaping hole the shotgun had made in the ceiling, at my gun lying halfway down the hallway, at the razor pinned in the wall above my head. Outside, the police sirens had become very loud.

Lonnie, I said to myself, fuck you.

XVI

My first impulse was to tell the cops everything I knew. I was that frightened and that furious. But as my pulse slowed down and my temper cooled, I started thinking clearly enough to realize that telling them everything meant telling them about the Encantada and Claude Jenkins. It meant explaining why I hadn't reported the murder on Friday night. It meant dragging Karen into it. And it meant putting Lonnie back in jail—this time, probably, for good.

Not that I felt that Lonnie didn't belong in jail. He did. He was too fucking stupid to be running around on his own. And apparently he was still doing just that. At least according to Bo, he was. If Lonnie's idea of a "big score"— of going off to Fire Lake—was to deal cocaine with folks like Bo, Maurice, and the guy with the shotgun and then to leave me and his wife holding the bag, he deserved to be betrayed to the cops.

But I didn't do that. I couldn't do it. Instead I ended up making excuses for him, like 1968 all over again. I told myself he must have been at the end of his rope. He had to be at the end of his rope to grab at the cocaine deal to begin with. I told myself that he couldn't have known that in signing my name on that motel register, he was signing me up for a visit from Bo and the boys. I told myself that, in spite of everything, in spite of what had gone on between Karen and me, he was still a friend—a friend who had turned to me when he'd had nowhere else to go. And you don't betray your friends.

So when the cops finally came piling up the Delores's stairs—six of them in close order, their faces cocked like their guns—I made out that I had been assaulted by three strangers, when I'd walked in on an attempted burglary of my apartment. I figured that the fact the three felons had been blacks would be enough incentive to keep the beat cops from asking too many embarrassing questions about the way my apartment had been torn up. But the cops weren't nearly as stupid or as racist as I'd expected them to be. And then I hadn't counted on what Bo or one of his friends had left behind him on the living room floor.

A little tube of crack had fallen out of somebody's pocket and landed in front of my rolltop desk. Just a few rocks, but enough to catch one cop's attention. I saw it, too, a second after he did. But by then it was too late. The beat cop immediately called in two investigators from narcotics. The narcs listened to my explanation of what had happened and took down my descriptions of Bo, Maurice, and the guy with the shotgun. Then they took a look at the tube of crack and at the way the stuffed furniture had been ripped open, and spent an hour trying to get me to admit that *I* had been involved in a drug deal that had gone awry.

About half past three, I realized the narcs weren't going to go away. Like Bo, Maurice, and the guy with the shotgun, they wanted the lady and they wanted me. In covering up for Lonnie, I'd put myself back on the spot. I didn't know how long the narcs were going to keep badgering me. They did have the tube of crack as evidence. But they didn't have my fingerprints on it. And given the circumstances, my story—that one of the burglars had dropped the tube during the fight—was as good as any. Good enough to stand up in court. But I couldn't help thinking it was a very lucky thing that the narcs didn't know about my bloody footprints in the Encantada office, or about my name on the motel register. If they ever made those connections, I was going straight to jail.

My clothes had been pretty well powdered over with plaster dust, after the scuffle in the hall. And that turned out to be a break. The dust prevented the cops from noticing the bloodstains on my pants cuffs. It also gave me an excuse to wash up and change my clothes. While I was in the bedroom, I phoned Karen at the hotel and told her, as delicately as I could, that there had been some trouble at my apartment.

"Are you all right?" she said anxiously.

"Yes," I said. "But I think maybe you'd better come over here."

"Why?" she said.

I didn't tell her the truth—that I was afraid to leave her alone in that hotel, with Bo and his friends still on the loose. Instead, I said, "I need you."

"I'll be right there," she said immediately.

"Karen," I said. "Don't make any side trips, okay? Just go down to the lobby, have the doorman hail a cab, and come straight here." I gave her the address on Burnett.

As soon as I got off the phone and came back in the living room, the narcs started in on me again. They were playing the old Ike-and-Mike game—the vicious cop and the pally one. If I hadn't just been shot at and threatened with emasculation with a razor, I might have been impressed. As it was, I was only irritated. And the longer they kept it up, the angrier and more short-tempered I became. I'd had enough excitement for one afternoon. I figured the narcs should have known that.

They *were* good at their act, especially the butch cop—a muscular, middle-aged sergeant named Jordan. Jordan had a walrus mustache, straight brown hair that looked as if it had been trimmed with a hatchet, acne-scarred cheeks, and the droopy, pitiless eyes of a predator. He didn't know I'd been a cop myself once, because I hadn't played that card yet—I was saving it for the station house, if it came to that. But I'd heard a story about Jordan once when I was working for the D.A.'s office.

He had been a vice cop before he went to narcotics. And in this town, vice meant rousting whores and homosexuals. The whores could usually buy themselves out of a bust with a blow-job. But the fags were out of luck. Inevitably, they got kicked around—sometimes pretty badly kicked around. Jordan, especially, had a reputation as a fag-hater. The story I'd heard was about a drag queen whom Jordan had busted in a club by the river. Instead of taking him to the station house, Jordan took the queer down beneath the Suspension Bridge. Jordan beat the guy up pretty badly. Then he drew his pistol and threatened to kill him if the queen didn't jump in the river and start swimming. It was Jordan's idea of a joke that the guy should swim over to Kentucky and never show his face back in Cincinnati. Jordan actually fired a couple of shots at the poor bastard to get him moving. The fag was so frightened that he jumped in the Ohio and started to swim.

It would have been a typical rogue-cop story if the fag hadn't drowned. But he did. His body washed up on a bridge pylon downriver a couple of days later. Jordan's partner covered for him. And the death was ruled a suicide. A few months after that, Jordan was transferred to narcotics.

I hadn't heard any other stories about him. But getting transferred obviously hadn't changed his personality. From the moment he stepped in the door, he started baiting me.

There was nothing subtle about his tactics. Jordan thought I was a drug dealer and he told me so. He called me a lot of other names too. His technique was so crude that it would have been laughable, if I'd been in the mood to laugh. But I wasn't in the mood. And after an hour or so of being pushed around by that tough bastard with the dead eyes, I lost my cool completely. I started shouting back at him, while his partner stood by with a weary, witless smile on his face. The partner, a cop named Lewis, was about ten years older than Jordan and a lot less energetic about the interrogation. He gave up playing his nellie part about halfway through the hour and just stood there and watched as Jordan and I went at it.

Jordan and I kept yelling and jockeying with each other, until we were very close to throwing punches. Even Lewis sensed it. He moved a little closer to where we were standing and kept his hand close to the gun in his belt.

"I'm taking you downtown, cocksucker," Jordan finally shouted, and jabbed his right fist into my chest. "You're connected and I know it." He jabbed me again, hard.

"Connected to what, asshole?" I said, slapping his hand away—hard. "I've given you a description of three drugged-out scumbags. Why don't you go after them, for chrissake? They can't be that hard to find."

"And get the niggers off your back, huh, Harry?" Jordan said. "Why should we do you any favors?"

At that moment, Karen walked in.

Jordan gave her a withering look. "Who's your cunt friend, Harry? Another junkie?"

Karen blanched.

I stared at Jordan for a long moment. I wanted to throw that punch at him. He wanted me to try.

"Read me my rights or get the hell out of here," I said through my teeth.

"What's *your* name, lady?" Jordan said, turning to Karen.

"Her name is none of your business," I said, stepping between her and him.

"I think she's holding," Jordan said to his partner. "Don't you, Carl?"

Lewis looked unimpressed. Jordan turned back to me with a vicious smile.

"I think we're going to have to take her downtown for a strip search, Stoner." He turned to Karen and grinned. "Unless you'd prefer I do it here, honey."

"Son of a bitch!" I said, and threw that punch.

It was a stupid, stupid thing to do. Stupid for me; stupid for Karen. I knew it while I was doing it. But I just didn't have it in me to pull the punch.

Jordan was facing Karen when I let go, so he didn't have a chance to do anything more than turn his head into my fist. And the whole thing happened too quickly for his partner to get in between us. I put my whole body behind a straight right hand and hit Jordan squarely on the chin. He went down in his tracks, like he'd been standing under a piano. Karen let out a little yip, as if I'd stepped on her toes, and jumped back toward the door.

Lewis, the older cop, jerked out his pistol and stuck the barrel in my nose. "That was *really* stupid, buck-o," he said in a level voice. He glanced down at Jordan, who was sitting on his butt. "You okay, Glen?"

Jordan didn't answer for a while. After a time, he nodded weakly and looked up at me. His eyes hadn't cleared, but they were already filling up with hatred. "You're going to regret that," he said, rubbing his chin. He held out his hand to Lewis and said, "Help me up."

Lewis pulled the gun out of my face and lifted Jordan to his feet. Jordan was still shaken by the punch, but he didn't want me to see it. "Cuff him," he said to Lewis. "I'm going to clean up in the john."

He walked unsteadily down the hall to the bathroom, went inside, and slammed the door behind him.

"You got a good lawyer, buck-o?" Lewis said, pulling the cuffs from his belt. "Or a relative on the force?" He holstered the pistol and cuffed my right wrist.

"I used to work for the D.A.'s office," I said to him.

"You were a cop?"

I nodded.

"You might have said something earlier," he said, glancing down the hall. "It would have saved us all a lot of trouble. I'm never going to hear the end of this." He pulled my left arm behind me and cuffed my hands behind my back. "He's going to try to kill you when he comes to. You know that, don't you?"

I nodded again.

"Even if you can get bail tonight, you're going to take a beating."

"I know that," I said. "What would you have done?"

Lewis laughed grimly and said, "One thing I wouldn't have done is mess with Jordan."

"About the girl . . ." I said, glancing at Karen, who had been taking all of it in with a horrified look on her face.

"She's free to go," Lewis said.

I turned to Karen. "Go home," I said to her. "Go back to St. Louis. Tonight."

She stared at me as if I were out of my mind. "And leave you to these bastards?" she said, staring right at Lewis. The old cop ducked his head.

"Karen," I said softly, "whether you stay or not isn't going to make any difference where they're concerned."

"How about where you're concerned?" she said angrily.

"I can't look after you from jail," I said.

"I can look after myself."

"You don't know what's going on here," I said helplessly. I wanted to pull her aside and explain it to her—about Bo and his pals and the cocaine. But there was no way to do it without letting Lewis in on it too.

I heard the john flush. "Please," I said again. "Go home."

Karen shook her head. "I don't understand this, Harry. Any of it."

Jordan stepped out of the john into the hall. He walked up to us and said to Lewis, "You take him in. I've got a couple of things to take care of." He didn't even glance at me—just walked out the door.

"C'mon, Stoner," Lewis said, jerking me by the handcuffs. "Let's get this over with."

He led me out of the apartment and down the hall. I

glanced back at Karen. She was standing in the doorway, staring after me with a stunned look on her face.

"Go home, for chrissake!" I shouted back over my shoulder. Lewis jerked the cuffs again and we started down the stairs.

XVII

Before they locked me up in the Central Station holding tank, I got to make my one call on the pay phone. I called Laurel Gould, my lawyer, and told her I was in trouble.

"What are the charges?" she asked.

"I'm not sure yet," I said. "But they may throw the book at me. Possession of cocaine. Possession for sale. Assaulting a cop."

There was a dead silence on the line. "You assaulted a police officer?" Laurel said, as if I'd told her I'd boarded a flying saucer.

"I lost my temper."

"You've lost your mind," she said sharply. "Assaulting a cop can be a nasty charge, my friend. And possession for sale is no day in the country. Where are you going to get the money to raise bail for all this?"

"From pushing drugs," I said acidly. "Just get me out of here, Laurel. I mean it. This cop I punched . . . he's very bad news."

"It's that way?" she said with concern.

"Very likely," I told her.

"I'll be down there in ten minutes," she said. "With a photographer."

"Good," I said, and hung up.

As they were closing the cell doors on me, I called Lewis over to the bars.

"Do me a favor and tell Lieutenant Al Foster that I'm down here?" I said hopefully.

Lewis walked away without saying anything.

After he'd gone, I wandered back to the rear of the tank. There were a couple of cellblocks inside the tank, rows of six-foot by three-foot walk-ins, sided with bars on three sides and stone on the fourth, like animal cages in the zoo. I walked into one of the open cells and sat down on the steel bench suspended from the wall. To the right there was a tiny porcelain toilet smelling of urine and Pine-Sol, with a roll of oatmeal-colored paper tissue sitting beside it. I reached down and picked up the tissue. Tearing off a dozen sheets, I wadded them up and formed them into a mouthpiece. It wasn't much protection—a toilet-paper mouthpiece. But it was better than nothing at all.

I sat there for a few minutes, staring at the graffiti on the wall: naked women with huge breasts and ash marks, where cigarettes had been stubbed out, for vaginas; a dagger with the slogan "Born to lose" bannered above it; a motorcycle wheel pouring smoke; a skull. A couple of the other inmates walked past the cell and tried to bum cigarettes from me. I didn't even have to ignore them. My mind, my whole being, was centered on one thing. It wasn't long in coming.

About five minutes after Lewis had booked me, I heard the jailer call out my name. I fitted the toilet-paper mouthpiece around my teeth, stepped out of the cell, and walked slowly up to the holding-tank bars. Just a little piece of me was hoping that it was Laurel and her photographer. The rest knew better. And the rest was right.

I could see Jordan plainly as I rounded the cellblock. He smiled at me as I walked toward him, crooking a finger and making a come-hither gesture. The jailer opened the barred doors and I walked out. A desk sergeant came out of the jailer's cage and cuffed my hands behind me, while Jordan looked on.

"We've got some unfinished business, Harry," Jordan said, giving me his graveyard stare.

I didn't say anything. I didn't want him to see the mouthpiece I'd fashioned from the tissue.

Jordan grabbed my arm and pulled me toward an elevator. I looked around to see if his partner was coming with us. But Lewis wasn't there, and the desk sergeant had already returned to his cage. It was just Jordan and I. Just the way he wanted it.

He took me down to the sub-basement. There were a couple of unused cells down there—dark, empty holes lit by hanging lamps and full of old, dusty office furniture. Jordan pushed me into a cell that was filled with ancient wooden chairs. He pulled one of the chairs from a pile and plunked it down in the middle of the room.

"Sit down," he said casually.

I sat on the chair and watched Jordan as he took off his coat and rolled up his sleeves. "You shouldn't have sucker-punched me, Harry," he said, turning to me with a pleasant smile on his mouth. There was a half-dollar-size bruise on his chin where I'd clipped him. The rest of his face was as dead as his eyes.

Jordan stared at me for a long moment, then reached behind him and pulled a four-ounce leaded sap from his back pocket. He slapped it against his palm. It made a full, rich sound in his hand, as if he'd slapped a loaf of fresh dough.

"I'm going to give you a good beating, Harry," he said. "Then we're going to talk about the crack. Okay?"

He looked at me as if he expected me to agree with him.

Jordan started toward me, waving the sap in his fist. As soon as he got close, I kicked at him. But Jordan was prepared for me this time. He juked to his right and brought the sap down hard against my upraised leg. It caught me on the left shin.

The pain was excruciating. I doubled over on the chair; and he brought the sap down even harder—on my spine. I snapped upright, throwing myself backward with so much force that I cracked the back of the chair and went sprawling onto the floor—my legs still crooked over the broken chair seat.

"Get up!" Jordan roared, yanking me to my feet by my shirtfront and throwing me against the bars of the cell.

I kicked at him again, with my right leg, missing badly. He countered by driving the sap deep into my belly. I doubled over again and sank to my knees with a groan. My face turned red and sweat poured out of me. I could feel it running down my cheeks, down my arms, as if I'd been doused with water.

Jordan stood over me for a moment, breathing hard.

"Tell me how you're connected, Harry," he said. "Save yourself some pain."

I looked up at him from where I was kneeling. The pain in my gut was intense. But I could feel the indignity just as intensely. My face started to burn with shame. The toilet tissue had turned to mush in my mouth. I spit some of it out on the floor, started choking on some more of it, and then vomited up the rest.

"You better kill me, fucker," I said between heaves.

For the first time, Jordan smiled at me with genuine amusement. It lit up his whole face, even his dead eyes. "I think I can manage that," he said.

He raised the sap over his head and slammed it across my right arm at the shoulder. I shrieked and Jordan barked with laughter. My right arm went numb, all the way to the fingertips.

"Did that hurt?" he said, pressing the sap against the bruise.

I shrieked again and writhed against the bars behind me.

He slapped me with the sap a few more times—little stinging snaps on my chest and thighs. He wasn't using all his strength, like he had on my shin, my back, my shoulder, and my gut. But the blows still hurt. And after a half dozen or so of them, the pain began to accumulate.

I started dreading the next slap, flinching before he hit

me, as if I were being whipped. I knew he was setting me up for another big one. And I told myself to save my strength for what was ahead. But each time he flicked that piece of lead against me, I lost a little more willpower and cowered a little more openly against the bars.

"Enough fooling around," Jordan said, when he'd gotten me good and scared. "This time, we go for the head." He dangled the sap in my face. "Give you a walleye and a drool for the rest of your life." He lifted the sap above his head, and I felt something inside me just give out.

"Don't!" I screamed.

"What was that?" Jordan said, pressing his face close to mine.

"Don't!" I said, begging him. "Please, Christ, don't!"

"That's a little better," he said, backing away with a satisfied look. He slapped the sap against the bars of the cell. They rang like a bell and I cringed. "You going to tell me about your connection now, Harry?"

I nodded weakly.

"I can't hear you," Jordan said.

"Yes!" I shouted. Yes, yes.

"All right," Jordan said with satisfaction. He smiled at me, almost paternally. "No hard feelings, Harry. That's the way it's done. You remember, don't you?"

He lifted me up to my feet and brushed some of the dust from my jacket. I could barely stand on my ankle; my back hurt up and down the spine; my right arm was useless; and the pain in my gut was like a knife wound.

"You think you can make it upstairs, tough guy?" Jordan said.

I leaned against the bars, unable to speak, barely able to stand.

"Just remember, Harry," Jordan said, poking me gently with the sap. "If I don't hear what I want to hear when we get up to the interrogation room, we're coming right back down here. We haven't even begun to party yet."

XVIII

Jordan left me in the holding tank while he arranged for an interrogation room and a stenographer. I barely made it into one of the little cells. I collapsed on the steel cot and lay there for what seemed like an hour, smelling the stink of my own fear and humiliation. I'd been unmanned before. In the war and afterward. It had happened. But even though I'd come close in the past, it had never actually happened at the hands of a cop, in the basement of a police station. The pain would go away. I knew that. I could live with the pain. What I couldn't live with was the way the pain had made me behave.

I wanted to kill Jordan for what he'd done to me. I wanted to kill him more than I'd ever wanted anything else in my life. And then I wanted to kill Lonnie. For the shame he'd brought down on my head, for the shit I'd had to eat to protect him. I'd had to grovel in front of an enemy. I'd almost been killed earlier that day by another enemy. And on both occasions, *I was the wrong goddamn man!* The injustice of it plagued me almost as much as the beating I'd taken.

Jordan hadn't been wrong. I was *connected,* all right—to an absurd, dangerous idea, to a fellowship out of the sixties that had been ambiguous to begin with and was now turning lethal. What killed me was that I'd brought part of it on myself. I hadn't just been victimized by Lonnie. I'd been victimized by my own need for . . . what? For something better than what I had now, I guessed, for what

Karen and I had briefly shared. For that feeling of connection itself.

I tried not to think about Karen. I just hoped she'd taken a plane back to St. Louis. There was nothing I could do for her from jail.

I sat in the cell for a long time. It was an even longer time before it dawned on me that Jordan hadn't come back. I'd been more than ready to talk in that deserted sub-basement. I'd been almost eager to betray Lonnie when I'd first been brought back up to the holding tank. But as the minutes went by, my resolve faded in and out. I started telling myself things—stupid things, like, "I'll be goddamned if I let that son of a bitch break *me* down." I'd say it, then I'd start feeling the pain in my ankle or in my back. And that would cool me off.

I really didn't know what I was actually going to do or say, right up until the moment when the jailer called my name again. Even though my shin was swollen like a balloon, I got to my feet and hobbled up to the bars. To my surprise, Laurel Gould was standing there, with Al Foster standing behind her. Jordan was nowhere to be seen.

Laurel looked as if she'd had a very long day. Always immaculately dressed in a business suit and white silk blouse, she was as raw and wrinkled as I'd ever seen her. Her pretty, careworn face turned purple with rage when she spotted me. I was a gruesome sight—hobbling on one leg, my back bent, my shoulder hunched, dried vomit all over my shirtfront. Laurel turned to Foster with a snarl and said, "You bastards!"

"Easy, Laurel," Al said. "Remember our agreement."

"That was before I'd seen what you did to him," she shouted.

"*I* didn't do anything to him," Al snapped. He gave me a concerned look. "Are you all right?"

I laughed. "How do I look to you, Al? All right?"

Foster's long, solemn face went blank. He'd seen what

Jordan had done, but he *hadn't* seen it. He couldn't afford to look too closely.

"I need to talk to you, Harry," he said. He gave the jailer a quick, angry look and said, "Let him out, for chrissake!"

The jailer opened the door and I hobbled into the anteroom.

Al looked down at the floor—to keep from looking at me. "All charges against you are being dropped," he said. "In return, you're going to agree not to press charges against Jordan."

"Who says that, Al?" I said through my teeth.

"Your lawyer and I came to an agreement."

I glanced at Laurel. She sighed and nodded.

"So we all forgive and forget, is that it?" I said to Al.

He didn't say anything.

"Where's Jordan?" I said.

Al shook his head. "Just let it alone, Harry."

"Sure, Al." I brushed past him, took Laurel by the arm, and walked out of the station house.

Outside it was fully night—cold, blue-black, filled with wintry stars. After several hours in the overheated jail, I felt the icy air like cold rain on my face. I shivered beneath my topcoat and wrenched my back.

"He did all he could for you, Harry," Laurel said, coming up beside me.

"Foster?"

She nodded. "There was really nothing I could have done without his help. Jordan had listed you as being transferred to the Justice Center. I didn't know you were actually still here, until Al stepped in." She smiled wearily. "I tried to find you, though. Believe me, I tried."

"I believe you, Laurel."

"You better go to the hospital, don't you think?"

I nodded. "I guess I should."

"I'll take you," she said. "My car is right across the street."

We walked over to her BMW. It was parked beneath a

fluted black gaslight. There was a police cruiser parked in front of the BMW. I glanced into the cruiser as we passed it, half expecting to see Jordan inside. But the cruiser was deserted.

Laurel gave me an anxious look. "Al was right, Harry," she said nervously. "You've got to put this behind you. You're never going to be able to touch Jordan, legally. And if you lose your temper . . . nobody's going to be able to get you out a second time."

"Let me worry about that," I said sharply.

"You don't know all of it," she said. "Al really had to push to get you out at all. Jordan is trying to connect you to a murder in Miamiville."

I shivered again and winced. "How?" I said uneasily.

"Apparently your name was found on the register at a motel where a murder was committed. Jordan is trying to make a case that the murder was done over drugs. I'm not supposed to know this, but apparently they found some crack on the scene. The same batch that they found in your apartment."

"Jesus," I said.

"Al and I know you're not involved in this. But Jordan isn't convinced. As far as he's concerned, you're still the main suspect in the murder." Laurel shook her head ruefully. "You shouldn't have punched him, Harry."

"I should have killed him," I said grimly.

It took me a full minute to get into Laurel's car. As I settled down gingerly on the seat, I said, "Do you mind making one stop before we go to the hospital?"

She shrugged. "It's your body."

"Let's stop at the Clarion, then. I want to check on a friend."

She started the car up, drove onto Central and circled back to Plum. We followed Plum down to Fifth. Even though it was Saturday night, the streets were deserted. The cold had kept everyone inside.

Laurel parked in front of the Clarion. I worked my way

out of the car and into the lobby. Several couples in evening clothes stared after me with horror. I pulled my topcoat tightly over my grimy shirt and went up to the front desk.

The night clerk eyed me with distaste, as if I were a dog running loose in the lobby.

"I want to know if someone checked out," I said.

"Who?" he said disdainfully, as if he could scarcely credit the idea that someone who looked like me could have a friend who stayed at his hotel.

"Her name is Karen Jackowski." I gave him Karen's room number.

He flipped through an index on his desk and said, "She checked out at five forty-five this afternoon."

He glared at me as if I were the reason why.

Feeling relieved, I hobbled back out to the car. Karen had shown good sense, after all. I figured she wouldn't have checked out unless she was leaving town. If she'd caught an evening flight, she was already back in St. Louis, with her kids. And that was where I wanted her to be—out of harm's way. Because, like it or not, I knew I was still going to have to deal with Bo and his friends. They weren't just going to forget about me or Lonnie or the cocaine. They'd keep coming back, until they got what they wanted or until Lonnie and I were dead. So would Jordan. He was like a pit bull. Once he got his teeth in, he'd never let go. I was going to have to run Lonnie down before Bo or the cops got to him. I was going to have to find out what had really happened to the cocaine. Then, somehow, I was going to have to make things right with Bo's boss, even if I had to feed Lonnie to him in the bargain. Jordan was a different question. He'd have to be dealt with too. I didn't know exactly how, although I knew what I wanted to do to him.

One thing was certain, I was tired of being taken for someone else. And I was deadly tired of being a friend to Lonnie Jack.

XIX

Laurel drove me to University Hospital on Goodman Street. She wanted to stay with me in the examination room, but it was a busy night at the hospital and I knew I was in for a long wait. I told her to go home.

"Is there anything you want to tell me?" she said, giving me her lawyer's clear-eyed look.

I thought about it for a moment. "Not now."

"You're sure?"

I said that I was sure.

She patted me on the shoulder and stood up. "I'll call you tomorrow, in case you change your mind."

She walked out of the examination room, leaving me alone.

It took me over three hours to get X-rayed and examined. Either I'd been lucky or Jordan had been more skillful than I'd thought, because nothing was broken. The intern wrapped my ankle in an Ace bandage, drained the bruise on my shoulder, gave me a steroid shot for my backache, and a bottle of muscle relaxants and painkillers to get me through the night.

I stared at the bottle of painkillers and asked, "Am I going to be mobile tomorrow?"

The intern smiled. "It depends on what you mean by mobile. You'll be able to move, but don't count on doing any lifting, running, or fast walking. In fact, if it's at all possible, you should stay in bed for a few days."

"It's not possible," I said.

"Then keep taking those muscle relaxants and the codeine."

I thanked him, picked up my coat, and hobbled out of the examination room. The muscle relaxant made me feel as if I'd been working out—loose-limbed, buoyant. But the feeling was illusory. If I stepped the wrong way or made any sudden turns, a sharp pain shot up my leg and through my spine like a jolt of electric current. Even with the codeine, the pain was bad enough to make me catch my breath.

I called a cab from the emergency room lobby and had it take me back to the Delores. I didn't really want to go home, but I couldn't think of anywhere else to go on a dismal December night. Besides, I didn't feel like wandering around unarmed, and I'd left the Gold Cup in the bedroom when I'd changed clothes.

The cabbie let me out in front of the Delores's courtyard. After I paid the fare, I stood on the sidewalk for a long time, watching the cab's red taillights disappearing down Reading Road, as if I were bidding adieu to a friend. There wasn't another car on the street and just the faintest glow from the traffic lights on Reading, flashing in the bare branches of the maples like Christmas tree ornaments. It started to rain as I stood there on the sidewalk, a cold drizzle mixed with flakes of snow. When the rain started to come down harder, I turned away from the street and stared at the apartment house. It was so quiet in the courtyard that I could actually hear the rain falling, a shushing noise like silk rubbed against silk. All told, I don't think I'd ever felt more lonely in my life.

I took a breath of the cold night air and started across the courtyard to the front entrance, walking carefully through the slush. I made it to the lobby without slipping.

Inside the lobby, the little coiled radiator opposite the mailboxes was hissing like a viper. I stared up the stairs with foreboding. It wasn't just the climb. God only knew who was waiting for me in my apartment this time. And this time, I was virtually helpless. Unarmed. Unmanned. Unable to react.

I climbed the stairs a step at a time. When I got to the landing, I peered down the hall. The wreckage from the afternoon had been cleaned up and someone had nailed a piece of plywood over the hole in the ceiling. I walked slowly down the hall, keeping my eyes fixed on the door to my apartment. There was a note taped to the door.

I thought maybe it was a message from Karen—a good-bye note. But it turned out to be an eviction notice from the management. I crumpled the paper up and shoved it in my coat. The last straw.

It took me a couple of minutes to fish my keys out of my pocket. I fitted them in the lock, turned the handle, and let the door fall open—resigned to anything that was in store.

At least, I *thought* I was resigned to anything. But when I saw Karen, curled up in my pieced-together armchair, I almost wept. She stirred as I came into the room, stretching her arms and smiling at me sleepily.

"I thought I told you to leave," I said with a stab at sternness. But my heart wasn't in it.

"Actually," I said, hobbling over to the couch and lowering myself in stages to the cushions, "I've never been happier to see another person in my life."

"Christ, what did they do to you?" Karen said as she watched me sit down.

"Oh, a little of this and a little of that."

Karen got up, walked across the room, and sat down beside me on what was left of the couch. She put a hand to my face and stroked my cheek gently. Her lip trembled as if she was going to cry. I studied her turned-up lip and smiled.

"It's not as bad as it looks," I said, laying my hand on top of hers.

"Poor bear," she said softly.

She tried to pull me to her. When I groaned, she jerked her hands away as if she'd burned them.

"I'm sorry," she said, looking pained for me. "I'm so sorry."

"You're here," I said. "No need to be sorry."

"Couldn't leave you in the lurch," she said with a smile.

"Yes, you could have. You should have—for your own sake. But I'm very glad you didn't."

"You need some rest," she said. She stood up. "Let's get to the bedroom. I've flipped the mattress over. It's thin, but it's sleepable."

"I'm afraid I'm not going to be much fun for a while," I said with a sigh.

"You're not going to do anything—for a while," Karen said, holding out a hand to help me up. "Let Karen do all the work."

I took her hand in mine. "Thanks," I said gratefully.

XX

Pain woke me up, around nine that Sunday morning. Pain that had circled around the bed all night long, and in the morning light had driven its beak into my back, my shoulder, my leg, my gut. I didn't know where to reach first. As the sleep left me, the throbbing became even more intense. I bit my lip to keep from groaning out loud and waking Karen, who was still sleeping soundly beside me.

I tried getting out of bed, but for a full minute I simply couldn't move. I finally managed to push myself upright and swing my legs to the floor. The effort made me break into a sweat. I wondered despairingly how I was going to make it through the day. In the movies, when a guy got beaten up, he was as good as new the next morning, except maybe for a few painted-on bruises and contusions. In real life, the pain stayed with you, like a lesson that was memorized by your body and that was relearned, minute by minute, with every breath you took. In fact, that lesson was the whole point of the beating. Jordan had done a good job.

Just the thought of that vicious, dead-eyed son of a bitch made me start to tremble with anger. As I was falling asleep the night before, he was all I could think about, in spite of Karen. He was all I could think about at that moment. I wanted to pay him back so badly, I could feel it in my flesh, like another bruise.

And at the same time, I knew, in my head, that Jordan was only one of my problems. Fantasies of revenge weren't going to get me out of the trouble I was in with Bo and his boss or with the police. Only Lonnie could do that. Finding Lonnie was the key. Only Lonnie could tell me what had happened to the lady. With Jenkins dead, only Lonnie could tell the cops that he had registered at that motel using a false name—my name. It was a good thing that Karen had relied on her heart instead of her head the previous afternoon. Without her around to point the way to Lonnie's old friends, I didn't know how I would have begun to hunt for him. To be perfectly honest, without her around, I don't know how I would have gotten through the night.

I stared at Karen, sleeping on the bed—at her long brown hair, her upturned mouth, her tan shoulders, her breasts—and knew that I was falling in love with her. It was that simple. Only it wasn't quite that simple.

I wanted and needed to protect what I loved. Banged up the way I was, I wasn't sure I could do that. I wasn't sure I could be there if Karen needed me, the way she'd been there when I'd desperately needed her. And then there was Lonnie.

I'd wanted to kill him the night before. I still hated him for senselessly involving me in his drug deal. But in the cold light of a winter Sunday morning, I knew that I couldn't fairly blame him for the beating I'd taken. Nobody had made me hold out on Lewis and Jordan. Nobody had made me a friend to Lonnie. I'd chosen that part myself.

I stared at Karen again and wondered if I was showing loyalty to him to make up for the way I felt about her. If I was, it could lead us both into trouble—following Lonnie's road to Fire Lake. My guilts could get us both killed.

I managed to make it down the hall to the john. I took a couple of muscle relaxants and a double dose of painkiller, then stripped down and stepped into the tub. I stood under the shower head for a long damn time, letting the hot water pour down my back and legs. Gradually the painkillers kicked in, and I didn't feel so bad anymore—about my aches and pains, about Lonnie, about anything. Then Karen came into the shower and I felt better still.

We switched places under the shower head. She stood facing the shower for a moment. When she turned back to me, her pretty face was beaded with water, her tangled hair was jeweled with it. She smiled her pouty smile and I felt like taking her right there—in spite of my bruises.

We switched again and she picked up a washrag, rubbed soap into it, and began to wash my chest. She washed my arms, carefully avoiding the multicolored bruise on my shoulder. She washed down my stomach, scarcely touching the blood bruises on my chest and gut. When she got to my groin, she held me for a moment. I grew hard in her hand.

"Karen," I said plaintively, over the hammering noise of the shower. "You're torturing me."

She stroked me and sank to her knees. Karen looked up at me, through the spray of the shower. Her blue eyes were dark and drunken-looking. She shut her eyes sleepily and I shut mine.

After the shower, Karen fixed coffee, eggs, and toast for us in the kitchen. The place smelled of coffee, browned bread, and butter. Karen found some paper plates and plastic ware, left over from a New Year's Eve party, and, naked, we ate breakfast on the living room couch. It still felt like the sixties to me, casually eating breakfast across from my naked lover. And the way the room was disarrayed, the patchwork chair, the confetti cushions, the way the winter sunlight lit up the floor and walls, the shivery coolness of the room, only added to that larkish feeling of freshness, of impulsiveness. Except we were grown people, not college kids, and we had a lot more to think about than making love again.

"That was very nice," I said, sipping the coffee.

"I liked it too," she said, and her eyes wrinkled up with pleasure.

"You know, I've never understood that. I mean, what's to like?"

"Giving pleasure to someone you care for is . . . sexy."

"You're sexy," I said.

"I used to think I was," she said sadly.

"What changed your mind?"

"I had to do some things," she said, "when Lonnie and I had habits. It kind of turned me off to sex."

I reached out and touched her leg. "You've made a spectacular recovery."

She laughed. But the sadness stayed with her.

"I wish we'd met a long time ago," she said.

I didn't say anything.

After a moment, Karen shook off her mood. "Are we going to go look for him today?"

"I am," I said.

"Meaning what?"

"Meaning," I said, "that I still think you should go home to St. Louis."

To my surprise, Karen didn't immediately disagree. Instead, she asked a very sensible question. "What happened yesterday before the police came?"

I told her the whole thing—about Bo, Maurice, and the guy with the shotgun.

"They were looking for cocaine?" she asked when I was done.

I nodded. "My guess is that whoever they work for fronted Lonnie some crack, and he lost it."

"Who was he supposed to sell it to?"

"I don't know, Karen. Somebody at that motel, maybe. Maybe the bikers. Jenkins said they dealt dope. They might have beaten Lonnie up and taken him off, with Jenkins's help."

"And then he tried to kill himself."

"It might have seemed like the only thing to do. Look what happened to Jenkins."

"Poor Lonnie," Karen said, shaking her head. "He never did have any luck."

I laughed mordantly. "That's what he said when I pulled out of the motel. That he had no luck, at all."

"You think those black men killed the clerk?"

"I'm sure of it," I said.

"But he didn't have the crack."

"No," I said. "They think Lonnie still has it. That I helped him rip them off."

"I guess we have to talk to Lonnie to find out what really happened."

"We?" I said.

She held up her right hand before I could finish objecting. "Harry, I've got to stay. The people you want to talk to don't know you. They barely know me. But they'll talk to me."

I thought it over. If I hadn't been beaten up, if I had more time, I could have managed on my own. I'd have to lean on people, but I could get them to talk. Under the circumstances, however, Karen's logic was indisputable.

"So, it's settled?" she said, getting up from the couch and starting down the hall to the bedroom.

I said yes. But she didn't hear me. She was already in the bedroom, getting dressed.

XXI

I loaded my pants pockets with muscle relaxants and pain-killers, before making my way slowly down the stairs. I also pulled the Gold Cup and a spare clip out of the drawer of the bureau and stuck them in my pea coat. Karen had gone down ahead of me, to warm up the car. I wasn't going to be able to drive—at least, not without working up a sweat. Besides, she knew where we were going and I didn't.

Outside it was a bitterly cold December morning. High clouds chased across the blue sky, giving the daylight the changeable, uneven quality of light before a storm. It would snow before the day was out and long before Karen and I were done with our search. I hobbled past the ice-shagged dogwoods and down the concrete steps to the lot.

By the time I finally made it into the passenger seat of the Pinto, I'd worked up a sweat. I knew I'd loosen up as the day went on, and my muscles warmed up, although bouncing in and out of the cold wasn't going to do me much good. At that moment I was glad Karen was with me.

I stared at her for a second. She was wearing her tatty fur jacket and blue jeans. With her hair in that bun and her face made up, she looked older and less vulnerable than she had in the apartment. More like the off-duty elementary-school teacher she really was.

"Ready?" she asked cheerfully.

I nodded.

Karen put the car in gear and backed slowly out of the

lot onto the side street running parallel to the Delores. She drove up to the corner of Burnett and pulled to a stop.

"Where to first?" I said as we poised there at the corner.

"St. Bernard, I think," Karen said.

"What's in St. Bernard?" I asked.

"A music store where Lonnie used to hang out. His old manager, Sy Levy, owns it and a little recording studio behind the store. Lonnie made his first tapes in Sy's studio."

"What makes you think Lonnie might have contacted Levy?"

"Before Lonnie got hot and went off to Hollywood, he and Sy were very close." She ducked her head and added: "Sy was very good to me, too. When Lonnie and I were down-and-out in St. Louis in '73, Sy sent me money to keep us going. It wasn't like he could spare it, either. He runs a shoestring operation."

"You think Lonnie might have touched him up?" I asked.

"My guess is that Sy would be the first person Lonnie'd run to, if he needed money or a shoulder to cry on. Sy's a warmhearted man. That's why his business has never gone anywhere. He always thinks about his musicians before he thinks about himself, and he never forgets an old friend. He's just the opposite of the kind of sharks Lonnie tied up with in L.A. It took Lonnie a long time to learn the difference. He thought all managers were like Sy, nice men who'd look out for him and do the right thing by him." She laughed bitterly. "Christ, was he ever wrong." She glanced over at me. "You want to give Sy a shot?"

"Sounds promising," I said.

"Then give me some directions," she said. "It's been a while."

I gave her directions to St. Bernard. Karen turned left onto Burnett and we were off.

* * *

We found Sy Levy's Music World on Vine Street in the ground floor of a long two-story red-brick apartment building on the southern fringe of the old blue-collar, good Catholic neighborhood of St. Bernard. Karen let me out in front of the store, while she went to find a place to park.

I'd kept an eye on the rearview mirror as we were driving over, just in case we were being tailed. But if Bo and his friends were following us, they were following from a distance. And if Jordan was dogging me, he was in an unmarked car. Still, I didn't let Karen out of my sight as she pulled around the corner and parked the Pinto in front of an old clapboard KOC hall. When I saw her get out of the car and start walking toward me, I took my first look at Levy's shop.

From a distance, his store was indistinguishable from the half-dozen other shops lining the block—just one more storefront on the ground floor of the apartment building. To my surprise, there were no instruments hanging in the window—no saxophones dangling like salamis in a butcher shop, no drum sets with their sparkling cheerleader trim and big white bellies. Instead, Levy had hung dozens of old 45's from wires. They ran in rows from the top of the window to the casement, like a curtain of hot wax.

I examined the titles while I waited for Karen. There was Elvis singing "Mystery Train." There was Nervous Norvus doing "Ape Call." There was Fess Parker and "The Ballad of Davy Crockett." Jerry Lee. Little Richard. Carl Perkins on the Sun label. There were a few artists from the sixties, too. Otis Redding, Wilson Pickett, Sam and Dave. And a couple of rockers from the seventies. But from the preponderance of the evidence, it was clear that Sy Levy had lost his heart to rock 'n' roll about 1956.

I peered through the curtain of records, into the shop itself, hoping to catch a glimpse of Sy. All I could see were peach crates full of records—some of them arranged on tables, with index and artist cards in them, some of them stacked on the worn wooden floors. A few microphones, angling from stands, were scattered among the crates. And a couple of big black Fender amplifiers, with finned horns on the high end, were sitting in opposite corners. There were more 45's glued to the walls, along with several album covers, including Elvis's first EP for Sun.

Karen caught me peering through the window. "See anything you like?" she said with a smile.

"Christ," I said, "it's like a birth-of-rock 'n' roll warehouse. Some of those records are worth a fortune."

"That's Sy," Karen said. "That's his whole way of life you're looking at. His whole treasure. Wait till you see the studio."

She opened the shop door, and a little bell on a spring jingled tunelessly. Karen stepped in and I followed her. There was no one in the shop itself. No one guarding the old NCR register, sitting on a glass display case by the door. I glanced at the display case. It was empty, save for a dozen red plastic inserts for 45's. The glass panels were clouded over with dust and grease. The whole store smelled of dust, mildewed cardboard, and damp, radiated heat.

"Where is he?" I said, glancing at Karen.

She pointed to a corridor on the far side of the room. "In his studio. Can't you hear it?"

And all of a sudden I could hear it—a faint tinny sound of music, like the high-pitched buzz you pick up when you pass someone wearing headphones.

Karen smiled nostalgically. The close, dead-end atmosphere of the shop clearly had a different meaning for her than it did for me.

"This is where Lonnie made his first record," she said, looking a little dreamy. "This is where we had some good times."

She smiled at me, and I smiled back at her.

"Is it okay to go back?" I asked.

"Sure," she said. "Sy loves company."

I followed her across the room and down the hallway at the far end. The hall was lit from above by a string of bare bulbs and lined on either side with Steelcase shelves, empty save for a couple of reel-to-reel tape boxes and a few coils of coax cable. As we walked down the corridor the tinny sound of music got louder and fuller. I couldn't make out the melody—the drums were masking it—but it was definitely three piece, fifties-style rock 'n' roll.

There was a steel door at the end of the hall, with a conical bulb above it set in a wire cage. Karen glanced up at the bulb and said, "It's okay. We can go in. He's not recording now or that bulb would be lit."

She opened the door and I followed her into a small wainscoted room, with a glass window and another door on the far wall. There was a pair of speakers built into the wall to our left, blaring the music we'd been hearing. On the wall behind us, a huge bank of half-inch tape machines and line amplifiers, racked in metal cases, was lit up like a Christmas display. The VU meters were all pegged. And to our right, sitting on a castered chair behind a twenty-four-track mixing console, was a balding, paunchy, elfin man with a Reds cap on his head and earphones over the cap.

For a second, Sy Levy didn't realize that we'd come into the room. His eyes shut, he bobbed his head, drummed his fingers, and tapped his feet to the sound of the music coming through the headphones. He was wearing a white dress shirt open at the collar, a ribbed, high-necked undershirt, a red cardigan sweater, and baggy chino pants. A pair of steel-rimmed bifocal glasses were lying on the console in front of him. I could still see the indentations they'd made on either side of his nose. His face was tanned, plump, and kindly-looking. Tufts of gray hair jutted out of each side of the Reds cap, like the wings of a petasus. With the earphones on his head and the gone

grin on his face, he looked like a weird cross between
Timothy Leary and your uncle in Miami.

"Simon!" Karen shouted at him.

The old man blinked his eyes. When he saw Karen, his
face lit up like his console. "Karen!" he shouted. "How the
hell are you!" He had a high, cheerful voice that fit his elfin
look. "Pull up a chair and sit down!"

Levy'd forgotten he had the earphones on, and he was
talking at the top of his lungs. Karen pointed at her ears,
and Sy Levy made a questioning face, then smirked. He
pulled the earphones off.

"Goddamn things," he said, tossing the headphones on
the console. He looked up, with a start, at the speakers on
the far wall. "Who turned *them* on?"

"You did," Karen said with a laugh.

He shook his head, as if it were an old joke, and flicked a
switch on the console. The room went quiet, except for
the swish of the tape machines. Simon Levy leaned back in
his chair, fitting the cap down over his smooth bald head
with his right hand. "It's been a long time, Karen," he said,
eyeing her affectionately. "You still look the same. Better."

"Bullshit," she said, grinning at him. "I'm an old lady
now, Simon, with two kids."

"Two!" he said with wonder. "Nobody'd guess." He
glanced over at me. "Who's your friend?"

"Stoner," I said, holding out a hand. "Harry Stoner."

Levy leaned forward and shook with me across the console. "I'm Simon Levy," he said warmly. "Last of the beat-
niks. That's what I call myself, anyway. My ex-wives
would tell you nudniks. But who's asking them?" He
looked back at Karen. "How come Lonnie's not with you?"

Karen shook her head. "We're not together anymore,
Sy."

"Since when?" Levy said with surprise.

"A long time," Karen said.

"How come he didn't tell me that?" he said in a pained
voice.

"You've spoken to Lonnie?" I asked Levy.

He nodded. "He came to the store just last Wednesday." Levy glanced from Karen to me then back at Karen. "Is there something I should know about?"

"We've been looking for him, Sy," Karen said. "Lonnie's in some trouble."

"What kind of trouble?" Levy said with alarm. He gave Karen a searching look. "What's wrong here, Karen? What's Lonnie gotten himself into?"

"It's a long story, Sy," she said.

"I got time." He stood up and came out from behind the desk. "Time is all I got. We'll go to the studio, get a cup of coffee. Talk it over."

Karen glanced fondly at the little glass window in the far wall. "Does it look the same?"

Levy laughed hoarsely. "On my budget, how could it look different?"

XXII

Levy picked up a placard that was sitting on the floor beside the console. "You go on ahead," he said to Karen. "Help yourself to coffee. I'm going to put this sign in the window and lock up."

He flipped the placard over. *Back in an hour* was written on it in pen.

"I don't know why I bother anymore," he said with a shrug. He tucked the sign under his arm and ambled off down the hall.

Karen watched him disappear down the corridor, then glanced at me.

"What do you think?" she said, arching a brow.

"We'll find out," I said. "I have the feeling your friend likes to talk."

She smiled. "He's a good talker, all right." She pointed to the door in the far wall. "Let's get some coffee."

Karen opened the door and we walked through it into a large open room, with peeling off-white walls and ratty green carpeting. An ancient upright piano was sitting beside the far wall, elevated off the floor on a riser. Two microphones were set up next to it—one by the keys, and the other peering straight down into the sounding board like a bird standing on one leg. Several other microphones were standing next to empty risers scattered around the floor; thick black microphone cables ran in coiled tangles everywhere. A tiny sealed-off sound booth with smoked-glass windows took up one corner of the room. I could see a drum set sitting inside the booth. Beat-up plastic couches and chairs lined each of the walls.

Karen took it all in with that same look of nostalgic pleasure that she'd had on her face when we'd first stepped into Levy's shop.

"Believe it or not," she said, "a lot of good music was made here."

"I believe it," I said.

She shook her head. "No, you don't. You couldn't know just by looking at it. You would have had to have been here in '69, when Lonnie was really cooking."

"I've heard him play," I reminded her.

"I know you have," Karen said. "But it was different here, Harry. He was better here. With Sy and his friends and me. He was at home. We weren't really into smack yet. And he'd sworn off speed. Or so he said. All he wanted to do was play his music. And man, he could play. He had a real hot band then—Flower Power." She laughed at the name. "Flower Power. Can you believe that?"

I smiled.

"Flower Power," she said again, staring around the room.

A coffee machine was burbling on a little stand by the door. Karen walked over to it and poured two cups of coffee. She handed one to me.

"The last time we stopped back here was in '70," she said, sipping the coffee. "After our stint in Hollywood, on our way to New York. We had a kind of reunion—a jam session with Pete and Alex and Norvelle. Guys from the old band. God, that party lasted for days. People just kept coming to the studio, like it was an open house. Sy loved it. He was so happy for Lonnie, because he'd made it big. He never said a word about Lonnie dropping him as his manager. He was just happy for his friend." She put the coffee cup down, walked over to one of the microphones and pushed it with her hand. It wobbled on its platter stand, like a dumbbell, then snapped upright.

"If we'd known then what was in store, we'd have never stopped partying," she said, her back to me. Her voice had grown heavy with nostalgia. "Because it was all downhill, after that. That week was like the crest of a wave—the height of something. It was never that good again. That new. That full of promise. New York turned out to be a nightmare. Then Chicago. Philly. East St. Louis. After that, it was all . . . Fire Lake."

I walked over to her and pulled her close. She looked up at me with tears in her pale blue eyes. "I'm not crying for him, Harry," she said apologetically. "Just for the way it was."

"It's all right." I stroked her brown hair and brushed the sidelocks from her wet eyes. "We'll find him."

She shook her head. "Too late."

Levy walked into the room, and we both glanced at him. Karen wiped the tears from her eyes with her fingertips and smiled bravely.

"I'm just feeling sad about the old days, Sy," she said with a broken smile.

" 'S all right," he said, waving a hand at her. "I feel sad about them all the time. Feeling sad about the past is my business."

Karen smiled. "The studio really hasn't changed, has it?"

Levy looked around the decrepit room, with just a touch of pride on his face. "Nope. It's still a mess. But this room has history in it. The wallpaper may be peeling, but there's music in that plaster. Lots and lots of music. And Lonnie made his share."

I had the feeling he was saying it for my benefit. I smiled at him and said, "I wish I'd been here then."

"Where were you, kid?" Levy said in his sprightly voice. "We'd have taken you in, wouldn't we, princess?" He smiled at Karen, and she nodded. "We were a family."

Levy walked over to one of the plastic couches and sat down.

"About Lonnie," Levy said, folding one thin leg over the other and cupping his hands on his paunch. "What kind of trouble is he in?"

Karen glanced at me and I said, "Tell him."

She ducked her head. "Drugs."

"Son of a bitch," Levy said with a sigh, as if that's what he'd been expecting to hear. "Is he in jail?"

Karen shook her head. "But he might be better off in jail. He's botched up a drug deal and gotten in trouble with the man."

Levy winced with pain. "How could he do that?" he said, staring at Karen helplessly. "A kid like him. With all that talent. How can he keep destroying himself this way?" He shook his head mournfully and tsk-tsked with his lips. "Stupid, stupid."

"What did he talk to you about on Wednesday?" I asked Levy.

"He asked me for a few bucks."

"Did you give him money?"

Levy blushed for an answer.

"How much money?"

"How much I had on me," he said, shoving his hands in his pockets, as if he were hanging on to what was left. "Not much. Thirty, forty bucks." He jiggled the change in his pants pockets, making his trousers flutter loosely about his legs.

"Did he tell you why he needed the money?" I asked.

Levy shook his head again. "We didn't talk money. Money don't mean nothing. We talked old times. We talked music. Mostly we talked about you, sweetheart," he said to Karen.

Karen put a hand to her mouth. "What about me?" she said timidly.

"About bringing you back to Cincy," Levy said. "He didn't tell me you two were separated. He just said he had high hopes about relocating and starting fresh. He had a plan. He was going to get back together with Norvelle Thomas. Remember Norvelle?"

Karen nodded, her hand still over her mouth as if she were afraid to make a sound.

"He was going to start a new band with Norvelle. Rehearse out here, in the studio. He was going to get back on track. Then he said he was going to bring you here to live with him. We were going to have another reunion, once you got here. Like the one back in '70. One big family again. Remember?"

Karen stared at Levy with a heartbroken look on her face. I put my arm around her and pulled her against me.

"I can't," she said, shaking her head. "I just can't, Harry."

She broke away from me and walked quickly out of the room.

Levy stared after her piteously. He took his glasses off and wiped his eyes. "Life isn't fair," he said—to no one, to the walls with the music in them. "You should have seen her in 1969. She was the most beautiful child. So loyal to him, so full of spirit, so full of hope. And Lonnie . . ." His tired eyes went out of focus, as if he were reliving it in his mind. "He was the best I ever had. And I helped a lot of kids. But Lonnie was special, and you don't ever stop being special."

I stared around the forlorn studio and ducked my head.

"He still loves her, you know," Levy said sadly.

I kept staring guiltily at the floor. "This Norvelle you mentioned. Do you know where he can be reached?"

Levy nodded. "Leanne Silverstein gave him a handyman job at that theater she manages. For old times' sake. Except for pickup work, Norvelle hasn't really played steadily for years."

"Leanne Silverstein?" I said.

"That's her married name," Levy said. "Ask Karen. Tell her Leanne Gearheart. She'll know."

"Where is the theater?" I asked.

"Downtown. On Fourth Street. The Bijou."

I thought of the ticket I'd found in Lonnie's clothing. It was a connection. Not a big one, but it gave me the feeling that Karen and I were on the right track.

"Thanks," I said to the old man. "You've been a help."

I started for the door.

"Mister?" Levy said.

I glanced back at him over my shoulder.

"Look out for her, won't you?" he said with feeling. "She didn't deserve the break she got. She never did."

"I'll do my best," I promised.

"And mister . . ." He put his glasses back on and stared at me. "Look after him, too, if you can."

I told him I'd try.

XXIII

I had a brief moment of panic when I stepped out of Levy's Music World and couldn't find Karen on the street. Then I looked over at the Pinto and saw her sitting behind the steering wheel, fixing her makeup in the rearview mirror. I walked slowly over to the car. My back was beginning to hurt again, but I didn't know what to do about it—except take another pill.

"Are you all right?" I said, easing into the seat beside her.

She glanced over at me as she blotted her eyes with a wadded-up tissue. "I'm sorry for that scene in there," she said, blushing.

"It's okay," I said gently.

Karen stared at herself in the mirror. "No, it's not okay. I don't like to get like that. It's not good for me. It puts bad ideas in my head."

I eyed her for a moment.

"You still love Lonnie, don't you?" I said, perhaps because Levy had just said that Lonnie still loved her.

"I don't know," she said with a doomed look on her beautiful face. "I guess a piece of me does. In spite of all the shit, I guess part of me will always love Lonnie."

I must have winced a little, because Karen reached out quickly and touched my cheek. "I'm falling in love with you, too, Harry. Don't misunderstand. But you're still new to me. Being in a relationship is new to me. We hardly know each other yet." She dropped her hand and stared vacant-eyed at the car seat. "Seeing that studio . . . it made me realize how many years had gone by. Wasted years. Dreadful years. But it also made me realize that there had been a good time too." She looked up at me again, uncertainly. "I can say that, can't I?"

"Sure," I said.

She shook her head. "Maybe I can't say that. Maybe it's crazy to say that. Maybe I ought to go back to St. Louis now and forget this whole goddamn thing."

"I think you should, although I'd miss you."

"I'd miss you too. That's the bitch of it." She turned back to the steering wheel. "No," she said decisively, "I won't run out on you, Harry. I just don't know how many more of these trips down Memory Lane I can stand. I don't want to lose my balance again and start falling."

A few drops of rain dashed against the windshield. Karen started up the engine and switched on the wipers.

"I don't know where Norvelle lives, but I guess we should find out," she said, straightening up the rearview mirror.

"That's the good news," I said. "Levy told me that Norvelle was working in a theater downtown—the Bijou. When I found Lonnie at the motel, he had a ticket in his pocket from that theater; so he must have gone there, after visiting Sy."

"He and Norvelle were always tight," Karen said.

"Who is Norvelle?" I asked.

"A tall, gangly black kid who played bass in Lonnie's band. Flower Power—the group I told you about."

"He's working for someone named Leanne Gearheart now."

Karen winced, as if I'd pricked her with a pin. "Another name from the past," she said, although I could tell from the pained look on her face that it wasn't a name she was fond of.

"You don't like her?"

"It's not that I don't like her," Karen said, pretending indifference. "She went with Lonnie before I did, and we just never got along. You know, there was a lot of jealousy there. And then she took it hard when Lonnie broke up with her. I always felt kind of guilty about that."

"Do you think Lonnie might have looked her up?" I asked.

Karen shrugged. "Sure. It's possible, although she might not have been all that happy to see him. Norvelle is a better bet."

"Why?"

"He's a junkie," Karen said. "Or at least he used to be. And after getting out of jail, Lonnie may have been looking to get high."

"Norvelle is connected?" I said with interest.

Karen nodded. "Norvelle is the dude who taught Lonnie how to shoot up. He's a ghetto kid, and smack's a ghetto vice. At least, it used to be back when we got into it. I used to kid Lonnie about being half black himself; but it wasn't really a joke. For a few years there, we lived in the ghetto. All our friends were black. It just came with the habit."

"Maybe Norvelle was Lonnie's connection on the cocaine deal," I offered.

"Maybe," Karen said absently, "although Norvelle was into getting down—not up."

"It's still worth a look-see," I said, trying to sound positive. "You've got to start thinking like a detective."

"I don't think I like being a detective, Harry," Karen said as she guided the car back out onto Vine Street. "It hurts too much."

"Tell me about it," I said with a laugh.

The Bijou theater was located on Fourth Street, on the first floor of a converted brownstone office building. The brownstone was right on the edge of what had become the gallery district—a block of trendy, hi-tech art emporiums. I could remember when that same block had been the wholesale clothing district. When I was a kid, my grandfather had jobbed menswear from the second floor of one of the brownstones.

It gave me an odd feeling to be wandering near his old warehouse. In fact, I found myself staring nostalgically at the tall windows of the building that used to house his company. I'd spent a lot of hot summer afternoons in that warehouse. It was a printing outfit now.

As we walked down Fourth, Karen seemed to be lost in thought too. I figured she was still brooding about Lonnie. It didn't make me happy to know that. I didn't know quite how it made me feel. Guilty, jealous. A little of both. More jealous than guilty, finally. I'd already started thinking of her as my own.

The Bijou was still a very new place and trendy, like the arty shops around it. There was no old-fashioned marquee, running with light bulbs, above the doors—just a neon sign on the bare brick wall reading "Bijou" in fancy script. The lobby was tiled in parquet. The walls were decorated, like a gallery's, with works of local artists; and there were several abstract-looking metal sculptures dotting the floor. One of them reminded me of the fish statue in front of the futuresque house in Jacques Tati's *Mon Oncle*. In fact it would have been a funny allusion, if the rest of the theater hadn't reminded me of the house itself. It seemed as if someone had gone a long way out of his or her way to make the Bijou look like anything but what it was. The only bows to tradition were the chrome-and-glass refreshment stand on the right and the little ticket booth built into the wall on the left. And when I took a closer look, I realized that the refreshments at the stand consisted of hot cider and espresso. No popcorn machine. No Milk Duds. No orange drink.

In the rear of the lobby, a guy who was trying very hard not to look like an usher was standing in front of a pair of polished wooden doors leading to the theater. He was a white college kid, a DAAP student from the look of him. And the girl in the ticket booth looked just as white and collegiate. It seemed like an odd place for a black junkie to be working.

"I guess we're going to have to ask about Norvelle," Karen said, glancing around the lobby. "I don't see him here."

I nodded and walked over to the ticket booth. The girl inside smiled at me with polished insincerity.

"Two?" she said sweetly.

I shook my head and her face fell. "I'm looking for one of your employees. Norvelle Thomas."

"I don't think Norvelle is working today," she said.

"Is there someone here I could talk to about Norvelle? It's really important that I get in touch with him."

The college girl gave me a skeptical look. I could hardly blame her. Norvelle Thomas didn't seem like the kind of guy with a guest register.

"I guess you could talk to our manager, Leanne," the girl said. "If it's *really* that important."

"Oh, it is," I said, looking serious and concerned.

"There's a door on your right," she said. "Just go through and tell the secretary you want Leanne Silverstein."

"Thanks."

There *was* a door on the right, but it took me a few seconds to find it. It had been made to look like part of the wainscoted wall.

I opened it up and ushered Karen through.

We walked down a little corridor to an anteroom full of sleek Italian modern furniture and framed movie posters. A secretary, another college girl, was kneeling in a backless chair in front of a lacquered desk so smooth and angleless it looked as if it had been poured from a jar. Soft rock music was being piped in from speakers concealed in the ceiling.

"Yes?" the secretary said, looking a little alarmed at the company.

"We'd like to speak to Leanne Silverstein," I said.

"I don't know if she's in," the secretary said.

"Tell her Lonnie Jackowski's wife, Karen, wants to see her," Karen said.

The secretary got out of the chair as if she were dismounting a horse. She started off down another hall, looked back nervously, and said, "Just stay there, okay?"

Karen nodded, and the secretary walked off.

"Christ," Karen said with a scowl, "this is going to be awful."

"I'm kind of curious," I said. "Why would a woman with this kind of job hire a black junkie?"

"Old times, probably," Karen said. "I think she and Norvelle used to sleep together, after she broke up with Lonnie."

"Is she black?" I asked.

"Half-and-half. Her parents were a mixed couple—solidly middle-class. Her father was a GP. Her mother was a social worker. They raised Leanne like a white kid, and she was so light, she could pass. Then the sixties came along, and passing for white suddenly didn't seem as good a deal as it once did. Leanne went through a hell of a lot of changes about that. She and her dad used to get into real screaming matches about the race thing and about Lonnie. I saw them fight, once—at Sy's studio, actually. It was awful. I mean, I think he would have hit her if the band hadn't been standing around. I think he hit her a lot, anyway. Her dad was a real hardworking black man, who was proud of what he'd accomplished with his life. And, man, he did not like what Leanne was doing with hers."

"How did she end up with Lonnie?"

Karen smiled. "Lonnie had his good points, Harry."

"I remember," I said.

"I don't just mean sex. He was also a very sympathetic guy. Completely nonjudgmental. He more or less took people at face value—took them for what they wanted to be. He was like a very flattering mirror, if you understand what I mean."

"Better than you think," I said, remembering the way Lonnie had helped me when I'd first met him.

"I guess Leanne just connected with him at the right time. From what Lonnie told me, she'd been an art student when the black power thing started up. Sometime in the mid-sixties, she dropped out of DAA and tied up with some local black activists. Those dudes were really into macho, and they ended up treating her like shit. When Lonnie met her at the end of '68, she was very confused about her race and her sex and her folks, who couldn't understand why she wasn't happy being the white girl they'd raised her to be. Lonnie was a good listener. He helped her out. He lived with her until he met me, in '69."

Karen glanced nervously down the hall.

"It has been close to twenty years, Karen," I said. "She's probably forgotten the whole thing."

"You don't understand," Karen said, shaking her head. "Leanne tried to kill herself after Lonnie broke up with her. She took some pills. That's not something you're likely to forget, even if you wanted to forget it. And Leanne didn't want to. For a year or two after that, she'd send Lonnie these pathetic letters about how her life was over and how he'd ruined her for other men. She laid a real guilt trip on him, and on me."

The secretary came back into the anteroom—a smile on her face. "Follow me, won't you," she said. "Leanne's office is in the back."

Karen glanced at me nervously as we followed the secretary down the hall. "I'm not looking forward to this," she said in a stage whisper.

I patted her back and said, "If it gets us closer to Lonnie, it'll be worth it."

XXIV

We followed the secretary up to a door at the end of the hall.

"Through there," she said, smiling cordially.

I opened the door, guiding Karen in ahead of me.

It was a tiny, dry-walled office—not much bigger than the anteroom and furnished in the same chic, gallery style with posters and sleek Italian furniture. On the far side of the room, across from the door, a very pretty woman in a pale gray silk dress was sitting behind a white lacquered desk. The woman had a round, high-cheeked, light brown face, and curly, dark brown hair cut short and tinted with henna. She'd made herself up expertly—pale blue eye shadow that gave her black eyes an almost Egyptian look and bright red lipstick that made her large, sensuous mouth gleam like cut strawberries. There was something not quite sober about the woman's beautiful eyes. They were slightly unfocused-looking, as if she'd been drinking. But nothing else about her suggested that she was drunk. She smiled at us as we entered the room.

"Hello, Karen," she said in a sweet, lilting voice. "It's been a long time."

"Hello, Leanne," Karen said with a stab at a smile. "You look prosperous."

"That's what I've become," Leanne Silverstein said with an abrupt laugh. "Prosperous."

"You're not complaining, are you?" Karen said sarcastically.

Leanne Silverstein shook her head. "No. It's just that

prosperity wasn't all I expected, if you can dig where I'm coming from. How about you?" She stared at Karen with open curiosity. "How did things work out for you and Lonnie?"

Karen sighed heavily. "Not so good," she said with an effort. "We're not together anymore. And neither one us is . . . prosperous."

The two women stared at each other silently for a long moment. Karen glanced at me uncomfortably. She wanted out—I could see it in her face and so could Leanne Silverstein. I felt a little embarrassed for both of them. I also felt distinctly like a third wheel.

Leanne Silverstein leaned forward, planting her elbows on the desktop and resting her lovely face in her hands. A strand of pearls she was wearing at her throat fell forward and clicked against a gold bracelet on her right wrist. "You're still mad at me, aren't you, Karen?" she said, stating what was obvious.

Karen looked nonplussed, then said, "Yes. A little. Aren't you mad at me?"

"A little," Leanne admitted. "But I can handle it. The older I get, the more important friends become to me. I can't afford to hold grudges anymore. It's just too damn cold outside."

Karen half smiled at her.

"Who is your friend?" Leanne said, glancing my way.

"I'm Harry Stoner," I said.

"Sit down, Mr. Stoner. You, too, Karen." She gestured to two handsome chairs in front of her desk. When Karen hesitated, Leanne added: "Please."

We sat down across from her.

Leanne kept staring at Karen in a wistful, vaguely remorseful way.

"Are you in town for long, Karen?" she said. "I'd like you to come out to our farm if you have the time. We call it the farm, although it's just a house and a duck pond."

"We?" Karen asked.

"I've got a husband now and a couple of sons. I married Jon Silverstein. Remember him?"

Karen looked surprised. "Jon the Postman?"

Leanne nodded her head and mugged long-sufferingly. "Jon the Postman. He doesn't deliver mail on Calhoun Street anymore. He's got his own real estate business. I manage this theater and a small gallery around the corner. We do all right, I guess. But it's tame, compared to the old days."

Karen smiled. "Sometimes I think tame is better."

The two women eyed each other again, a little less tensely.

Leanne leaned back in her chair. "I guess I owe you something like an apology," she said, after a time. "I mean, for the way I carried on after Lonnie and I broke up."

Karen shook her head. "What's the point? We were different people then."

"Still," Leanne said. "I shouldn't have put you through all those changes. I just didn't have anyone but Lonnie to hold on to."

"Did you ever make it up with your folks?" Karen asked.

Leanne nodded. "Eventually. I guess we all do, eventually. As soon as I got a job and started making some money, they took me back in the fold. And, of course, I married a honkie. And that pleased Dad."

Karen smiled, but Leanne didn't look particularly happy about the dispensation.

"Dad and I still don't see eye to eye on most things. But he's older now, and I'm older too. So . . . it doesn't seem to matter like it used to. He and Mom stay out at the farm, now that they're retired. In fact, the place really belongs to them. Jon and I just go out for dinner every once in a while and on the weekends. Mom's got a garden. Dad does some hunting and fishing. They seems to like it out there, especially when the kids come out to visit, although Dad's still kind of hard-nosed when I'm around."

Leanne Silverstein got a troubled look on her face, as if talking about her father had upset her.

"Last I heard, you and Lonnie were in Hollywood," she said, abruptly changing the subject.

"That was a long time ago," Karen said.

"You know, I was out in L.A. for a while, too, back in '71 and '72. I did some graduate work at UCLA. Spent most of the time stoned out of my head. Made a lot of guys. It was my last fling before I came limping back home to Cincinnati and got reformed. I didn't know I was going to get reformed. I just thought I was paying the folks a visit. Looking for a little TLC and some home cooking. Looking to get my head straight after L.A. But the weeks stretched into months. And the times . . . they do keep changing. And here I am. Still." She looked thoughtfully at her desk. "I kept thinking maybe I'd run into you or Lonnie out in L.A. After I came home, I used to brood about that a lot. It was like a chance I'd missed—a chance to patch things up."

"We weren't there for very long, Leanne," Karen said. "Things didn't go well for Lonnie in L.A. We moved to New York at the end of '70. After that, we drifted around."

Leanne nodded. "How is Lonnie?" she said delicately. "I mean, is he all right?"

"I don't know," Karen said with a frown. "That's why I'm here. We're trying to find him."

"Find him?" Leanne said, looking confused. "Is he lost?"

"Lonnie's still a junkie, Leanne," Karen said flatly. "He was in Lexington for the last two years. He was released a couple of weeks ago, and apparently got himself involved in a drug deal here in Cincinnati. Something went wrong, and now he's in trouble."

Leanne put her hands to her face and pulled down on either cheek, stretching her mouth into a ripe red grimace. "Lonnie's in trouble?" she said with real pain in her voice.

Karen nodded. "Harry and I are trying to bail him out— if it's not too late."

"Jesus," Leanne said, looking horrified. "How can I help?"

"You've got a guy working for you here—Norvelle Thomas," I said. "We'd like to talk to him."

"Norvelle?" she said. "Why Norvelle?"

"Lonnie might have been in touch with him," Karen said. "Sy Levy said that he was talking about paying Norvelle a visit, last Wednesday. Something about getting the band together again."

"I'm off on Wednesday," Leanne said with an uneasy look. "And I haven't talked to Norvelle in a couple of weeks." She dropped her hands from her cheeks and sat up in her chair. "Do you know anything about the drug deal that Lonnie was involved in?"

We both looked at her uncertainly.

"I have a reason for asking," Leanne said, when we didn't answer her right away.

"It was crack," I said. "And it must have been a sizable amount, because the folks Lonnie was dealing with want it back in the worst way."

"Which folks?" Leanne said.

"We're not sure. But they're young and they're black and they're tough."

Leanne nodded angrily, as if I'd confirmed what she'd been thinking. "That fucking Norvelle!"

"You think he was involved in this?" I asked.

"Of course he was involved." She glared at me as if *that* should have been obvious. "I never should have given him a job. If it hadn't been for old times, I wouldn't have. God damn him."

"Norvelle deals crack?"

"Norvelle does anything for a dime bag," she said. "He's been strung out so long, it isn't funny. He's one of those guys from the sixties who just never made it to the other side of the decade. I hate to say it, but he probably put Lonnie in touch with the man."

"It would help if we could get Norvelle's address."

"He used to live on Cross Lane in East Walnut Hills. Last house on the left. But a guy like Norvelle usually goes where the action is—where the junk is. And I don't know where that would be."

"Is there any way we can find out?" I said.

Leanne started to answer me when a tall, red-haired man with a drooping mustache walked into the room. He had a pleasant, horsey face—ruddy, freckled and lit up with the sort of toothy, feckless grin you see on rookie ballplayers. Although he was dressed in tailored business clothes, the outfit didn't suit him. He moved inside his pinstripes as if he were wearing a spacesuit, as if he could hardly wait to doff the woolens and pull on a pair of jeans.

Leanne looked startled by the interruption. She put both hands on her desk and stared at the man coldly.

"Don't you ever knock?" she snapped.

The man shrugged good-naturedly. "Can't I pay you a lunchtime visit?" he said with his loopy smile. "After all, I own the joint."

"You own it. I run it. This is my office, and I expect some privacy. I thought we'd agreed on that. God knows I get little enough of it everywhere else."

The man's big grin just disappeared, as if all of his teeth had fallen out on the ground in front of him. "Jesus, Leanne," he said, looking embarrassed and bewildered. "It's not as if I'm a stranger."

Leanne stared at him for a second, as if that were precisely what he was to her—a stranger. Then she made her beautiful face over into a mask of amiability. "I'm sorry, Jon. Karen and I have been talking over old times, and I guess it's got me a little rattled."

Jon Silverstein went behind Leanne's desk and put a comforting hand on her shoulder. Leanne sank beneath it, as if he held the weight of the world in his palm. Silverstein sighed and took his hand away.

"Hello, Karen," he said, glancing red-faced at us. "Remember me? Jon the Chauvinist?"

Karen smiled at him affectionately. "Of course I remember you, Jon."

"You look great, Karen," Silverstein said. He stared at me blankly.

"Stoner," I said, reaching across the desk to shake with him. "Harry Stoner."

Silverstein shook with me. The encounter with his wife had unsettled him, because his palm was sweaty and his hand was trembling. "You two are . . . ?"

"Friends," Karen said.

Silverstein nodded. "So where's Lonnie?"

"That's what we're trying to find out," Karen said.

Silverstein looked confused. "He's not with you?"

"We're separated, Jon."

"I'm sorry to hear it," Silverstein said, looking down at Leanne, "although that does seem to be the way it is with our generation. Nobody stayed together very long. In fact, none of our friends from the sixties is still married. Except for us."

"And we're getting a little rocky," Leanne said pointedly.

There was a momentary lull, in which everyone in the room looked off in a different direction. It was clear that the Silversteins' marriage was more than a little rocky. I felt bad for the man, mainly because he looked as if he was still in love, where Leanne looked as if she'd stopped caring.

"I guess it didn't work out the way anyone expected," Jon Silverstein said, filling the silence.

"Why don't you and Mr. Stoner go out in the hall, Jon," Leanne said suddenly. "Karen and I have some girl talk to finish."

"Sure," Silverstein said. All of the boyish energy in his face and voice had vanished in the course of the conversation. He literally dragged himself across the room and stepped into the hall.

I followed him, closing the door behind me.

Silverstein leaned against a wall and sighed. "Women,"

he said, trying to make light of the scene in Leanne's office. "I guess she's had a bad day."

I smiled at him. "I guess we didn't help."

"You two were . . . you're looking for Lonnie?"

I nodded. "He's gotten himself into some trouble."

Silverstein laughed coarsely. "That's all he's ever been—trouble." He said it bitterly. But then, I'd seen the look on his wife's face when she heard that Lonnie was missing; I'd heard the history of her relationship with Lonnie. I guessed Jon Silverstein had had to live with that history for too long, even if Lonnie had once been a friend of his. Frankly, I could feel for him.

"You haven't seen him this week, have you?" I said.

Silverstein shook his head. "I haven't seen Lonnie or Karen in almost nineteen years."

He reached into his jacket and pulled a cigarette out of a gold case. I hadn't noticed in the office, but the man was wearing a good deal of gold jewelry—rings, a Rolex. He'd obviously made some money and liked to show it off. Maybe that was what his wife held against him.

Silverstein lit his cigarette with a gold lighter. Inhaling deeply, he blew a huge cloud of smoke out of his mouth. "What kind of trouble is Lonnie in?"

"Drugs," I said.

He nodded. "It figures. And I guess you told Leanne about it?"

"Yeah."

"That explains it. Lonnie's always been a god to her. A fucking god." He dropped the cigarette onto the carpet and crushed it angrily with his shoe. Bending down, he plucked the butt off the floor and stuck it in his jacket pocket, then toed at the carpeting until the ash mark had been rubbed away.

The office door opened and Karen and Leanne stepped out.

"I'll be in touch if I hear anything," Leanne said to her.

Karen said, "Fine." She turned to Jon. "The last time I

saw you, you were delivering mail on Calhoun Street and hawking concert tickets on the side."

Jon Silverstein ducked his head. "That was ages ago."

Karen smiled and touched Jon gently on the arm. "It's good to see you."

Silverstein looked up at her and smiled back. "It's really good to see you again too." A bit of enthusiasm returned to his face. "Maybe we could all go to lunch. I've got the four fifty outside. We'll hop in and drive over to the Maisonette. Talk over old times. I'll treat. Or we could go out to the farm. Have Grandma make us some grub."

Leanne Silverstein turned abruptly on her heel and walked back into her office.

Silverstein's face fell again. "Maybe not," he said with a long sigh. "Good luck to you, Karen. I hope you find Lonnie."

He followed his wife into the office and closed the door behind him.

XXV

It began to snow again as we walked up Fourth Street. At first there were just a few flakes, then it started coming down like a hard rain. For several minutes the snow fell so thickly that it was impossible to see. I pulled Karen into an alcove in front of a shop window, and we stood there for a while, watching the snow sweep in wind-driven sheets up the deserted street.

"Did Leanne tell you anything else?" I asked.

Karen shook her head. "She just wanted a moment to collect herself and to cry on my shoulder a little about Jon."

"Not a happy marriage," I said.

"No," Karen said sadly. "It's weird, but I kind of feel for her. Even though I don't like her, I feel sorry for her." She laughed mordantly. "Christ, she's wearing pearls and I'm feeling bad! I don't know why it is that Leanne can always manage to make me feel guilty."

I laughed. "I felt sorry for him."

"Don't," Karen said. "In spite of the way it looked in there, Jon's nobody's victim. He could always take care of himself. Even when he worked as a postman, he had a knack for turning a dollar. And it looks like he's still doing a pretty good job of it. But Leanne . . . it seems like she's been hanging by the same thread since the day I met her. It's no surprise that it's finally wearing through." Karen sighed. "Oh, for God's sake, what do I care? So she's rich and unhappy. So what? She's got her life. And I've got mine. Jon was right—none of it worked out the way anyone planned. The important thing is to keep moving forward, like the Marine Corps manual says."

I smiled at her. "How do you know about the Marine Corps manual?"

"My brother, Tom, was a Marine," she said with a touch of pride. "Tough Tom. Tough guy."

Karen stared out at the snow. There was snow all over her jacket, in her hair, on her face. I brushed some of it off with my hand.

"Give me a kiss, huh?" she said, turning toward me. "I could use one."

I kissed her.

When the storm let up for a moment, we walked quickly up to the parking lot where we'd left the Pinto. Once we got inside the car, I took the bottles of muscle relaxant and painkiller out of my pocket and swallowed a couple of pills—dry.

"You hurt?" Karen said, eyeing me with concern.

"I'm all right," I told her.

She started up the car and pulled out of the lot onto Fourth.

"Do we have a plan?" she said.

I shrugged. "Go see Norvelle, I guess."

"He isn't likely to tell us anything we want to know, is he?" Karen said. "I mean, if he's dealing drugs . . ."

"I'll persuade him," I said dryly. "The important thing is to find Lonnie and to find out what happened to the crack."

I didn't say it to Karen, but it was also important to find out who Norvelle's connection was, assuming that Thomas was the one who put Lonnie in touch with the man. I was hoping that Leanne Silverstein could help us with that. If I got a name from her, I might be able to do a little business of my own with Lonnie's supplier. Once I got Bo and his friends off my back, I could deal with Jordan. And I planned to deal with him, in my own time.

* * *

Because of the blizzard, it took us almost thirty minutes to drive up Gilbert to McMillan. By the time we turned onto the little East Walnut Hills side street called Cross Lane, the streets and sidewalks were covered with several inches of snow.

The house that Leanne Silverstein had directed us to was a ramshackle two-story frame Victorian, with a screened-in front porch and a turret window on the second story. It sat at the end of the block, on the verge of an empty lot. The porch screen was full of holes and several of the upper-story windows had been pasted over with cardboard. There was a single lamp on in the turret window, glowing a warm yellow in the blowing snow.

Karen parked in front of the house. Before she could get out of the car, I said, "Maybe you better stay here."

She turned on the seat and gave me a questioning look. "But you don't know him."

"He's a tall black junkie," I said. "I'll find him."

"I mean, you won't know him to talk to," Karen said.

"I don't think old times are going to get us anywhere with Norvelle. You said it yourself, Karen. He isn't going to want to talk about a drug deal, especially one that's gone as bad as this one has."

She looked down at the steering wheel. "You're not going to hurt him, are you, Harry?"

"I'm not planning to."

"Remember that he's a junkie. All he cares about is getting well and getting off. The most important person in his life is his connection, and he won't give the man's name up easily."

"What do you suggest?"

"That I come in there with you."

I shook my head.

"I can talk to him, Harry. I know where he's at. I've been there myself."

I stared at her for a second and sighed. "All right,

Karen. But for chrissake, if anything goes wrong in that house, just come back to the car and drive away."

"Without you?"

"Without me," I said.

"You're scaring me," she said with a shaken look.

I said, "Good. Because this is likely to be a scary place."

We got out of the car and walked through the blowing snow to the porch. As we stepped up to the front door, I caught the sound of heavy metal coming through the iced-over front window—Kiss, I thought. Inside that front room a girl laughed shrilly and shouted something obscene at someone else. I patted my coat pocket—the one with the pistol in it—and knocked on the paneled wooden door.

When no one answered, I pounded on the door with my fist. Someone turned the volume down on the stereo, and a few seconds later a short towheaded girl, with a pale freckled face and greasy pigtails, opened the door a crack and peeked out. She was wearing a blue gingham dress with a man's red cardigan sweater draped over her shoulders. An unlit cigarette drooped from her mouth.

The girl eyed me hostilely and shivered against the cold. She would have been pretty if she hadn't looked so strung out. Her arms were like sticks, and her face was careworn and darkly ringed around the eyes. She couldn't have been more than fifteen; but in most of the ways that counted, she'd never get any older than she already was.

"What do you want?" she said belligerently. Her voice had an Appalachian twang to it.

"I want to talk to Norvelle Thomas."

"Are you his social worker?" she said.

It looked like that might be good enough to get us through the door. I said, "Yes."

Karen glanced at me, then smiled at the girl. "We're friends of Norvelle's."

The girl stepped back from the door and pulled the sweater tightly around her chest. "Well, come in, then," she said. "I ain't gonna stand here catching pneumonia."

We walked into a tiny hall. The girl slammed the door behind us. I could see a living room through an archway to the left and an uncarpeted staircase to the right that led up to the second-story turret. Another short hall ran past the staircase toward a kitchen. An old blacklight poster for Jr. Walker and the All Stars had been taped to the wall by the front door. The concert was at the Black Dome. July 22, 1968. I smiled when I saw the poster. I'd been to the concert.

"You like Jr. Walker?" I said to the girl.

"Fuck no," she said.

Karen laughed.

Upstairs a phone began to ring. It rang twice, then someone picked it up.

I glanced up the staircase. "Is Norvelle up there?"

The girl shook her head, no. "Cal," she said.

"Where *is* Norvelle?" I asked.

"I don't know," she said sullenly. "You better talk to Cal." She nodded toward the living room. "Y'all wait in there till I come back." She started up the stairs, then looked back over her shoulder. "And don't touch nothing."

Karen and I walked into the living room.

Another teenage girl was sitting on the floor inside, leaning against a cushion covered with a paisley throw. The three pieces of furniture in the room—two chairs and a sofa—had also been covered with paisley throws. There were brick-and-board bookshelves along each wall, filled with science fiction paperbacks and record albums. Drug paraphernalia was scattered on top of the shelves—pipes, roach clips, glass hookahs. A forty-watt light bulb with a paper globe around it hung from the ceiling; a threadbare oriental covered the floor. Piles of dirty clothes sat in two of the corners. The room smelled like dirty clothes. It also smelled faintly of marijuana and sex.

"Who are you?" the girl on the floor said.

She pulled herself upright and stared at us curiously. She was about the same age as her friend, but she still had her baby fat. She was wearing jeans and a torn T-shirt. The T-shirt was draped at an angle across her chest, leaving one of her shoulders bare except for the strap of a black leotard that she was wearing as an undershirt. She'd cut her hair in a kind of spiky Mohawk and sprayed one side of it with blue glitter. She'd also made up her eyes with mascara and rouged her cheeks like a clown's. But in spite of the punk look, she was still obviously a little girl, dressing up like the big kids.

"We're looking for Norvelle," I said to the kid.

"What do you want with that nasty old nigger?" she said with a sneer.

"He lives here, doesn't he?" I said.

She gave me a bored look. "So? It's Cal's house. Cal's the man." She got a dreamy look in her eyes and let her head loll back against the cushion. "Cal's so cool."

"Are you his girlfriend?" I asked.

She nodded. "Me and Renee. He says we do him better than anyone."

"I'll bet," I said. "You live here too?"

"Renee does," she said a little sullenly. "But I'm going to move in soon. Living at home is a drag."

"Is Norvelle here now?" Karen asked the girl.

The girl shook her head. "I don't know. I ain't seen him."

I didn't feel much like sitting down on any of the furniture. There was something so visibly corrupt about the place that it affected me physically, as if I were staring at an accident.

I glanced at a huge beaten-tin ashtray, sitting on the floor by the couch. There were no butts in it—just torn-off cigarette filters and a couple of balls of cotton. Karen noticed it, too, and nodded, as if it meant something to her.

We stood there for a while, waiting for Cal. The girl turned up the stereo and went back to Kiss. I thought about going upstairs and searching the second floor. Then

Renee came into the room. The cigarette was still hanging in her mouth, unlit.

"Thelma," she said to the other kid. "Get your ass out of here."

Thelma made a sour face, but she got up and walked slowly out of the room.

Renee stared at us for a moment. "Cal's coming down," she said in a forbidding tone of voice, as if we'd awakened a monster. She turned on her heel and followed Thelma out of the room.

"You ain't no social workers," she said over her shoulder. "You're fucking narcs."

"Who told you that?" I asked her.

Renee walked down the hall without answering me.

I turned to Karen and asked her the same question, "Who told the kid we were narcs?"

Karen shrugged. "When you do junk, every stranger's a narc." She pointed to the tin ashtray. "You know what that shit is?"

I shook my head.

"You've got to filter junk, Harry," Karen said authoritatively. "After you cook it up, you've got to filter it before you shoot—to get rid of the impurities. Most of the time you use cotton balls as filters. You draw the junk up from the cooking spoon through the cotton into the syringe. If you don't have enough cotton, though, a cigarette filter will do the job nicely."

I stared at the ashtray and felt a wave of disgust pass over me like a flash of heat. "Those kids are junkies?"

She nodded. "The one with the sweater—Renee—has got railroad tracks on her right arm. She was trying to cover them up, but I caught a glimpse when she went upstairs."

I shook my head in despair. "This Cal must be a real charmer."

"He's probably just another user, Harry," Karen said coolly. "He pushes enough on the street to keep himself high and to pass out a few bags to his girlfriends—in return for favors rendered. It was no different in our day. You just didn't see it."

I stared at her for a moment. "I'm glad I didn't see it," I said angrily. "I'm fucking proud of it."

Karen wasn't impressed by my indignation. "Grow up," she said. She glanced around the corrupt little room. "This is the real world. It always was."

XXVI

As Karen and I stood there staring at each other, a tall, skinny, black-haired man walked into the room. We both turned toward him. He looked like a mean Harry Dean Stanton—long, thin redneck face, deeply grooved on either side of his tiny mouth, heavy-lidded blue eyes, sharply hooked nose, uncombed coal-black hair that fell in thick locks across his forehead. He was wearing jeans and an unbuttoned checked shirt that gave anyone who was interested a good view of his sallow, hairless chest and pudgy little belly. I put his age at about forty—the same as mine.

He stared at us for a moment, then passed a hand through his black hair and smiled. His mouth was rotten-looking—long decayed teeth, red-rimmed gums.

"You looking for Norvelle?" he said in a thick Appalachian drawl.

I nodded. "We're friends of his."

Cal laughed a nasty little laugh. "You told them girls you was his caseworkers."

When I didn't answer him, he said, "Well, which is it, mister?"

"Friends," Karen said quickly. "Norvelle used to play in a band with my husband."

"And who would he be?" Cal asked. "Your husband?"

"Lonnie Jackowski. Lonnie Jack."

Cal shook his head. "Never heard of him."

"You don't know where Norvelle is, do you?" Karen said.

"I hope he's dead," Cal said. "I done kicked him out of

here about a month ago. I got tired of that nigger freeloading on me. Eating up my food and shit."

"Do you have any idea where he might have gone?" Karen asked.

"Might try K.T.'s Barbershop on Forest. Norvelle used to hang out there."

Cal wasn't the kind to volunteer information, so I assumed he was lying. "We heard Norvelle was still living with you," I said, throwing him a hard look.

The look didn't faze him. He was used to that kind of look. He bounced it back at me, with a little extra spin of his own. "You heard wrong," he said icily.

"What if I wanted to look around?" I said. "How'd you feel about that?"

Cal tossed his head back and laughed—a single, contemptuous bark of amusement. When he leveled his head again, he stared right at me—his mean blue eyes full of fight.

"You're welcome to try," he said in a whisper.

"Harry," Karen said nervously. "Maybe we better get out of here."

"She's right," Cal said in that same whispering voice. "You *better* get out of here."

"Tough guy, huh, Cal?" I said, smiling at him.

"Don't you press it, mister," he said, smiling back at me.

"We'll check out the barbershop, Cal," I said, guiding Karen toward the door. "But if I find out you were lying to me . . . I'll be back."

"I'll be waiting," he said, with his rotten grin.

It felt good to get out in the cold again. I took a deep gulp of the snowy air and breathed it out in a cloud of steam, as if I were breathing out the corrupt atmosphere of that dirty living room. Karen ran down the walk ahead of me. She had already started the motor up by the time I got to the passenger-side door. I glanced over the car roof at the screened-in porch. Cal was peering out the front window, watching me closely.

"Why did you push him like that?" Karen said irritably, once I'd gotten in beside her.

"He's a junkie who runs a chicken ranch," I said to her. "Why should I coddle a piece of shit like that?"

"Aren't you forgetting that you're hurt?" she said, giving me an aggravated look.

"Hurt or not, if I can't take Cal, it's time for me to hang it all up."

Karen shook her head disgustedly. "That kind of macho bullshit may impress the hell out of your other girlfriends, Harry, but I think it sucks. That was a bad scene in there, man. Don't you know that a guy like that has nothing to lose?"

I smiled at her, soothingly. "I know more about guys like that than you think."

"I wonder," she said coldly. "I don't want to get killed so that you can prove a point about your manhood. I used to live around fuckers like Cal, and they are not fooling around. He's not another Lonnie, Harry. He doesn't mule for dope, or cash bad checks to score a bag. That man is a stone-cold dope fiend, for chrissake! He makes his buy money by ripping people off. Even other junkies are scared of him. He'd murder his mother for a big score. Man, he *likes* his work."

"You're really scared, aren't you," I said, patting her shoulder. "I'm impressed."

"You're crazy," she said, shaking off my hand. "And you're not listening."

Karen pulled out onto Cross Lane and turned around. "Are we going to try K.T.'s Barbershop?" she said in a calmer voice.

"Might as well," I said. "But I think the bastard was lying to us."

Karen nodded halfheartedly. "I do too."

I stared at her for a second. "If he was lying, you know I'll have to come back here."

She bit her pouty lip and sighed. "Maybe we'll get lucky. Maybe Leanne'll come through for us. Or maybe we'll find Norvelle on our own."

"Maybe," I said. "But don't count on it."

"Do you have a death wish or something?" Karen said.

I laughed. "Just picking up after Lonnie," I told her.

XXVII

K.T.'s Barbershop was located on Forest, about a half block from Burnett, in a part of South Avondale that had once been a prosperous Jewish neighborhood. The area had long since gone downhill. The houses and apartments, those that were still standing, were dilapidated turn-of-the-century buildings, red-brick and frame, with sprung porches, peeling paint, and broken doors and windows. Many of the oldest structures had been torn down and replaced with two-story, tar-papered storefronts. K.T.'s Barbershop was one of the storefronts. It stood in the middle of the block—a little concrete building spackled with windblown snow.

From where Karen had parked across Forest, I could see halfway into K.T.'s through its plate-glass front window. The shop looked deserted—the old-fashioned leather and steel barber chairs standing empty on their porcelain pedestals.

This time I managed to talk Karen into staying in the car. She took one look at the run-down tar-board building and nodded at me.

"I'll wait here. But for my sake, Harry, please be careful."

I told her I would.

I got out of the Pinto and walked across Forest, through the ankle-deep snow. As I got closer to K.T.'s front window, I could see farther into the shop. It wasn't completely empty. A middle-aged black man in a white smock was sitting on one of the barber chairs at the back of the room. He was resting his head against the headrest and was holding an *Ebony* magazine tented above his face. A second black man was sitting in a cracked leather chair across from the barber. He was an old man, in a tattered topcoat. A beat-up felt hat was tipped back on his head. He was staring stupidly at the checked tile floor, his hands cribbed between his legs.

I went up to the shop door and walked in. The mirrors behind the row of barber chairs were chipped and cracked; in several spots, they'd been worn down to the black mica under the glass. The porcelain toiletry counter underneath the mirrors was worn away in black spots too. The tile floor beneath it was thick with grime and unswept clippings. A half-dozen patchy armchairs sat on the left side of the room, with stacks of dog-eared magazines piled between them for waiting customers. The room smelled of hair oil and sweat.

As I came in the barber put down his magazine. He was a middle-aged man with processed hair, a trim black mustache, and a shiny, acne-scarred yellow face. He didn't make any move to get up. He just stared at me from where he sat in the chair. The old man stared at me too. His face was deep black and heavily wrinkled. His bloodshot eyes looked unfocused, as if he were very old or very drunk.

"What can I do for you?" the barber said, as if he knew perfectly well there was nothing he could do for me.

"I'm looking for an old friend—Norvelle Thomas."

"Don't know no Norvelle Thomas," the barber said.

"Cal told me I could find him here," I said, with a smile.

"Don't know no Cal," the barber said. "You sure you in the right place. K.T.'s Barbershop?"

"That's where Cal told me to look," I said, with an exaggerated sigh. "Norvelle used to play bass in a band that I managed. I was thinking of using him again. I mean, if he's straight and I can find him."

The barber stared at me for a long moment. "You a promoter?"

"Something like that."

"Don't look like no promoter." He glanced at the old man. "He look like a promoter to you, Lyle?"

The old man shook his head savagely. "Uh-uh," he said. "Don't look like no promoter I ever seen."

I reached into my pants pocket and pulled out my wallet. "I think I have a card in here," I said. I opened the wallet wide enough to let the barber, and the old man, get a look at my stake. "I guess I ran out of cards."

I pulled a couple of twenties from the wallet, instead. The old man licked his lips.

"I sure would like to find Norvelle," I said, holding the money out.

"I sure would like to help," the barber said. He eyed the bills for a moment and shook his head sadly. "But like I told you, I don't know no Norvelle Thomas."

I was certain that he was lying. But then I was certain that Cal had lied to me too. There was no sense in muscling both of them. I figured Cal was the better bet. I thanked the barber for his time and walked back out into the snow.

As I started across Forest to the car, the old man, Lyle, came scurrying out of the barbershop.

"Whooa up, there!" he shouted at me, over the wind.

I stood on the curbside as Lyle came up to me. I figured he was going to hit me for a handout—to buy a drink or a fix. I'd seen the way he'd looked when he spotted my bankroll.

"Heard what you was saying in there," he said, working his lips slowly, as if he were trying to get some spit.

A sudden gust of wind lifted his hat off his head. He pinned it in place with his right hand and tried to hold the skirts of his tattered topcoat together with his left. The wind kept blowing straight at us, kicking snow up like a passing truck. It made the old man's eyes tear and his black face tighten into a grimace, as if someone were yanking on his hair.

"You know where Norvelle Thomas is?" I asked him.

"I maybe might," Lyle said.

I pulled the two twenties out of my pocket. The breeze made them snap in my fingers like pennants.

"Oh, Lord," the old man said. "Don't let them blow away." He laughed hoarsely, but it wasn't a joke to him. He wanted to reach out and grab them before the wind did, as if they were his own children.

"You can have them if you tell me where Norvelle is," I said to him.

He eyed the money hungrily, then eyed me. "You say you a promoter?"

I nodded.

"Well, I guess it'll be all right."

So much for his scruples, I thought.

"You know that Cal you done talked to?" the old man said. "Norvelle live with him. Over to Cross Lane."

"He told me Norvelle had moved."

"Shee-it." The old man let go of the skirts of his coat and threw his left hand at me contemptuously. "If'n you believe anything that boy tell you, you crazy. He's a *mean* boy, that boy is. He treat Norvelle like dirt. Ain't but one reason he keep him around."

"And what's that."

Lyle put a liver-colored finger to his nose and sniffed dramatically. "Norvelle get him that candy. That boy do like candy."

"Why should I believe you?" I said to him.

"What reason I got to be lying to you," the old man said, looking a little outraged. His coattails were snapping around his legs like a wild dog. "Shee-it, out here in all this cold and snow." He put a pitiful look on his face and grumbled some more, under his breath.

"I was just over on Cross Lane," I said, "and Norvelle wasn't there."

The old man looked puzzled. "Well, I don't know," he said slowly. "Norvelle be there most of the time. But some-

time he hang around the chili parlor, down here to Vine
Street."

"Which chili parlor?" I asked.

"LeRoi's Silver Star," Lyle said.

"Why does he hang out there?"

The old man gave me a dirty look. I was making him
work too hard for his money, and it galled him. Before he
could get his scruples back, I pulled another ten out of my
pocket and added it to the two twenties in my hand. It was
just enough to put him back on track.

"LeRoi be the man," Lyle said.

"Which man," I said, playing dumb.

"The man, fool. The candy man."

I handed him the fifty bucks. He snatched it out of my
hand and tucked it deep in his pants pocket.

"*Don't* you say where you heard that," Lyle said, with a
warning look.

"I won't."

"And don't you turn your back on that boy Cal. He rob
you blind."

The old man turned around and walked back into the
barbershop—his head bent against the wind.

XXVIII

When I got back inside the car, Karen asked, "Who was that old guy you were talking to?"

"That was my good friend Lyle," I said to her. "C'mon, we've got another place to visit."

Karen started the car up and pulled out onto Forest. "The old man told you something?"

I nodded. "He told me where to find Norvelle's connection. And maybe Norvelle, too."

"Where?"

"A chili parlor, down on Vine Street."

"Then Cal wasn't lying to us," Karen said, with a touch of surprise.

"Oh, yes, he was," I said. "And we're going to pay Cal another visit, too. A little later. He didn't kick Norvelle out —he didn't dare."

"Why?" Karen said.

"Because Norvelle is Cal's connection. And Cal likes his cocaine."

Karen glanced over at me. "You got all that from the old man?"

"He was thirsty," I said. "I bought him a few drinks."

"Nice job you've got," Karen said sarcastically.

For some reason, the crack pissed me off. "You feeling sorry for Lyle? Or for yourself? You know, I told you to go back to St. Louis. You can still go, if you want. I didn't make any of this happen. It was wished on me by your ex-husband."

Karen ducked her head. "I'm sorry, Harry. It's just so

fucking dirty—all of it. I thought I'd had my share of this scene. I thought I'd worked out that karma. But I guess I was wrong."

I felt the anger drain out of me. "Look," I said, glancing at my watch, "it's been a long day already. Once we're done at the chili parlor, we'll go back to the Delores. Plan some strategy. Take a little R and R."

"That sounds very good to me," Karen said with a smile. "The R and R part. You think you're up to it?"

"There's more than one way to skin a cat," I said with a wink.

We found LeRoi's Silver Star chili parlor on Vine Street, a few houses up from the Mitchell intersection—right on the borderline between South Avondale and St. Bernard. Like K.T.'s Barbershop, it was nothing more than a concrete-block storefront, with a flat tar roof, a picture window, and wavy canary-yellow aluminum siding in front. A cracked neon sign hung above the door.

I made Karen drive past LeRoi's a couple of times, before we parked down the block from it on Vine. Unlike K.T.'s, the chili parlor was doing business in spite of the cold. The counter on the left side of the joint was lined with a dozen stools. Half of them were occupied by customers. I saw one of them—a middle-aged black man in a sweater cap and a raincoat—pour half a bottle of sugar into his coffee. You didn't have to be a genius to know that he was stoned. They all looked stoned—heads bowed or bobbing like the heads of those plastic dogs you see in the rear windows of old Chevys.

"That's a drug store, Harry," Karen said, staring through the car window. "And they don't just push cocaine. The guys in there are junkies."

"I know."

"You can't walk in there and start asking questions," she said, glancing back at me. "Not unless you have a badge."

"Do you see Norvelle in there?" I asked her.

She peered out the window and shook her head. "I can't tell from here. I'll have to go inside."

"You're not going in," I told her.

"You don't know what he looks like," she protested.

"Just stay in the car, Karen," I said in a no-nonsense voice, and got out onto the sidewalk.

The salt trucks had already hit Vine, and the snow on the street had turned to blackened slush. I waited for the traffic to slow, then walked across the boulevard to LeRoi's chili parlor.

It was hot inside LeRoi's, and the whole place stank of that peculiar mixture of cumin, rosemary, and grease that passes for chili in this chili-crazy city. A wall hanging was nailed beside the door—an Arabian scene full of camels and turbaned men, like an exotic postcard for the junkies to nod over. There were a few empty booths to the right, and the luncheon counter on the left, with its row of stools leading back to the kitchen. Behind the counter, a grill boy was standing in front of a tureen, ladling soup into a bowl. He had his back to me as I walked into the room.

The men on the stools glanced up at me as one. They all looked the same—black men in raincoats, with lean, hostile faces and bleary eyes. A couple of them started snorting, as if they had bad head colds. All of them eyed me with hate. I surveyed their faces, but I wouldn't have recognized Norvelle if he'd been sitting in front of me. None of those hardened junkies was going to talk to me. I began to think it had been a mistake to walk in there.

I knew it was a mistake when I turned toward the grill behind the counter. The grill boy was staring at me with surprise, the soup ladle still in his hand. He didn't have his sunglasses on, this time, or his camel's-hair coat or his plantation hat. He was wearing a chili-stained cook's apron, tied over a white shirt and black pants. But I recognized his curls and his milk mustache and his high-yellow face instantly. When he smiled, I saw the diamond in his teeth twinkle like a signet.

"Homes!" Bo said, as if we were old friends.

Seeing Bo, standing there smiling, infuriated me. I got so angry so quickly that my hands started to shake. In the back of my mind, I knew I couldn't pick a worse spot to make a move. But the adrenaline had already started up. And I owed Bo. For what he had done to my apartment. For what he had tried to do to me. For what he might try to do again, if I gave him the chance.

I didn't think about my injuries. I didn't think about Karen, waiting in the car. I didn't think about anything but Bo's razor and the wild, drugged-out look in his eyes when he'd come at me in my living room. Before he could open his mouth again, I reached into my coat pocket and pulled out the Gold Cup, unlocking it with my thumb.

A couple of the junkies cried out, "No, man!" And one of them jumped up and ran toward the kitchen at the back of the room.

Bo stared at the pistol with horror, transfixed by it for a split second. Before he could react, I reached across the counter and grabbed him by the front of the apron, pulling him right up to the barrel, so that the front sight pressed against his lips. He dropped the ladle on the floor and started trembling. His eyes crossed, trying to stare down the gun barrel.

"No!" he shrieked in his girlish voice. "Oh, Jesus, don't!"

I yanked him over the counter, knocking over coffee cups and sugar bowls. Hot coffee flew everywhere. The junkies nearest to where I was standing jumped off their stools. One of them fell off his, and went crawling backward on his hands toward the far wall.

I pulled Bo to his feet and pinned him against the wall by the grill, so I could see the whole room in front of me. No one went for a gun or a knife. No one was going to try. I could see it in their faces. All they cared about was not getting hurt by the wild honkie with the automatic.

I ground the gun barrel into Bo's face.

"You going to do some cutting, Bo?" I said to him.

His eyes rolled back and he screamed. He tried to pull away, his feet flying around on the linoleum floor as if he were on roller skates. But I had a good grip.

"Where's your boss?" I said to him, and smacked him on the scalp with the gun.

He shrieked again. And I hit him again.

His scalp started pouring blood. It spurted over his apron and over me. I wanted to hit him a few more times. I would have—I was that enraged—if someone with a deep, calm voice hadn't called out: "That's enough, brother."

I looked away from Bo toward the counter. A tall, good-looking black man in another apron was standing in the aisle between the stools and the wall. He had a shotgun in his hands. For a second, I thought I was dead. Then I realized the man wasn't training the shotgun on me—he was cradling it in his arms, as if it were just for show. Still, I almost shot at him. I was that close to gut reaction.

"No, no, no," he said softly, as if he were reading my mind. "Ain't gonna be no shooting."

I took a deep breath and let Bo go. He slipped to the floor at my feet, groaned, and started to crawl around on all fours. I stared at the man with the shotgun, trying to figure out why he hadn't shot me. Unlike the junkies in the chili parlor, he was stocky, almost healthy-looking. His face was light brown, handsome, with something unexpectedly gentle about his large black eyes.

While the guy with the gun and I were staring at each other, Bo managed to crawl around in a full circle at my feet. He grabbed at my trousers legs, pulled himself up, and stared at me desperately, as if he thought he'd found help. When he wiped the blood from his face and focused his eyes, he shrieked and let go of my pants. One of the junkies laughed shrilly, like a mynah bird. I pushed Bo away and he fell on his back. He just lay there pawing the air, like an upturned bug.

I stared at Bo for a second then looked back at the black

man with the shotgun, to see how he'd react. He didn't do anything. I still couldn't figure out why he hadn't shot me —a wild-eyed white man waving a pistol and beating up his friend. Then it dawned on me that he must have known who I was and that he didn't want me dead—at least, not until he'd gotten his goods back.

"You're LeRoi, aren't you?" I said to him, lowering my pistol but keeping my finger on the trigger.

"I'm LeRoi, man," he said, in his deep, soft voice—a choir bass.

"You're his boss?" I asked, pointing with the gun at Bo, who had flipped himself over and was now making his way on hands and knees down the aisle.

"He work for me some, yeah."

I raised the pistol and pointed it at LeRoi's head. LeRoi blanched.

"Wha'chu doing?" he said with a questioning look.

"Put the shotgun down," I said to him in a tough voice.

He hesitated a moment, then laid the shotgun on the lunch counter.

"Now, you think I've got something of yours, LeRoi," I said. "But I don't"

"I don't know what you talking about," he said icily. The gentle look in his eyes had disappeared. Replaced by something tough and controlled—something much tougher than the stuff that Bo was made of.

"I think you do," I said. "If you want to talk about it, you give me a call tonight. You know my number and my address. If you forgot, ask him."

I kicked Bo in the butt and sent him sprawling on his face. I backed toward the door, keeping the pistol trained on LeRoi. He didn't take his eyes off me. I opened the door and walked outside, pocketing the pistol as I left.

XXIX

It wasn't until I started back across Vine Street that I began to pay the price for my hijinks. My hands wouldn't stop shaking, and as the adrenaline washed away, my spine started to hurt like a son of a bitch. I'd wrenched it, pulling Bo across the counter. The spasms were bad enough to make me take small steps and pause in between them.

Worse than the pain was the effect my antics had had on Karen. I'd forgotten that she could see partway into LeRoi's chili parlor from where she was sitting in the car. I hoped she'd missed the worst of it—the tussle with Bo and the business with the shotgun. But there was little doubt in my mind that she'd seen some of what happened and that it had probably terrified her.

I knew my suspicions were right when I saw her jump out of the car as soon as I'd crossed Vine. She came running up the snowy sidewalk toward me.

"What happened in there?" she said breathlessly, giving me an anguished look. "I couldn't see through the window. You disappeared inside. Then people started running around, and I had no idea what was going down. I almost called the cops, for chrissake!"

I could see from her face that she was close to tears and very angry.

"I'm all right," I said, trying to smile reassuringly.

"All right!" she shouted. "You've got blood on your cheek!"

I wiped my cheek and glanced back over my shoulder at LeRoi's Silver Star. "Let's just get out of here, okay?"

She eyed me furiously. "You son of a bitch!" she said. "Don't you care about yourself? Don't you care about me?"

Her pouty lip started to tremble, and she turned away and walked stiff-legged back to the Pinto.

When I got inside the car, she was holding her hands over her face, breathing heavily. I stared at her guiltily.

"Karen . . ." I reached out to touch her.

She dropped one hand and pushed me away. "Don't you touch me!" she shouted.

She covered her face again. I knew she wasn't just crying over me. It was the whole day—the toll it had taken. It was her past coming back to haunt her. It was that bad karma she hadn't worked off. It was Lonnie. But it was also me, and I felt bad about it.

"I'm sorry, Karen," I said heavily.

"At least I knew where I stood with Lonnie," she said bitterly. "At least I could predict what he was going to do." She took a couple of deep breaths.

"All right," she said, her hands still tented over her eyes. She pulled her hands down to her mouth and rested them against her lips. "What happened?" she said, staring at me over her fingertips.

"The guys that Lonnie got the crack from live in that chili parlor," I said. "One of them was the kid who tried to carve me up in my apartment. When I saw him . . . I lost my temper."

"You're hurt!" she said through her teeth. "You're supposed to lay off for a while. You crazy bastard."

"It wasn't all bad," I said, blushing. "I made an impression on LeRoi. And LeRoi is the man we're going to have to deal with."

She shook her head, helplessly. "What about Norvelle? Did you forget about him?"

"I think we're going to have to talk to Cal about Norvelle."

She dropped her hands to her lap and gawked at me. "You *are* crazy."

"I told you before, Karen. I didn't make this scene. I'm just trying to survive it."

"Sure you are," she said, shaking her head.

She started the car up and headed south on Vine. As we passed LeRoi's, I glanced into the chili parlor window. The junkies were sitting at the counter again, their heads bobbing like plastic dogs.

It was almost four-thirty when we left the chili parlor, and the sun was already low in the sky, setting in a band of orange behind a bank of dark gray storm clouds. It was going to snow some more in the night. And after the chili parlor and the scene in the car, I was too cold, too hurt, and too generally dispirited to face Cal before nightfall. I told Karen to drive us home—back to the Delores.

She had just turned left on St. Clair, when I happened to glance in the rearview mirror. There was a late-model gray Ford, a cop car, on our tail. At least, I thought it was on our tail. When we got to Burnett, the Ford turned with us, and I was sure he was following us. I was also sure that it was Jordan behind the wheel.

Karen turned into the Delores's parking lot, with the Ford right on her bumper. Before she could turn off the engine, he'd turned on his siren.

"Harry," Karen said, giving me a sick look.

"Yeah," I said, "I know."

"The whole block knows," she said over the howl of the siren.

"That's the way he wanted it." I got out and walked slowly to the rear of the car. Jordan had parked behind us, on an angle—as if he were blocking off a felony suspect.

I peered through his front window, waiting for him to come out. He just sat there, for a good three or four minutes, watching me shiver. He left the siren running, too—long enough so that everyone in the apartment house had time to plaster themselves against their windows. People on the street had stopped, too, peeking over the snow-covered hedges into the frozen lot.

When Jordan was satisfied that he was commanding sufficient attention, he turned off the siren, got out of the Ford, and walked slowly up to me, a dead grin on his dead-eyed face. He knew how badly I wanted him, and he was enjoying making me squirm in front of the home folks, in front of Karen.

"How ya doing, Harry," he said. "How's the back?"

I straightened up. "What do you want, shithead?"

"Nice talk," Jordan said, shaking a finger at me. "Saw where you paid a visit to your pal LeRoi. He's an old friend of mine, too. I've seen lots of him downtown, Harry. You know about downtown, don't you? Where we keep the bad guys?

"You know, Harry," he said, staring at me hard. "It's a good thing you've got friends on the force or you'd be in slam right now. I got your name on the Encantada register. I got a few rocks from the motel. I got the crack from your apartment. I got a Polaroid of you going into that chili parlor. And before too long I'm going to have a witness, Harry, who saw what you and your pal were up to at the Encantada on the night that Jenkins was killed. And when I get a deposition . . ." He whistled like a fast freight. "We're going to take another trip downstairs. And this time, no one's going to stop us."

"You'll have to kill me before I give you another chance like that, Jordan," I said.

"Then that's what I'll have to do," he said, nodding as if the matter were settled. "You called the shot."

"Don't count on it being easy," I said with a smile.

"You pack your bags, Harry, and kiss the little woman good-bye. It won't be long." He waved at me with the fingers of his right hand. "See ya."

Walking back to the car, he got in, turned around, and pulled back out of the lot, spinning his tires on the ice and throwing up a plume of dirty snow in his wake.

XXX

What Jordan had said had shaken me up, especially the part about a witness to the murder. I could explain away the rest of it—the name on the register, the crack, LeRoi and Bo. But if someone had seen me coming out of the Encantada office on Friday night, I was in serious trouble. Accessory after the fact, concealing evidence, at the very least. If they really wanted to get ugly, it could be as bad as aggravated homicide. The first thing I did when I got upstairs to the apartment, was phone Al Foster at CPD.

"I just ran into Jordan," I said to him.

"You're talking to me again, are you?" Al said in his wheezy, high-pitched voice.

"I guess I am," I said. "I guess I forgot to say thanks yesterday too."

"Forget it," Al said. "What did Jordan want?"

"To put me in jail. He claims he's got a witness to what went down at the Encantada Motel, the night that the clerk was murdered."

"What do you care? You weren't there, were you?"

"I just want to know who the witness is—if there *is* a witness, if Jordan's not just jerking me off. You think maybe you could look into it for me?"

"I'll get back to you," Al said.

I stared at the phone for a moment, after I'd hung up. Karen came up beside me and put a hand on my shoulder. I patted her hand idly.

"Maybe I should take a trip out to the Encantada," I said, half to myself.

"It's past five," Karen said, staring out the window at the twilight settling on Burnett Avenue. "Don't you want to rest?"

I looked up at her with a smile. "I thought you were mad at me."

She shrugged. "I'm mad at the world. I just want this thing to be over with, without either one of us getting hurt."

I stood up and took Karen by the hand. "Let's go to bed," I said, staring into her pale blue eyes.

She smiled at me uncertainly. "You sure you want to? I said some lousy things to you, this afternoon."

"I've got a thick hide," I said, pulling her to me and guiding her down the hallway.

Our lovemaking wasn't explosive, like it had been in the hotel room. The urge was there, all right, but I could only move awkwardly, because of my back. For the most part, I just lay there and let Karen do the work. She didn't seem to mind.

After we'd made love, we huddled under the covers for a time, watching the snow blowing outside the bedroom window. The ground cover was reflecting streetlights and car lights, lending the night sky a warm, yellow cast. The bedroom was dark and quiet, save for the wind whistling in the casements. Karen traced a fingertip around my lips, then laid her head on my chest.

"I'm sorry about this afternoon," she said softly. "I mean about the chili parlor. I wasn't just mad at you." She raised her head and slapped my chest lightly with her palm. "Although that was pretty stupid, what you did."

"Pretty stupid," I agreed.

She put her head back down. "That place reminded me of another place, in East St. Louis. For almost a year, all Lonnie and I did every day was go down to the junkie restaurant and hang out—nodding off, talking shit, waiting to score. It was a very bad time in my life—maybe the worst, all told. Some awful things happened in the back room of that restaurant."

She shivered under the covers and I stroked her head, running my hand down her long, smooth neck. "We don't have to talk about it. I shouldn't have lost my temper in the chili parlor. It *was* stupid." I grunted. "In fact, I don't think I've done one smart thing since Lonnie stepped back into my life, except for making love to you."

I couldn't see her face, but I could feel her smile against my chest. She stirred under the blankets, pressing herself against me.

"There was something else about this afternoon," she said in a whisper. "I realized it when I was sitting in the car, waiting for you to come out of that chili parlor."

"What?" I said.

"I was afraid," she said guiltily.

I pulled her tight against me. "You had a right to be afraid. It was a scary situation."

"That's not what I meant," Karen said. "I wasn't just scared for you, although I *was* scared for you. What I realized was that I'd been afraid for a long time. Ever since I left Lonnie, really. I've been holding my breath for two years."

"I think what you did after you left Lonnie was pretty brave," I said to her.

She shook her head. "Sure, I uncomplicated my life. But I stopped loving, Harry. I stopped trying to love and started trying to get by. Sometimes in St. Louis I'll wake up alone in the night, and it's like Lonnie never happened to me, like I have no past at all. When I feel like that, I have to get up and go look at the kids, just to reassure myself that I do have a history. And then every once in a while, I'll hear an old song or see an old movie like *Woodstock* and it'll all come back. I'll think, my God, that was me, that was my generation. It's like, in trying to forget Lonnie, I've been hiding out from a whole decade."

"You kept going forward," I said. "Like the Marine Corps manual says."

She laughed feebly. "Sometimes I want to go back. I want to share that with someone. I don't want to be afraid of my own past."

"You can share it with me," I said.

"For how long, though?" she said uncertainly. "*He'll* always be there—for both of us."

The phone jangled on the nightstand.

"Don't answer it," Karen said with foreboding.

"I think I better," I said. "It might be Al."

I picked up the receiver and pressed it against my ear.

"Stoner?" an unfamiliar voice said.

"Yes."

"LeRoi say to tell you he be paying you a visit tonight. 'Bout midnight. He say to tell you there ain't gonna be no trouble. He just wanna talk."

"He's coming here?" I said.

The black man said, "Yeah. Your crib."

"You tell him if he isn't alone, there *is* going to be some trouble."

"Bet, man," the black said with a chuckle. "You a tough fucker, ain't you?"

"You just tell him," I said, and hung up.

Karen pulled away from me in the bed. "The nightmare's starting up again, isn't it?"

I didn't know how to answer her. I didn't know what LeRoi had in mind. I'd gotten what I'd wanted—a meeting with the candy man. Only I didn't know what had happened to the candy. And that was all he cared about.

"It'll be all right," I said reassuringly. "Maybe LeRoi can tell us what happened to Lonnie."

"Do we really want to know?" she said in a distant voice. "What happens when we find out?"

To be honest, I didn't know how to answer that, either.

XXXI

I told Karen I'd take her out for supper. While she was in the shower, the phone on the nightstand rang again. I hesitated for a moment before picking it up, wondering what I was going to say if it turned out to be LeRoi again. This time, it was Al.

"Jordan's partner, Lewis, tells me he's been talking to some biker who hangs out at the Encantada bar. The guy's a regular at the bar, and he's got some information that Jordan thinks is crucial."

"Information about what?" I asked.

Al said, "I don't know, Harry. About the murder, I guess."

"Do you have a name for this biker?" I asked him.

"Sonny Carter. Lewis says he's a big guy with a black beard. Wears a chain vest. That sort of thing."

"Thanks, Al," I said.

"Harry," Foster said in a concerned voice. "If you haven't come clean with me about that motel murder, I think now is the time. I've got my neck stuck out a mile for you, pal. And Jordan would like nothing more than to chop it off. If he nails you, he'll nail me too. You can count on it."

I should have told him the whole story. After what he'd done for me the night before, he deserved to hear it. But I didn't. Partly because it seemed too complicated to explain over the phone. Partly out of stubbornness, out of a stupid desire to show Jordan up, without help from anyone. And, in spite of everything, partly because of Lonnie.

"I've got nothing to tell you, Al," I said.

He grunted. "You always play it your own way, don't you, Harry?" He started to hang up, then said, "Oh, by the way, that guy you asked us to find? That Jackowski guy?"

"Yeah?" I said.

"Jordan's looking for him too."

"Why?" I asked.

"You tell me, Harry," Al said with bitterness. "You could, if you wanted to. Couldn't you?"

"Al . . ." I said.

"Fuck you, Harry," he said, and hung up.

Great, I said to myself. I was in no position to alienate one of the few friends I had left, and I knew it. I picked up the phone—to call Al back. Then I started thinking about Jordan, about what he would do to Lonnie if he got his hands on him, and I put the phone back down. Having been through it myself, I simply couldn't do that to Lonnie. I couldn't do that to any man.

I sat down on the bed, listening to the sound of the shower pounding against the stall. For a moment, I almost felt panicky—the way Karen had said she'd felt, waking up alone in the middle of the night, trying to block Lonnie out of her mind. Out of nowhere, out of the night, he'd come back into my life. Spent one day in my apartment. Then disappeared again, into the darkness, leaving me to pay the price for his mistakes. Leaving me fighting for my life.

There was something so bizarre about his visit, so inexplicable, that it truly frightened me. It was like he wasn't real. Like he was some manifestation of a bleak, joking providence. An incarnation of a zeitgeist, a phantom from the raucous, irresponsible past—from the wild old days that Leanne Silverstein had said she regretted and that Karen was trying desperately to forget—come to teach me a lesson, about nostalgia and brother's keeping.

But that was giving Lonnie much more than his due. All he really was, I told myself, was a stupid junkie trying to get to Fire Lake. A kid playing with matches in a motel room, setting blazes in wastebaskets and running away. That's what I told myself. But for a few moments I stayed scared.

Karen came out of the shower and walked into the bedroom—naked, her hair dripping wet. "Where are your towels?" she said.

I pointed to the bottom drawer of my dresser.

Karen bent down and opened the drawer, pulling a towel out.

I sat there, staring at the floor—still thinking about Lonnie. "We've got to stop him," I said, without realizing that I'd said it.

"Who?" she said, wrapping the towel around her as she stood up.

"Lonnie," I said, looking up at her.

"Are you okay?" she said, eyeing me critically. "Who was that on the phone?"

"It was Al."

"And?"

"And I'm going to have to go out to that goddamn motel again."

"Christ," she said. "What happened?"

"Jordan may have a witness to the murder. A biker at the motel."

"But we already know who killed Jenkins," Karen said. "It was that black kid, Bo. Wasn't it?"

"Yes," I said.

"So why do you have to talk to the biker?"

"I was there, for chrissake!" I said, and I could hear the panic in my own voice. "My name's on the Encantada register. I left my footprints on the fucking floor. I took Lonnie's license out of the office. I didn't report the murder. I'm involved. What if the son of a bitch biker saw *me* coming out of the office?"

"Christ," Karen said, paling. "I didn't think of that."

"Jenkins had been dead for a while," I said, thinking about the way the blood had coagulated on his body, thinking about the terrible smile on his face. "At least an hour or more. That would put the murder around two or earlier. I didn't get there until close to three."

"So you're in the clear?" Karen said hopefully.

"If the biker remembers the time right," I said without much confidence. "An hour isn't a lot of leeway." I slapped my knee with my palm. "What the fuck was he doing out there anyway, in the middle of a freezing cold night? The bar was closed. The motel was deserted."

"Maybe he was waiting for somebody?" Karen offered.

"Who?" I said.

"I guess we're just going to have to find out." She picked up her duffel bag and walked back toward the john. "This better end soon," she called out. "Or my kids are going to start wondering what happened to me."

We grabbed a bite to eat at McDonald's and ate it in the car as we headed out Columbia Parkway to Miamiville. I drove this time. The aches and pains hadn't gone away. They just didn't seem that important anymore. The important thing was getting a lead on Lonnie, before midnight, if I could manage it. I wanted to give LeRoi something—something to get me off the hook.

I could have paid Cal another visit. It probably would have been the smart move, especially if Norvelle had come back home. But I knew that my next visit to Cal was going to end in violence—he'd made that clear. And, unless it was necessary, I didn't want to put Karen through that scene again. Actually, I didn't want her along on the trip to the Encantada. But there was no place to hide anymore. No place that was safe. Even if I'd stuck her in the Clarion, I knew that she was still vulnerable to LeRoi or to Jordan.

It was close to eight when we pulled into the Encantada lot. This time the bar was wide open. A row of bare yellow bulbs surrounded the Quonset's door, winking alternately, like the entrance to a peep show. You could hear the roar of laughter, music, and talk from where we'd parked, a good hundred yards away from the hut. I stared at the row of motorcycles parked in front of the entrance. They were all chopped, forks extended and dressed with chrome. The bar lights played on the fenders, making them look as if they were spangled with oil.

"This is going to be fun," I said.

Karen smiled bleakly. "What are you going to do?"

"Whatever it takes," I said grimly. "First I've got to find the guy."

"And then?"

I turned on the car seat. "Lonnie made his connection with LeRoi through Norvelle. Then he came out to this motel, presumably with the crack. There had to be a reason why he did that."

"You think he was going to sell it to the bikers?" Karen said, staring at the row of Harleys.

"It would explain why he was here."

"Then he got ripped off and tried to kill himself, right?"

I nodded. "By Jenkins, I think. That's what LeRoi must have thought, too, or else he wouldn't have sent Bo out here to kill him."

"But Jenkins didn't have the crack," Karen said.

"Nope. Somebody else's got it."

"You think Jenkins had a partner?"

"Lonnie *was* beaten up by a biker, before he tried to kill himself," I said. "It could have been a coincidence, but I kind of doubt it."

"So you think one of the bikers has the lady?" Karen said.

"The guy that Jordan was talking to had to have some reason to be hanging around out here in the middle of the night. Maybe he got to Jenkins before Bo and his pals did. Maybe he got the crack before Jenkins got offed. Maybe he thinks he can pin the whole thing on me or Lonnie and still keep the dope."

"It makes sense," Karen said. She glanced at the bar. "He's not likely to want to talk to us."

I laughed. "I'd say not."

"So how do we do this?" she said, turning to me.

"Let's find him first," I said. "Then we'll worry about getting him to talk."

XXXII

Karen and I got out of the Pinto and walked across the lot to the Quonset hut. The closer we got to the door, the louder the bar sounds became. This was no neighborhood saloon; it was a raucous, redneck hangout. Just the ticket for an evening's fun.

The wind was blowing loose snow from the Quonset's roof. It trailed from the eaves like a banner, fluttering in the air above the lighted entrance. I brushed the snow out of my eyes and opened the door. A cloud of cigarette smoke came pouring out of the bar, as if the whole place were on fire.

"Jesus," Karen said, swiping at the smoke and the snow. "It looks like hell in there."

"Pretty close," I said. "When we get inside, just play along with whatever I say. Can you manage that?"

Karen laughed. "I'm good at playing along, Harry. I've had years of training. For a couple of months in a row back in '72, Lonnie and I didn't tell the truth once. Not even to each other."

"Sounds like you qualify," I said, guiding her through the door.

The smoke was like a river fog inside the bar. And the place was even noisier than I had imagined. A jukebox beside the door was blaring country music through four speakers hung from the rafters, and the bar talk was being carried on at the top of everyone's lungs. Even the clink of mugs and pitchers seemed too loud, as if for every beer that was being poured, someone was breaking a bottle.

A couple of dozen round wooden tables were set up in the center of the room—all of them occupied by bikers and their women. A few strangers were sitting in booths on the left wall. At least, I assumed they were strangers from their cowed faces. They looked like travelers who'd wandered into the Twilight Zone from the highway and who didn't know how to get back out again.

A long polished-wood bar ran the length of the room on the right, with a mirror behind it and rows of liquor bottles stacked beneath the mirror. An overworked-looking barmaid in jeans and a lumberjack shirt was standing at the end of the bar, waiting for the bartender to fill an order. She was resting her elbows on a cork-lined tray. She'd lost a barrette at one temple, and wisps of loose brown hair were hanging down over that side of her face. As I walked up to her she blew the hair back and smiled at me wearily.

"Busy night?" I said.

"Every night's busy around here," the barmaid said.

"You always get the same crowd?" I glanced at the bikers in their chains and leathers.

She nodded. "They ain't as bad as they look," she said, a touch defensively.

"I didn't mean to sound smart," I said quickly. "In fact, we're looking for a guy. We're supposed to meet him here."

"Who?" she said.

"Sonny Carter," I said, glancing around the room. I pointed to one of the tables in the distance. "Isn't that Sonny?" I glanced at Karen. "Isn't that Sonny over there, hon?"

Karen pretended to peer through the haze. "I don't know," she said, swiping at the smoke. "I can't make him out."

The barmaid shook her head. "That ain't Sonny over there. Sonny's up in the corner with Duke."

"Which corner?" I asked, looking confused.

She pointed to the right.

I sighted across the room, my hand over my brow. "Oh, yeah!" I said cheerfully. "I see him now."

The barmaid glanced at me and Karen uncertainly. "You all friends of his?"

"Yeah," I said, smiling at her. "Me and Sonny go way back."

The bartender came up and slapped four margaritas on the barmaid's tray.

"Go on," he said, giving her a stern look. "You got tables to wait."

She snarled at him, picked up the tray, and wandered off into the maze of tables.

I pulled Karen away from the bar. "What do you think?" I said.

She stared at Sonny—a big, bearded lummox in a sweat-shirt, grimy blue jeans, and a chained leather vest. Twenty-five, twenty-six years old. Six-two. Two-hundred-eighty pounds. Lank, uncut black hair that hung down to his shoulders. Porcine face. Teeth missing on either side of his mouth. Huge, bulging belly. Huge arms, dripping fat like an upturned skillet. Tattoos on either forearm. A folding knife hanging from a chain on his belt. He was a prize.

Karen shook her head. "He's a monster."

"Yep," I said. "And probably mean as a snake."

"What do *you* think?" Karen said.

"Well, we've got to get him out of here—that's for sure. He's enough of a handful on his own. We don't want his pals stomping us too."

Karen glanced back at Sonny. "If he does have all that crack, maybe he'd be willing to sell some to me."

"To a stranger?" I asked dubiously.

"I don't have to remain a stranger," she said, giving me a wink.

I stared at Karen. "You'd make a play for . . . that?"

"I've done a lot worse," Karen said casually.

"I don't think I want to hear about it," I said.

"Tell you what," Karen said. "You go out to the car. In

due time, I'll come out with Sonny. I think that one's up for something kinky. Maybe we can get him to take us home and feed us some crack. You think *you* can play it by ear?"

"Play what?" I said.

"A swinger," she said with a laugh. "I mean, it's casting against type, but . . ."

"Jesus, Karen," I said, "I don't know."

"You have a better idea on how to get him out of here—alone?"

"I guess not," I said.

"Then leave it to mama." She unzipped her fur jacket, roughed up her hair, unbuttoned the top two buttons on her blouse, and walked off toward Sonny's table.

I watched her for a time from the bar rail. Karen sat down at Sonny's table and started talking to him. I couldn't hear what she said, but after a minute or two, Sonny called the barmaid over and ordered a couple of drinks. Karen kept talking to Sonny, leaning across the table to give him a look at her breasts. A minute or two after the drinks arrived, Sonny told his friend Duke to blow. Duke, a biker as skinny as Sonny was fat, grinned salaciously and took his drink to another table. Sonny scooted over toward Karen, patting her hand with one of his paws. She smiled at him encouragingly.

I started to feel a little sick.

When I couldn't stand to watch him drool over her anymore, I walked out of the bar into the cold. I stood in front of the door for a long time, counting seconds like a timekeeper. When Karen didn't come out right away, I wandered back to the car.

I wouldn't have gotten in the car, if the cold hadn't been so fierce. But ten minutes of shivering made my back start to ache. I climbed in the front seat, behind the wheel, turned on the engine, and turned the heater up to high. I opened the vents and sat there, with the heat pouring over me, until I broke into a sweat. And still she didn't come out.

I glanced at my watch. It had only been twenty minutes. I knew I was behaving like a kid. I knew she was only doing whatever she was doing in there for me—to get me off the hook with LeRoi. But some chauvinistic fold of my brain simply couldn't handle the thought of Sonny Carter touching her, even if it *was* only an act. The longer she stayed in that bar, the angrier I got. By the time she and Sonny came out the door, I was livid. I wanted to tear that fat cocksucker to pieces—to cut off his hands and nail them to the fucking wall.

Karen came bouncing over to the car, a half-dozen yards ahead of Sonny. She knocked on the window, and I rolled it down.

"We got us some real action here, Harry," she said, loudly enough for Sonny to hear her.

Then she took a look at my face and whispered, "What the hell is wrong?"

"I don't like this game," I said through my teeth.

"Don't be an asshole, Harry. Play along. I've got the bastard hooked."

I took a deep breath and nodded. But I was still gritting my teeth.

Sonny came ambling up behind Karen. He pulled her back to him and ran his huge hands up the front of her blouse to her breasts, squeezing them tightly. Karen laughed, as if she were drunk. Glancing over her shoulder at me, Sonny said, "I hear you're into threesomes."

"Is that what you heard?" I said coldly.

Karen gave me a warning look. "Lighten up, Harry," she said. "Sonny's going to party with us."

Sonny gave me a long look. He had piggish eyes, and what I could see of his mouth through the curly black beard was red and wet. For a moment, I wondered whether he'd remember me—from Friday. But there wasn't a hint of recognition on his stupid face. He was just staring hard at me because he liked to stare hard at strangers—because he was big enough to do it and to get away with it. I started to wonder why Jordan considered him a key witness. If Carter didn't know me, and he didn't seem to, then I had no idea whom or what he'd seen at that motel.

Sonny kept staring at me coldly. "If you're not man enough to handle this scene, maybe I'll just take her off on my chopper." He squeezed Karen's breasts so hard, she winced. "This bitch is hot."

I forced my mouth into a smile. "I'm ready to party. Any time. Any place."

Sonny grinned and wiped his red, dripping mouth with the back of his hand. He said to Karen: "Let's go back to my crib. Get naked. Do some bad things." He turned her face to him roughly. "I got a video camera back there, baby, and a fourteen-inch dildo your ass will just love. We can make movies."

"I want to get high," Karen said with a pout of her pouty lip.

"I told you," Sonny said. "I can handle that too. I got a connection."

Karen got in the backseat and Sonny piled in behind her. The car shook when he got in, as if someone had dropped a boulder in the bed of a pickup truck.

"Let's go, boy," he said.

"Where?"

"Just a few blocks up the road. Miamiville Apartments."

"What about your chopper?"

"It ain't going anywhere. Let's move."

I started the car up and pulled out onto Wooster Pike. It was only a couple of blocks to the apartment complex, like Sonny had said. Just the same, I didn't dare look in the rearview mirror on the way.

XXXIII

Carter's pad was on the third floor of one of those jerry-built apartment complexes that promise you wall-to-wall carpeting, equipped kitchens, balconies with a view, and air-conditioning—all for under two hundred dollars a month. What they are, are dry-walled rattraps, with Astroturf on the floor, a disposal bolted under the sink, a two-foot by four-foot balcony overlooking a highway, and an 8000-BTU air conditioner rattling in the wall.

I followed Sonny from the parking lot to a concrete stairwell and then up to the third floor. He'd kept Karen with him, as if he'd taken possession of her for the night.

When we got to the door of his apartment, he let her go for a moment. While he was fiddling with the locks, she gave me a sick look, as if to say, "What now?" It was clear that she was as tired of the game as I was. Plus she was getting frightened. It was party time, and Sonny wasn't likely to waste much time on foreplay. He'd had foreplay in the backseat of the Pinto.

Sonny unlocked the door, opened it, and grabbed for Karen's arm.

I pulled her over to me before he could get a grip. "Easy, Sonny," I said with a smile. "Let's take this slow."

He gave me a vicious look. "I don't know if I want to party with you, boy. You're too square."

He stared at Karen, cowering behind me. She was looking scared; she just couldn't hide it anymore. And Sonny could see it. He wasn't a smart man, but he was street smart. And Karen and I were beginning not to add up.

"I don't know if I want to party at all," he said slowly.

"I want to get high," Karen squeaked, from behind my back.

"We all want to get high, lady," Sonny said.

He stood in the doorway to his apartment—his hand on the knob—squinting at us for a long moment. "Uh-uh," he finally said, looking directly at me, "you ain't party material."

He turned his back to us and started to close the door.

Before he could shut it completely, I braced my hands against the wall behind me, raised my right leg, and kicked Sonny in the small of the back—kicked him as hard as if I was trying to kick down the door itself. The kick hurt me as much as it did him, sending a fierce pain shooting up my spine. But it had its effect. Carter fell forward through the doorway with a thud, landing on his face—hands outstretched, arms outstretched, as if he were lost in the desert.

In spite of the ache in my back, I followed him right through the doorway, pulling the Gold Cup from my coat pocket. After the way he'd pawed Karen, I wanted to hurt the son of a bitch. I wanted to castrate him.

Luckily the only light in the room was coming from the hall, and it was illuminating the spot where he was kneeling. He couldn't see me, but I could see him fine. He started to get to his knees, huffing and blowing like a walrus, and I cracked him on the temple with the gun barrel. The first shot just seemed to make him mad. He snarled and swung one of his huge arms out at me blindly. I wrapped both hands around the gun barrel and whipped the butt across his face like a baseball bat, breaking his nose. He spit out some blood, wobbled on his knees like a tenpin, then fell over on the carpet, in the middle of that square of light.

I raised the gun a third time and Karen cried out, "No!"

I turned toward her with a snarl of my own. "I'm going to kill the fucker," I said.

"That's going to do us a lot of good, isn't it?" she said.

For a second I felt like hitting her. Karen could see it, too, and she took a step back toward the hall.

"Harry?" she said in a frightened voice. "You're scaring me."

"I hated that whole scene in the car," I said fiercely. "I mean I *hated* it."

"You think I didn't?" she said, staring at me with a shocked look on her face. "You're the first man I've felt anything for in two years, you crazy bastard. Or do you think I was born to swing?"

I felt my heart sink. "I couldn't stand to see him touch you," I said.

"A lot of guys have touched me, Harry," Karen said, giving me a softer look. "I thought you understood that."

"I guess I didn't," I said heavily.

"Can you live with it?"

I nodded.

But she didn't look convinced. "We're pretty different, you and I. More different than I thought. I'm not the person you think I am, Harry. I've been around the block —more than once."

"It wasn't you. It was him," I said, staring at Carter's bloated body. "I'm never going to let that happen to you again. I shouldn't have gone along with it in the first place."

She shook her head. "My bodyguard, huh? You're a square, you know that? And a chauvinist."

"So?" I said without apology.

"So . . . I don't know. Under the circumstances, I guess I can handle it, but with that attitude, I honestly don't know how you ever survived the sixties."

Karen reached over and flipped on a wall switch. A lamp on a table by the door came on, lighting up the tiny living room. It was just what you would have expected from a guy like Sonny. A velvet hanging of a naked siren above a black plastic sofa. A pine end table littered with beer cans and brimming ashtrays. A couple of cardboard boxes full of oily motorcycle parts. A video camera set up by a dilapidated color TV. The room smelled equally of cigarettes, beer, and forty-weight.

Carter groaned dully and moved his head. It would take him a while to come around, and I wanted to be prepared.

"See if you can find something to tie him up with," I said to Karen.

The living room opened onto a tiny kitchen, just an alcove, really. Karen shut the front door and walked into the kitchen. She flipped on a light and went through several drawers.

"There isn't any rope in here," she said.

I glanced at the boxes of motorcycle parts and said, "We can use the chains."

I flipped Sonny over on his stomach and pulled an oily bike chain from the box. I managed to loop it around each of his arms, loop it through itself, then bring it back and loop it around each of his legs. The chain wouldn't have held him if he had had all his strength. But with a busted nose and a concussion, he wasn't going anywhere.

While I was hog-tying Sonny, Karen searched his bedroom, looking for crack. I knew that she'd found something when she made a little whooping noise. She came striding into the living room with a tube filled with rocks in her hand. It looked like the same stuff that Bo had dropped in my living room. Presumably the same stuff that Lonnie had lost at the motel.

She handed the tube to me.

"Was there any more in there?" I asked her.

She shook her head. "That was all I could find."

I stared at the tube. There were about twenty rocks in it. A couple hundred dollars' worth. Not enough to get anybody killed.

"Maybe I better take a look," I said, walking toward the bedroom. "You keep an eye on him."

I searched the bedroom for about ten minutes, turning

over everything I could find. Twice. There wasn't much to turn—a mattress and a box spring. A beaten oak dresser. A couple more boxes of bike parts in the closet. And a few pieces of clothing. When I couldn't find anything in the bedroom, I tried the kitchen. And then the living room itself. All to no end. If Sonny had the crack, he didn't have it in his apartment.

I was just sorting through the last box of bike parts, when he came around.

"Harry!" Karen called out.

I got up and walked over to where Sonny was lying facedown on the rug, his arms and legs chained behind him. I knelt next to him, took out the pistol, and pressed the barrel against the back of his head.

"You know what that is, Sonny?" I said to him.

He nodded weakly.

"Now you're going to answer a few questions," I said. "If you don't answer them, I'm going to kill you. It's that simple. No second tries. I'm just going to blow the back of your head off. You understand?"

He nodded again. "Yeah," he said groggily.

"Where's the rest of the crack?"

"What?" He started to cough and hack. "I gotta get a doctor, man. You broke my nose. And my bridge. You broke my bridge, man."

"The crack," I said again.

"I don't know what the fuck you're talking about," he shouted. "What crack?"

"The crack you took off that guy at the motel on Thursday night."

He didn't say anything for a moment. I tapped his skull with the gun barrel and he flinched, rattling the chains.

"I didn't take him off," he said in a frightened voice. "I swear to God I didn't."

"I don't believe you." I cocked the piece, pulling back the slide and letting it snap forward noisily.

"Christ, don't kill me!" Sonny cried out. "I'm telling you

I didn't take him off. Jenkins did. All I done was beat him up. All I got out of it was a few rocks, man. That's all. A few lousy rocks." He started to cough again, then to sob hoarsely. "Please. You gotta believe me, man. Jenkins come over to me at the bar and said he wanted to take this guy off. I was supposed to rough him up a little while he and his buddy did the job. That's all I did—rough him up."

"What buddy?" I said.

"That guy, man," Carter said. "That guy Claude hung around with. That's how Jenkins knew about the crack. That guy told him, man. He told him it would be going down."

"A black guy?" I said, thinking of Norvelle.

"No, man. A white dude. What the fuck's his name? A mean fucker. Does a lot of coke."

I glanced at Karen. "Cal?" I said.

Sonny nodded. "That's it. That's the one."

I stood up.

"You ain't going to shoot me, are you?" Carter said in a pleading voice. "I told you what I know, man."

"What about the night of the murder?" I said.

"What about it?"

"You told the cops you saw someone."

"Bullshit!" Sonny said. "I told the cops what I just told you. About how that guy got ripped off by Jenkins. I don't know nothing about no murder." He rattled the chains again. "Let me loose, man. I gotta call a doctor."

"Let's go," I said to Karen.

"What about him?" She stared at Sonny with disgust.

"He'll work himself loose in an hour or so. Or one of the neighbors will hear him bellowing."

We started for the door.

"Let me loose, man," Carter called out.

Karen and I walked out the door, locking it behind us. For a good way down the hall, we could still hear him hollering to be let loose.

XXXIV

It was close to eleven when Karen drove us out of the Miamiville Apartments' lot. I let her do the driving because my back was killing me. In fact, after the fight with Sonny, all my bruises had begun to ache. I barely made it out to the Pinto. As soon as we turned onto Wooster Pike, I swallowed two painkillers and a muscle relaxant, washing them down with the watery remains of a McDonald's Coke. I told Karen to head straight for the Delores—for our rendezvous with LeRoi.

If we'd had more time and I'd been in better shape physically, I might first have tried to check out what Sonny had told me. But checking out Carter's story meant a confrontation with Cal—a violent one. And the way I felt physically, I just wasn't up to taking Cal on. Besides, I figured that once I'd told LeRoi what Sonny had told us, taking on Cal would no longer be my problem. All I'd have to worry about was Jordan. And if Sonny Carter was Jordan's only ammunition, a grand jury would never indict me. Without an eyewitness, all he had on me was circumstantial evidence.

The highway was deserted between Miamiville and Fairfax, and for a while the only sound on the road was the tires singing in the snow. As we raced down Wooster Pike, I stared out the windshield at the snowflakes blowing toward us and thought of that Friday morning, three days before, when I'd driven that same stretch of road through the ice storm—not knowing what I was going to find, not really sure I wanted to know.

Poor Lonnie. He'd really let himself get screwed this time. Desperate to make up for all those years lost to drugs and prison and schemes that had gone nowhere, he had been an easy mark for Cal and Claude Jenkins. For all I knew, Norvelle had been part of it too. Lonnie's old friend from the sixties. Apparently, old friendship didn't count for much in the eighties—not with that crew.

After his visit to Sy Levy, Lonnie had probably gotten together with Norvelle at the Cross Lane house, on Wednesday afternoon—a couple of old dopers, sharing a pipe or a fit. A communal ritual, right out of the wild old days. Only it wasn't the old days anymore. Norvelle must have introduced Lonnie to his roommate, Cal. And Cal, who knew a desperate man when he saw one, could have sized things up quickly and formulated his plan over a little base or smack. All Lonnie would have to do to score quick and big was act as a mule, a role he'd played dozens of times before. Just transport some crack to this motel that Cal knew about and make the trade with the bikers.

I wasn't sure how Lonnie had managed to talk LeRoi into fronting him the lady without a down payment. Perhaps he'd done business with LeRoi before, back in the sixties or seventies. Perhaps Norvelle had vouched for him. More likely, Lonnie had promised LeRoi a bigger cut of the pie if he fronted him the dope to sell to the bikers. Ghetto blacks and redneck bikers don't mix—at least they don't in Cincinnati. So it wasn't the sort of deal that LeRoi could have managed on his own; and, if Lonnie had made it seem big enough, LeRoi might have gone along with him for the vig.

Once Cal had manipulated Lonnie into getting the crack and going to the motel, the rest had been child's play: he'd paid Carter off to knock Lonnie cold; and while Lonnie was out, Cal and Jenkins took him off for the crack. When Lonnie woke up, he discovered the bad news —that he'd been robbed of the lady and of his one last chance to make it to Fire Lake.

Neither Cal nor Jenkins had counted on Lonnie's trying to kill himself after that. The suicide attempt had been the only wrinkle in their scam, because if Lonnie had succeeded in committing suicide, there would have been no patsy to take the fall with LeRoi. Cal and Jenkins needed Lonnie alive. That was why Jenkins had ministered to him in that little storeroom. That was why Claude had solicited my help—to get Lonnie away from the motel and out of his life. That was why I had ended up a fall guy too.

"Sorry, Harry." I wondered if Lonnie had known, when he'd written that, how sorry both he and I were going to be.

Karen had just turned onto McMillan, when the painkillers kicked in. Worn down as I was, they hit me hard, and for a few minutes I felt as if I was just coming off an all-night drunk. I must have started singing to myself, because Karen glanced over at me with a smile and patted me on the leg.

"You okay, there, tough guy?" she said affectionately.

"Never better." I started to laugh. "The most important meeting of my life, and I'm not going to be there."

"*I'll* be there," Karen said, reassuringly.

"There could be trouble," I said, almost gleefully.

"Everywhere you go, there's trouble," Karen said. "I'm used to it. Besides, after what that creep Sonny told us, LeRoi should lay off."

I nodded. "He should. He certainly should."

"I'm going to get you some coffee," Karen said, pulling into the White Castle on Reading. It was just eleven-thirty, and we were exactly one block from home. So I didn't put up a fuss.

Karen parked in the White Castle lot and went inside—into that stainless steel and porcelain birthday cake. A few minutes later she came back out with three big cups of coffee in a sack.

For the next ten minutes I drank coffee, watched the

colorful White Castle traffic, and jabbered drunkenly. I'm not sure what I jabbered about, but it seemed to amuse Karen.

"You know what I don't understand?" she said, pulling a paper napkin out of the sack and blotting up some coffee that I'd spilled down the front of my shirt.

"I don't understand a lot of things," I said. "I don't understand why I'm sitting here with you right now."

"I mean about what Sonny said."

"What don't you understand about what Sonny said?" I asked.

"If Cal and Jenkins ripped Lonnie off, why didn't LeRoi know that?"

I swallowed some more coffee and said, "I don't follow you."

"Well, LeRoi must have suspected Jenkins, right? I mean he had him murdered, didn't he?"

I nodded slowly.

"From what you told me, Bo and his friends . . . they tortured Jenkins before he died."

I nodded again. "Yes, they did."

"So why wouldn't Jenkins have talked?" Karen said, looking perplexed. "Why wouldn't he have told them everything—about Cal and Lonnie and you too?"

I stared at her for a long moment. Either the coffee was beginning to burn a hole in my stomach or what she'd said had had the same effect, because I started to feel sick.

"He *would* have told them," I said uneasily.

"Then why didn't he?" Karen asked.

"I don't fucking know." I glanced at my watch and then looked up the block, toward the Delores. "Christ," I said out loud, "we may be in big trouble."

"LeRoi wouldn't try anything in your apartment. Not twice in a row."

"Probably not," I said. "It's what happens after that, that worries me."

"All we can do is tell him the truth."

"If we know the truth," I said grimly. "If Sonny wasn't bullshitting us."

"I don't think he was bullshitting, Harry," Karen said. "He wasn't smart enough to think up a story like that. And we *didn't* find the drugs on him."

I sighed. "Something's missing, then."

Karen started up the Pinto and backed out of the parking spot. "Let's go find out what it is."

XXXV

The point that Karen had made sobered me completely. Why hadn't Jenkins told LeRoi's boys about the way he and Cal had double-crossed Lonnie? A man would have to be made of a lot sterner stuff than Claude had been to hold out on Bo with his razor. Moreover, I couldn't see why someone like Claude would have felt any loyalty to Cal in the first place. They'd run a dirty little double-cross —nothing worth holding out about under torture. All of which left me feeling uncertain about the scenario I'd spun on the way back from Miamiville. And even more uncertain about what I was going to tell LeRoi. As we pulled into the Delores's lot, I asked myself if I really wanted to go through with this meeting. Then I asked Karen.

"Do we have a choice?" she said. "If we don't go through with it, we'll be in even worse trouble."

"You're getting to be awfully goddamn logical," I said testily. But I knew she was right. Not showing up was just going to invite more visits from Bo.

Karen parked the Pinto by the stairs leading to the courtyard. After giving each other a nervous look, we got out into the cold and snow and walked slowly up to the lobby. The dogwoods were tinkling icily in the stiff breeze. The lobby itself was empty—just a warm yellow room with its brass mailboxes, its hissing radiator, its muddy tile floor. The dimly lit stairwell looked empty too. There was no way to see beyond the first landing, though, where either Bo or Maurice could easily be concealing himself. As

Karen opened the lobby door, I put my hand in my coat pocket and grasped the gun.

I stopped Karen with my left hand before she could start up the stairs. "Maybe you ought to stay down here," I said to her. "Better yet, maybe you should wait in the car."

I realized I was whispering.

Karen shrugged resignedly. "Harry, what's going to happen to us is going to happen—whether I'm here or there. I'm with you now, babe. For better or worse."

I smiled at her impromptu vow, although there was nothing funny about the situation. She knew it, too, in spite of her bravado. Her pretty, pouty mouth was set; but her pale blue eyes were restless with fear.

She'd been right about one thing. Whether she stayed in the car or came with me, she was still vulnerable to LeRoi. And alone, she wouldn't have a chance. I decided I wanted her with me.

"All right, Karen," I said, patting her cheek gently.

She pressed my hand against her cheek and smiled at me with everything but her frightened eyes.

"Ready?" I said.

She swallowed hard and nodded. "Ready."

I pulled the Gold Cup from my coat pocket and started up the stairwell, with Karen right behind me. We took the stairs one at a time. When we reached the first landing, I peeked around the corner—both hands on the grip of the gun, my finger on the trigger. There was no one there.

We went up the second flight of stairs, at the same snail's pace. When we got to the second-floor landing, I put my hand across Karen's chest, touching her breasts the way I had days before. We smiled at each other nervously.

"Let me take a look," I whispered.

I peered around the corner and down the second-floor hallway—the gun still tight in my hands. There was no one on the landing or in the hallway. I listened for a long moment, but I couldn't hear anyone moving around on the floor above us, either.

"Let's go," I said, giving Karen a little push.

We walked quickly down the hall to the apartment. I fumbled with the keys for a moment, cursed myself anxiously, then put the key in the lock.

"Stand over there," I whispered, pointing Karen away from the doorway.

Karen took two steps to her right and huddled against the doorway. She looked terrified, hugging herself tightly, as if she was trying to hold herself together by main force. I pulled the Gold Cup out and leaned against the jamb. With my left hand I turned the key in the lock and gave the door a gentle push, keeping the pistol at the ready in my right hand.

The door creaked and fell halfway open. From where I was standing by the jamb, I could see through the crack at the door's hinges. The living room looked empty. But just to be safe, I waited a long moment before putting both hands on the gun, easing around the jamb, and stepping into the living room. If someone *had* shown his head at that moment, I would have shot him without hesitating. I was that keyed up.

"It looks all right," I whispered to Karen. "Let me check the bedroom before you come in."

I walked down the hall to the bedroom, plastered myself against the jamb again, and, reaching around the corner with my free hand, flipped on the bedroom lights. The room was empty. I checked the bathroom. Then the kitchen. Then I called Karen into the living room.

I glanced at my watch—it was exactly twelve.

"We've only got a few minutes before he shows," I said.

She nodded and bit nervously at her lower lip.

I went over to the rolltop and unlocked the file drawer. There was a .357 Magnum inside the locked box—a little item that Bo and his friends had apparently missed when they'd searched my rooms. I unlocked the box, took out the pistol, and handed it to Karen. She held it up by the butt, as if it were a dead animal.

"Wait in the bedroom," I said. "If there is any trouble, protect yourself with that. Just cock it and pull the trigger."

She stared at the gun. "Am I supposed to save the last bullet for myself?"

"It's not funny, Karen," I said, giving her a look.

"I know," she said. "I'm just scared."

"It'll be all right."

Karen walked down the hall to the bedroom, closing the door behind her.

I sat down in the armchair and waited.

Around twelve-fifteen, I heard the sound of someone coming up the stairs. Whoever he was, he was wearing rubber boots, because I could hear them squeaking like frightened mice on the hall floor. He paused for a moment at the second-floor landing. I got up off the armchair and went through the archway into the kitchenette. I flipped off the kitchen light and settled in behind the archway wall. In the darkened kitchen, no one could see me and I would have a clear shot at anyone coming through the door.

I stood there for a long moment, listening for the sound of the guy in the boots. A minute later, I heard him start down the hall. He came up to the door and stopped again.

"Stoner?" a man said softly.

It was LeRoi. I recognized his choir bass voice.

I raised the Gold Cup and trained it on the door—both hands on the grip.

"C'mon in, LeRoi," I called out.

LeRoi opened the door slowly.

"No tricks now, man," he said as he took one step into the living room.

I could see him clearly from where I was standing—a tall, stocky black man with a gentle, big-eyed face. He was

wearing boots, a tweed topcoat, and a navy blue sweater
cap. He was not carrying a gun in his hand, although he
could have had anything from a revolver to a shotgun hidden under the long-skirted topcoat. I was struck again by
how healthy he looked compared to his help. Apparently,
LeRoi was smart enough not to use the shit that he pushed
—or, at least, not to use it regularly. There was nothing
crazed about his eyes. They were wide open and alert-
looking.

He glanced around the room without spotting me. Then
he saw the barrel of the Gold Cup, gleaming in the kitchen
archway. LeRoi flinched and took a step back toward the
door.

"You keep pulling guns on people, you gonna get hurt,"
he said nervously.

"Close the door," I said to him.

He hesitated for a moment. And in that moment it
dawned on me that I was as much of an unpredictable
quantity to him as he was to me. All he knew about me
was that I was a violent white man who had ripped him off
and then pistol-whipped one of his best boys. He must
have thought I could be reasoned with, or he wouldn't
have scheduled the meeting. Still, he knew I was dangerous. And he was treating me with due caution. I figured I
could keep him off-balance by playing it as tough as possible.

"Close the door," I said again, coming out from the
archway and pointing the gun at LeRoi's head.

LeRoi glanced nervously at the gun, then closed the
door by leaning back against it.

I said, "Stand away from the door. Put your hands up
and clasp the top of your head."

"I thought we was gonna talk," he said, without budg-
ing.

"Do it, LeRoi!" I snapped. "Or I'll blow your fucking
head off."

He scowled at me defiantly, but he stepped away from the doorway and put his hands on his head.

I walked over to the door and locked it. Then patted LeRoi down.

"You got some of your friends outside, LeRoi?" I said as I frisked him.

"Man," he said, giving me an icy look, "I told you I'd be alone. If I wanted you dead, homes, you *be* dead. And your bitch too."

"Yeah," I said with some ice of my own. "Your boys are topnotch."

I put my hand in the small of LeRoi's back and shoved him across the room toward the armchair. He didn't like being pushed. But I didn't care.

"Lay off me, man," he said, turning toward me angrily. "Don't nobody lay hands on me."

"Sit!" I barked at him.

He brushed the seat of the chair off with his left hand, then sat. "You gonna get burned down, fucker," he said, eyeing me with hate. "You keep pullin' attitudes on people."

I jerked the gun toward the door.

"If I hear anything out there, I mean anything, you are dead."

"Shit, man," he said, half rising out of the chair. "You know who you talking to?"

"Yeah, the nigger who's dumb enough to front crack to Lonnie Jackowski."

"Wha'chu talking about 'front,' sucker?" he said with outrage. "Your partner give me two grand for the lady. Say he give me the rest when he score."

"Where the fuck did Lonnie get two grand?" I said, giving him a disbelieving look.

"From you, homes," LeRoi said, throwing the same look back at me. "Who you trying to zoom, man? You jive-ass motherfucker! You fronted him the bread. Now, you lay the other ten on me, and we be square."

"He owes you ten?" I said.

LeRoi shook his head. "Wha'chu act like you don't know for?"

"Because I don't know." I sat down across from him on the couch. "I'm only going to say this one more time. I'm *not* Lonnie's partner, LeRoi. I'm just a friend."

"That's not what he say," LeRoi said coldly. "He say if anything go wrong I was to call you."

I stared at LeRoi for a long moment. I wanted to think that he was bluffing. But there was nothing about his face that suggested a bluff. Besides, I said to myself, what the hell would he be doing in my living room if he was running a bluff.

"Lonnie told you to get in touch with me?" I said, feeling it fully—the betrayal, the double cross. Feeling it but not understanding the reason for it.

"Bet, man. He say you be his partner."

"For chrissake," I said, saying it out loud, "he fucking set me up!"

LeRoi didn't look impressed by my outrage. And it was obvious that he didn't believe me. I couldn't really blame him. If I'd been lying, I would have said the same thing. And, thanks to Lonnie, he thought I *was* lying.

"You save that shit for somebody else, motherfucker. Give me the dime, like he say you would, and we be square. Give me the lady back, and we be square. One or t'other. Don't matter to me."

"I don't have the lady," I said with exasperation. "Didn't Jenkins tell you what was going down when you took him off?"

"Don't know nothing about that, bro'," LeRoi said, shaking his head.

I stared at him again, with that same twilight-zone sensation in the pit of my gut. "You're telling me you didn't take Jenkins off?"

LeRoi stared at me. "Wha'chu think? I just go 'round killin' folks for no reason?"

"Jenkins had your crack," I said to him. "A guy named Cal's got it now. They took Lonnie off at the motel."

"Then you better get it back, homes," LeRoi said, giving me a hard look. " 'Cause *you* be the man I'm dealin' with. I don't want to hear you tell me that other shit. I don't care. You get that crack back or you get me the bread. By tomorrow. Hear?"

He got up from the chair.

I pointed the gun at him. "What if I shoot you right now," I said to him.

He blanched, then smiled sleekly to cover his fear. "You ain't gonna shoot me, bro'. Shooting me ain't gonna do you no earthly good. Wha'chu think? *I'm* the man? Shit." He threw his hand at me contemptuously. "The man live out in Indian Hill. He got him a mansion and a Ferrari. You shoot me, and he just gonna send some other nigger to take you off. And, homes, he gonna burn you down big. You dig?"

He glanced contemptuously at the gun I was holding on him, then started walking slowly to the door. I stared at him dully as he walked by.

"You still got a day, man," he said as he opened the door. "You get the bread or the flake, and don' nobody have to get hurt. Just talk to your partner, man."

I laughed dully. "You don't know where he is, do you?"

LeRoi didn't answer me. "Call me at the chili parlor when you ready to deal." He stepped out the door, then looked back in. "And, homes . . . don'chu make me call you."

XXXVI

After LeRoi left I just sat there on the sofa, the gun dangling in my hands. Karen came out of the bedroom and sat down beside me.

"You heard?" I said, glancing at her.

She nodded. "Most of it."

"He set me up, Karen," I said. "Lonnie set me up."

"Maybe he didn't, Harry," she said gently. "Maybe he was just being Lonnie—playing all the angles, like a big shot."

"Big shot!" I said with a bitter laugh. "He told that bastard LeRoi that I was his partner. He signed my name at the fucking motel. He ran away from the apartment, after I'd saved his bacon, *knowing* that I'd have to take the heat."

"He also tried to kill himself, Harry," Karen said with a sad look. "He couldn't have known that all this was going to happen, before he went out to the motel—that Cal and Jenkins were going to take him off and that he'd end up owing his soul to LeRoi. He wouldn't have gone out there if he did. He's not that stupid."

"But why use my name?" I said, feeling the injustice like a biblical smoting. "Why tell LeRoi I was his partner?"

She shrugged. "Maybe he wanted to think you *were* his partner. Maybe it made him feel safer. He didn't really have a friend he could trust on this deal. He didn't know Cal or LeRoi or the bikers; Norvelle's been zonked out for years; and I wasn't around anymore to hold his hand. Maybe he got scared, afraid that something could go wrong while he was dealing with all those strangers. Maybe he thought that he might need an old friend to get him out of trouble. Or to bail him out of it. You're a tough guy, Harry. Lonnie always admired that. Deep down, I think he always wanted to be a man like you."

I didn't say anything, although I was mystified by the fact that she was defending him.

Karen stared at me for a moment. "Can you get the money?"

"If I have to," I said. "But I'll be goddamned if I'm going to pay for Lonnie's mistake anymore."

"Tell me about it," Karen said, with a hopeless look.

I suddenly felt embarrassed for the way I'd been grousing. I had a right to be mad, all right. But compared to Karen, I'd gotten off easy. She'd had fifteen years of Lonnie Jackowski. Fifteen years of Fire Lake. And in spite of all she'd been through, part of her still loved the amoral bastard.

"He's got to take care of himself now, Karen," I said, pulling her to me. "You can't do it anymore. And I won't."

She rested her head against my shoulder. "Then what are we going to do?"

"I don't know." I glanced at my watch. "It's a quarter to one. I'd like to pay Cal a visit and find out if he really does have the crack, but to be honest, I don't know if I've got the strength."

She smiled at me. "Even tough guys have to sleep."

"I don't know if I can do that, either," I said nervously. "Where the hell did Lonnie get two thousand dollars? Can you tell me that? And who the hell killed Jenkins?"

"LeRoi could have been lying," Karen said.

"So could Sonny," I said, feeling lost. "I don't know. I thought I had this fucking thing figured out."

"We'll figure it out, Harry," Karen said bravely. "Tomorrow."

* * *

I didn't realize how truly worn-out I was until I lay down on the bed beside Karen. I took a look at her lush body and wanted like hell to make love to her—to make up for the scene with Sonny. Karen knew that was what I wanted, but she also knew I was too dead tired to do anything but sleep.

"It's all right, tough guy," she said, hugging me tight. "Just get some rest."

I closed my eyes, and when I opened them again, cold sunlight was filtering through the bedroom window. I glanced at the clock on the nightstand—it was eight-thirty —and tried to sit up. The stiffness was still there, in my back and my shoulder. But the pain wasn't as bad as it had been the day before, and that cheered me.

I glanced at Karen's side of the bed. She wasn't there.

For just a second, I felt panicky—the way I'd felt waking from the dream in the hotel room. Then I heard her moving around in the living room, and my heartbeat slowed down.

"Are you up?" I called out.

"I'm making coffee," she called back.

I pulled myself out of the bed and stared out the window, squinting against the sunlight. It was a high blue winter morning without a cloud in the sky. It would have been a beautiful day, if it weren't for Lonnie. He'd spoiled too many days for me and Karen. The terror was going to end, I told myself. Today.

I picked up the phone on the nightstand and called George DeVries at the D.A.'s office.

He answered in a sleepy voice. "You're up mighty early, aren't you, Harry?"

"It's dues time, George."

"I haven't seen the yard yet," he said.

"Don't fuck with me, George. I'm in no mood to be fucked with by a cop."

"Yeah, I heard you had a little trouble with one of our finest."

"It's a continuing story."

"Glen's a vicious bastard, all right," George said merrily. "I kind of like him."

"You would," I said with disgust.

"About that problem you have?" George said. "I guess you already know that the motel murder was drug-related. You do know that, don't you, Harry?"

"Quit the clowning, George."

He laughed snidely. "Aside from you, Glen's only got one suspect. A guy named Jackowski. Some biker at the motel said Jenkins ripped Jackowski off for a shitload of crack. Apparently, Jackowski came back for his goods. You know what happened." George paused for a moment. "This Jackowski's a friend of yours, isn't he, Harry," he said in a vaguely calculating voice.

"Who told you that?"

"Somebody told Glen that—that you and Lonnie were good buddies."

"Who told Glen?" I said.

"An informer that Jordan uses. A junkie named Norvelle Thomas."

"Great," I said to myself. Another betrayal. It was getting to be monotonous.

"And Jordan believes him?" I said to George.

"Harry, if John Wayne Gacy told Fred that you were dirty, he'd believe him. He wants you, buddy. In the worst way."

"The feeling is mutual," I said angrily.

"This guy Thomas told Glen that your pal Lonnie was copping crack for a friend of his. And that that friend had fronted him the money to cop."

"And I'm supposed to be the friend?" I said disgustedly.

"That's the way Glen is reading it."

It all made a kind of hideous sense. In fact, it was virtually the same story that LeRoi had heard from Lonnie. For all I knew, that was where Norvelle had heard it too. From my good buddy, Lonnie. I'd fronted him two thousand dollars to buy me some crack. It was neat, all right. And without Lonnie around to explain the lie or the wishful thinking or whatever the hell he'd call it, it would be damn hard for me to prove differently.

"All right, George," I said wearily. "Thanks."

"Harry," he said, dropping the sarcasm. "I'd be careful this time. Really careful. Glen'll be tailing you pretty closely, and he's good at his work. When he wants someone as bad as he wants you, he doesn't fuck around."

"Neither do I," I said, and hung up on him.

I stared angrily at the phone. I felt like pulling it out of the wall. Instead, I cursed—at the top of my lungs.

Karen came running in from the living room. "Are you all right?"

I gave her a dirty look. "Hell, yes, I'm all right. What do I have to worry about?"

She sat down on the corner of the bed. "Tell me about it," she said.

She looked deracinated in the stream of white sunlight that was flooding the room. I closed the curtains and the color came back to her cheeks.

"Norvelle told Jordan the same story that Lonnie told LeRoi," I said, turning back to her. "That I was Lonnie's partner. That he was buying the dope for me. That I'd fronted him the two grand."

Karen dropped her head. "Christ, Lonnie must have told Norvelle, then, too."

"Maybe, Lonnie was copping for somebody else," Karen said, her head still bent to her chest. "And was trying to cover up his real connection."

"By using to me to do it?" I said disgustedly. "What a guy!"

Karen looked up at me suddenly, with a spark in her eyes. "He did go to that theater on Wednesday. What if he didn't just go to see Norvelle? What if he went to see

Leanne, too? I mean, he had to get that two thousand from somebody."

I shrugged. "She'd have the money all right. But why the hell would she want to buy twelve thousand dollars' worth of crack? And why all the comedy at the motel? If Lonnie was copping for Leanne, why didn't he just deliver at the theater? Or at her fucking farm?"

"I don't know about the motel business. But you'd be surprised who deals dope in the suburbs. I told you about that pharmacist in St. Louis, who used to send us to New York to cop smack. Christ, he was the most respectable guy you'd ever want to meet. Had a chain of drugstores around the city, a mansion in Forest Park, a social-climbing wife and four spoiled kids. It's just not that unusual, Harry, for your neighbors to be dealing coke—even your rich, respectable neighbors."

I gave Karen a dubious look. "Are you sure you're not letting your feelings cloud your judgment?"

"Meaning?" she said sharply.

"Meaning that you don't like Leanne Silverstein."

Karen gave me an angry look. "Do you have a better idea?"

"Sy Levy," I said. "He could have used the money from a score a lot more than the Silversteins could. And he might have been able to scrape together a down payment on the drugs."

"Sy would never do that," Karen said flatly.

"Why?" I snapped. "Because you like him, and you don't like Leanne?"

"Fuck you," Karen said bitterly.

I stared at her for a moment. "I'm sorry. I'm just pissed at Lonnie."

"I'm sorry too." She looked up at me apologetically. "I can't believe that Sy could have changed that much."

"Everything else has."

She nodded grudgingly. "So you think we should pay Sy another visit?"

I shook my head. "Not yet. I think we should talk to Norvelle first. Don't forget that he was working for Leanne and that he was a friend of Sy's. If either one of them did give Lonnie the money to cop, Norvelle could easily have heard about the deal, and then told Cal and Jenkins about it. Regardless of who fronted Lonnie the two thousand, I still think it was Jenkins, Cal, and Norvelle who ripped Lonnie off. I just don't know how they got him out to that motel. Or who ended up murdering Jenkins. Or why."

Karen laughed. "So we're going back to Cross Lane?"

"That's our first stop."

"What about Cal?" she said with a nervous look.

"He and Norvelle live in the same house, Karen. We've got to confront him sometime."

"Maybe he won't be home," Karen said, as if she were saying a prayer.

XXXVII

Karen and I walked down to the parking lot. There was a gray Ford sitting on the corner of Burnett—it was the first thing I noticed when we stepped out of the shadows of the Delores. I nodded disgustedly in the direction of the Ford. Karen shaded her eyes against the brilliant winter sun and sighted toward the corner.

"It's him again," she said, dropping her hand and turning to me with a fallen look. "It's Jordan."

"The son of a bitch," I said angrily. "He's not even bothering to conceal himself anymore."

"Is he going to stay behind us all day?"

"If it suits him," I said. "And there's nothing we can do about it. I just don't drive well enough to shake him. Plus there's snow on the street."

"But we're on our way to see Norvelle," Karen said, aghast. "A junkie."

"What the hell difference does that make? He already thinks I'm a drug dealer."

I walked quickly down the stairs and over to the Pinto, got in behind the wheel, and started the car. The engine turned over like a low-speed drill, sputtered a few times, then backfired and began to chug. Karen got in the passenger seat, slapping her arms against the cold.

"You know I'm with you, don't you, Harry?" she said suddenly, giving me a sweet, shivery look. "To the end."

I smiled at her with pleasure. "I do know that, Karen," I said. "But I'm glad to hear it anyway."

I put the Pinto in reverse and guided it out on the

street. As I headed up Burnett the gray Ford pulled out behind me—its tail pipes steaming in the cold. I could see Jordan in the rearview mirror. He waved at me with his middle finger.

I turned left on Taft and left again on Highland. The sun was very bright on the snow-banked sidewalks and on the salt-whitened street. I had to flip down the visor to cut the glare.

We turned east on McMillan, with Jordan still behind us. When we got within a block of Cross Lane, Jordan dropped back, pulling over in front of a bar—his engine still idling.

"He stopped following us!" Karen said excitedly, as if that were a triumph.

"He knows where we're going," I told her. "Norvelle is his snitch."

Her face fell. "Oh," she said with disappointment.

Cross Lane hadn't been salted by the city trucks. There had been so little traffic on the street that the snow looked as if it had just fallen, plumped up like meringue from one curb to the other. I inched down to Cal's house—the car grinding and sliding through the drifts.

"It's going to be hell getting out of here again," I said to Karen. "That's probably why Jordan stayed out on McMillan."

She pointed to a dark spot on the right, where a car had been parked overnight. "Pull in there."

I parked in the spot, with my rear wheels on what little pavement was showing through the ice.

We both got out into the brilliant sun and, hands over our eyes, stared across the street at Cal's turreted frame house. Two pairs of bootprints led away from the porch, down the walk to the street. They circled a spot where a car had been parked. Apparently, Cal and his friend didn't have much patience with the snow, because the area behind the car was deeply scarred with tread marks and gravel thrown up by spinning tires.

"Looks like someone was in a hurry to leave," I said to Karen.

"Maybe there's no one left at home," she said hopefully.

"We'll check anyway."

We crossed the street and walked up the sidewalk, past the bootprints in the snow. The prints hadn't frozen yet, which meant they were damn fresh—within the hour.

We stepped up on the porch, stomping our feet on the slats to shake the patchy snow off our pants legs. Karen glanced through the muslin drapes in the front window and said, "Looks empty."

I knocked on the door. When nobody answered, I took a credit card out of my wallet and slipped it between the door lock and the jamb.

Karen laughed nervously. "I thought only junkies knew how to do that."

"We detectives have our secrets." I fiddled with the lock until the door sprung open. *"Voilà!"*

I waved my hand through the doorway, and Karen walked into the hall. I followed her in, closing the door behind me. A loud plucking noise, like the sound of water dripping was coming from the living room. We both glanced through the archway.

Someone had left a record spinning on the turntable, and the needle was sticking in the last groove and being amplified through the speakers.

"Jesus," Karen said, "they did leave in a hurry."

I walked into the living room and lifted the tone arm off the record. There was something different about the room, but it took me a moment to realize what it was. The clothes that had been piled in the corners were gone. Just a couple of pairs of girl's underpants and a man's T-shirt remained on the floor, along with the lingering smell of dirt and sweat.

"Maybe they went off to do the laundry?" Karen said from the archway.

"Maybe," I said dubiously as I walked back into the hall. "Let's look upstairs."

Karen stared up the stairwell with foreboding. "Oh, Harry," she said faintly. "What if they come back?"

"I don't think they *are* coming back, Karen," I said, starting up the stairs. She fell in behind me.

The stairwell made one turn to the left, before ending in a short hall with three rooms running off it. There was a door at the head of the stairs on the left, one at the end of the hall, and one halfway down the hall to the right, which must have led to the turreted room. As I neared the top step I began to smell something—a charred chemical smell that I couldn't place.

"Someone's been cooking up," Karen said immediately.

I glanced back at her. "Smack?"

She nodded. "I ought to know."

I glanced at the door at the top of the stairs. The smell seemed to be coming from inside that room.

I pulled the pistol from my pocket and unlocked it with my thumb.

"Harry," Karen whispered, "be careful."

I walked up to the door at the top of the landing, put my hand on the knob, and turned it. As the door opened the chemical smell became much stronger, mixed with another powerful smell—one that I had no trouble identifying.

I turned immediately back to Karen, who was standing at the head of the stairs. "Go down to the hall," I said, giving her a grim look.

"What?" She stared at me with confusion.

I nodded toward the door. "Someone's dead in there."

She threw her hand to her mouth, and her face went white. "Oh, my God . . . Lonnie!"

Before I knew it, she'd pushed past me, running up to the door and throwing it wide open. She let out a shriek, then covered her face with both hands and began to cry,

leaning heavily against the doorjamb and rocking back and
forth as she wept.

I went inside the room.

It was a bathroom. A skinny, naked black man was lying
on the tile floor—his head propped against the pedestal of
the toilet, his arms akimbo, his knees bent, as if he'd tried
to get up and failed. His brown skin had turned a violent
purple. His face was bloated-looking—his cheeks puffed
out, as if he'd taken a breath and died before he could
exhale. There was urine and feces on the floor, where he
evacuated as he'd died. There was also a good deal of drug
paraphernalia scattered on the floor. A fit. A glassine bag
half filled with brown powder. A Bunsen burner. A
charred ice-cream scoop that he'd cooked up in. The rubber hose he'd used to tie off with was still draped loosely
around his left arm. I could see tracks all over him—on
every bend and joint of his arms and legs, as if he'd been
pieced together by a sewing machine. There were even
needle marks on the carotid arteries of his neck.

It looked as if someone had made a halfhearted attempt
to revive him. The bathtub was filled with water. And a
couple of trays of ice cubes, melted now, were lying by his
body, along with several damp, rolled-up towels.

I turned to Karen, who was still sobbing. "That's
Norvelle Thomas, isn't it?"

She nodded heavily, without looking back into the room.

I glanced again at his body. "The poor son of a bitch."

"Take me out of here, Harry," Karen said suddenly, in a
shrill voice. "Please, take me out of here. I can't stand it. I
can't stand it!"

I pulled her to me, guiding her away from the bathroom
and down the stairs. I took her into the living room and sat
her down on the dusty couch. I seated myself beside her,
holding her close until her sobbing began to die down.

"I never thought I'd see that again," she said, dropping
her hands from her face. She shook her head violently, as

if she were trying to shake the sight of Norvelle out of her memory.

I took a handkerchief out of my pocket and wiped off her face—gently, as if she were my child.

Karen bit down hard on her lower lip, her eyes still brimming with tears.

"That used to happen in shooting galleries," she said, trying to control her voice. "I *saw* it happen twice. The other junkies . . . they didn't care. They were bummed out because it spoiled their high. Maybe somebody would call the life squad. Maybe not. I was always afraid that Lonnie or I would end up that way. It was my worst fear."

"It's pretty scary," I said.

"You don't think . . ." She glanced at the stairwell.

"He's dead, Karen," I said.

"Dead," she repeated.

Someone jiggled the front doorknob. Both Karen and I jumped. Thelma, the teenage girl with the punk hairdo— the one who thought Cal was so cool—came stomping into the hall, shaking the snow off her high-heeled go-go boots. She was wearing a cloth coat with a fur ruff, buttoned at the neck. Under the coat, she was dressed like she'd been the day before—in a torn T-shirt, and a leotard, and a short leather skirt.

"Hey!" she said, staring at us through the archway. "I remember you." Her baby's face fell momentarily, as if she *did* remember us. "Cal said you were narcs."

"We aren't narcs," I said. "We're friends of Lonnie Jackowski's."

"Norvelle's old pal?" Thelma said, coming up to the archway and leaning against it. "The cute old guy that used to have the band, right?"

Karen straightened up on the sofa. "Do you know where he is?" she asked Thelma.

Thelma shook her head. "I just met him a couple of times. He came over here on Wednesday. I wanted to talk to him, but Cal took him upstairs. He and Norvelle and

Cal spent most of the afternoon up there, talking business." She made a face, as if she didn't like it when Cal
"talked business."

"How about the second time?" I said to Thelma.

"Huh?" She made a questioning face.

"That you saw Lonnie," I said, prompting her with a
smile, although she didn't seem to need much prompting.
She was much more of a kid than the other one, Renee.

"That was on Friday night," Thelma said. She gave
Karen a quick, nervous look. "He didn't look so hot.
Somebody'd beat him up and he was acting kind of . . .
you know, crazy."

Karen put her hand on my knee and squeezed hard.
"Do you know where he went after that?"

"Norvelle and Cal drove him out to meet somebody."

"Who?" Karen said breathlessly.

Thelma shook her head. "I don't know. It was out in the
country, I think. That's where he said he wanted to go,
anyway. Cal said they'd be gone for a while." The little girl
glanced behind her, at the stairs. "What's that smell?"

Neither one of us knew how to answer her.

She could see by the looks on our faces that something
was wrong. She stepped back toward the hall. "Where's
Cal and Renee? Where's Norvelle?"

I got up from the couch. "They're gone, Thelma. Everybody's gone."

She stared at me disbelievingly. "Bull!"

Before I could stop her she'd run up the stairs.

"Harry!" Karen cried out. "Don't let her see him!"

I bounded across the room after her. As I got to the hall
landing, I heard Thelma shriek.

I ran up the stairs to the john door. She was kneeling
against the doorjamb, holding her stomach. She'd thrown
up on the bathroom tile; her little girl's face was sick with
terror.

"Don't kill me!" she screamed when I walked over to

her. She scrambled away from me, backward on her
hands. "Don't kill me too!"

"Honey," I said gently, "I didn't kill Norvelle. He overdosed. We found him that way."

She stopped scrambling down the hall and settled back
against the wall. Her eyes began to glaze over—she was
going into shock.

"We were all going to get well," she said staring dully at
the floor. "Everybody was going to get well."

I picked her up from the floor and carried her down the
stairs.

When we got to the living room, I put her back on her
feet. Karen took her over to the couch, cooing at her
sweetly and holding her in her arms. "It's all right," she
said. "All right."

I left her consoling Thelma and went upstairs again to
check out the other rooms.

XXXVIII

The smell from the john was horrendous. When I got back upstairs, I closed the bathroom door, pulling it tightly shut. Then I walked down to the room at the end of the hall. The door was open and sunlight was pouring in through greasy, unblinded windows.

It wasn't much of a bedroom. Except for a peach crate with a lamp on it, and an unmade-up mattress beside the crate, there was no furniture. There were no decorations on the peeling walls either, no rug on the rough pine floor. A few clothes had been stored in the crate—a pair of jeans and some rumpled shirts. I checked the jeans and found a wallet in the back pocket. The only thing in the wallet was an identification card—the kind that comes with any wallet when you first buy the damn thing. It had *Norvelle Thomas* written on it. No address. No phone number. He didn't even have a social security card, much less a driver's license. And no photographs or mementos at all. By comparison, the stuff that I'd found in Lonnie's clothes seemed like a treasure trove.

The bedroom was so grim and empty that I didn't feel like searching it any further. It was clear that Norvelle's whole life—everything that mattered to him—had been arrayed at his feet, on that bathroom floor. Outside of smack, he just didn't exist.

But I went through the bed and bedclothes anyway. And, to my surprise, found seven hundred dollars rolled up in a wad and hidden inside the zippered pillow on the mattress. There were also several dozen glassine envelopes full of brown powder inside the pillow. About three thousand dollars' worth of drugs and money, all told.

I picked up one of the brown envelopes and stared at it. Mexican smack was brown, I'd read somewhere. Norvelle had had a hoard of it—enough to keep him happy for weeks. Enough to kill him.

I dropped the glassine envelope on the bed and walked back down the hall to the turreted room. Its door was closed. I pushed it open and stepped inside.

It looked a lot more like a bedroom than Norvelle's barren digs. There was a desk with a lamp and a phone on it on the right side of the room, a brass bed with a parachute hung above it on the left, an oak bureau on the far wall across from the door, and assorted blacklight posters on the walls. A threadbare brown oriental rug covered the floor. Just like the sixties.

I went over to the bureau and opened the top drawer. It had been emptied. So had all the other drawers. I opened each one and all I could find were the sort of tail ends— the unmatched socks, the faded sheets, the torn underwear—that people leave behind them when they move.

I went over to the desk—an old oak library table with one long drawer in front. Behind the desk, the turret's bay windows looked out on Cross Lane.

I pulled the drawer out, picked it up, and put it on the tabletop. It was filled with the usual items—pens, pencils, loose papers. I started sorting through the papers and found a school notebook with Hughes High printed on the cover, a math pad, a calendar. The notebook and most of the other items obviously belonged to Cal's teenage girlfriend, Renee. As I was thumbing through the math pad, a blue-and-white folder fell out.

At first I didn't realize what it was. I was about to toss the folder back in the drawer, unexamined, when I happened to turn it over and saw the greyhound printed on the front. Lonnie's bus ticket—the return ticket to St. Louis—was tucked neatly in its paper pocket.

I stared at the bus ticket for a long moment. Thelma had already said that Lonnie had returned to Cal's house on Friday night, apparently after he'd run away from my apartment. He must have taken the bus ticket with him when he'd run. It was logical to assume that he'd also taken his driver's license. And now the folder with the ticket was sitting in Cal's desk drawer. And the blood-stained license had been left at the scene of a murder, where it most certainly would have incriminated Lonnie, if I hadn't come along to pick it up.

I started to feel very bad about Lonnie. He wouldn't have left the damn ticket behind him, or the license, even if Cal and Norvelle *had* taken him to meet a friend in the country, as Thelma had said.

I tucked the bus ticket in my coat pocket and put the drawer back in the desk. As I was closing the drawer I happened to glance out the turreted window. Jordan's gray Ford was coming down Cross Lane.

"Jesus!" I said aloud.

I slammed the drawer shut, ran out of the room, and bounded down the stairs. If Jordan came in the house and found Norvelle in the john and all that smack in the bedroom, I was a deadman. I knew immediately that if he stepped through the front door, I was going to have to kill him or he would kill me just like he'd said he would. I'd already taken the pistol out of my coat.

When I got down to the living room, I went directly over to the front windows and peered through the curtains at the street. I didn't even give Karen or Thelma a glance.

"Harry?" Karen said with concern.

"It's Jordan," I said, still staring through the window.

She grasped the situation at once. "My God, what if he comes in."

I didn't answer her. But she could see the gun in my hand.

"You can't kill a cop, Harry," she said in a frightened voice.

"I can if he's planning to kill me."

The Ford was sitting in front of the house now, idling in a cloud of white exhaust. I could see Jordan squinting through the side window at the porch. He couldn't see me from where he was sitting because of the glare of the sun.

"Harry, the girl . . ." Karen said loudly.

I glanced back at Thelma. She had calmed down somewhat, but her face still looked a little stoned out, as if she couldn't fathom all that was going on around her. I stared at Karen, who gave me a desperate, pleading look.

"Please, Harry," she said, "there has to be another way."

I peeked through the curtains again. Jordan had pulled over behind the Pinto. As I watched him, he opened the Ford's door and stepped out onto the street.

"Is there a back door?" I said, not taking my eyes off Jordan.

When Thelma didn't answer me, I whipped around and glared at her. "Is there a back door!" I shouted.

Thelma shook as if I'd slapped her, and nodded spastically. "Down the hall in the kitchen," she said, pointing behind her.

I looked out the window again. Jordan was making his way across the street, toward the house.

"C'mon!" I said. "We're getting out of here!"

I ran over to the couch, jerked Thelma up with one hand and Karen with the other.

"Quick now," I said, pushing Thelma ahead of me. "Show us the way."

The little girl led us through the archway and down a short hall to the kitchen. There was a windowed door on the rear wall. I unlocked it, pulled it open, and ushered the two women out onto the back stoop, shutting the door behind me.

The stoop overlooked a snowy lot that ran between the back of Cal's house and the backs of the shops on McMillan Street.

"Go!" I said, pushing Karen and Thelma down the stairs.

Before leaving the stoop, I glanced back through the tiny window in the kitchen door. I could see all the way up the hall. When the front door opened, I skedaddled down the steps and followed Karen and Thelma, who were making their way across the snowy field to McMillan Street.

XXXIX

Once we got across the field, we ducked into a muddy alley between two brick buildings and followed it up to the south side of McMillan Street. The three of us stopped as one when we got to McMillan, leaning against the cornice of the building at the head of the alley, trying to catch our breath. Out on the street, cars drifted by, wreathed in exhaust smoke and drenched in cold white sunlight.

"The car," Karen said, huffing. "How do we get back to the car?"

I shook my head. For a second I couldn't find the breath to speak. "We don't," I finally said. "We can't risk it. We'll have to catch a ride with someone else."

"Who?" Karen asked.

I glanced at Thelma. "I don't suppose you're old enough to drive, are you?"

She shook her head. The run across the field had left her exhilarated, chasing away the last of the shock that had paralyzed her inside Cal's living room. She looked herself again—a fourteen-year-old kid with a punk haircut and a brazen attitude, for whom death, even the death of a friend, held no real meaning.

"That was a cop outside, wasn't it?" she said to me with excitement in her voice, as if the whole thing had turned to TV adventure in her mind.

I nodded. "Are you going to turn us in?"

"Shit, no," Thelma said, looking outraged. "I hate cops."

"What *are* you going to do?" Karen asked her with genuine concern.

Thelma's face knotted up momentarily, as if she'd taken the question to heart. "Now that Renee and Cal are gone . . . I don't know. Go home, I guess."

Karen smiled approvingly. "That's a very good idea. And stay there, honey."

Thelma nodded determinedly. But I could see from the slight restlessness of her eyes that her resolve wasn't going to last long. She'd probably have a few nightmares and swear off drugs for a week or two. But there would be another Cal within the month. For Thelma, there would probably always be another Cal.

"I guess I'll go, then," Thelma said regretfully, as if she were leaving a party too early in the evening.

"You can find your way?" Karen asked.

"Always," Thelma said, putting a very adult look on her kid's face. She gave Karen a quick hug, then walked off down the snowy sidewalk, toward Gilbert—her little butt swinging beneath the coat.

Karen stared after her for a moment, then turned to me. "I hope she'll be all right."

"She'll be fine," I said.

She looked back up the street, at Thelma's receding figure. "I was like that when I was her age."

"You were a little older," I said, "when you were her age."

Karen smiled and turned back to me. "Shouldn't we get off the street?" she said. The run across the field seemed to have exhilarated her, too. Or maybe it was the fact that I'd chosen to run rather than to confront Jordan.

I glanced across McMillan. There was a Frisch's a block up near Victory Parkway. "Getting off the street is probably a good idea." I nodded toward the restaurant. "Let's get something to drink."

We waited for a lull in the traffic, then dashed across McMillan and into the restaurant.

* * *

We sat in Frisch's for about a half an hour, drinking coffee. At first I let Karen do most of the talking—partly because I was trying to keep an eye on the street, in case Jordan blew by, partly because I didn't want to tell her about what I'd found in Cal's desk drawer.

"You know," Karen said, sipping her coffee, "while you were upstairs, Thelma told me a couple of things that might be important."

"Like what?" I asked.

"Like the fact that Cal and Norvelle had a big fight with another man on Friday afternoon. A skinny guy with red hair. The whitest guy Thelma had ever seen."

"That would be our friend Claude Jenkins."

Karen nodded. "That's what I figured."

"Did Thelma tell you what they were arguing about?"

"Selling some drugs," Karen said, giving me an arch look. "A lot of drugs that the white guy, Jenkins, was holding for them."

"Lonnie's crack from the motel," I said.

"It had to be. Cal and Norvelle wanted to turn the stuff over immediately."

"To whom?" I asked.

"To a friend of theirs. Thelma didn't know his name. But the other guy, Jenkins, thought it was too risky to move the crack right away. He wanted to hang on to it for a while."

"Until LeRoi caught up with Lonnie," I said. "Or with me. That's why Claude kept Lonnie alive on Thursday night; so he could play the fall guy with LeRoi."

"After Jenkins left, Cal and Norvelle kept arguing with each other. Thelma said that Norvelle was pretty strung out. He hadn't had a fix in better than a day, and neither one of them had any cash to cop."

I thought of all those glassine bags full of smack, hidden in Norvelle's pillow. And the seven hundred dollars wrapped in the rubber band. Between Friday afternoon and Monday morning, Norvelle had found a lot of dope and a lot of money. I imagined that Cal had found some, too, and taken it with him when he ran. It was obvious now how they'd scored—by taking Claude off the way Claude had taken off Lonnie.

"Thelma went home for supper," Karen went on. "When she came back that night, Lonnie was there. Later in the evening, the three of them drove off to a place in the country together—a place that Lonnie said he wanted to go to. When Norvelle and Cal came back home late that night, Thelma said their moods had changed completely. They were talking about partying. Everybody was going to get well, Thelma said."

I'd heard her say it myself—outside the john.

"Norvelle and Cal must have killed Jenkins that night," I said. "Taken the crack off him. Then sold the whole bundle to their friend the buyer. Whoever the hell he was."

"Maybe they didn't sell all of it," Karen said. "Maybe they just sold enough to party with."

"I found several dozen dime bags of smack in Norvelle's room, along with seven hundred dollars in change. That's not just party favors." I reached into my coat pocket and pulled out the bus ticket. "I also found this."

Karen picked up a paper napkin from the Formica table and dabbed it in a glass of ice water.

"What is it?" she said, wiping out her eyes.

"It's Lonnie's bus ticket," I said.

She stared at it for a moment curiously. "So?"

I explained it to her, trying my best to gloss over the worst of it. "When Lonnie ran to Cal's house on Friday night, Karen, he must have taken this ticket with him and his driver's license, too. Later that night, the license was planted in the motel office to incriminate Lonnie. Norvelle and Cal left it in Jenkins's office, along with a little crack. The murder was made to look like a revenge killing—like Lonnie had run amuck after getting ripped off for drugs by Claude."

"Cal or Norvelle could have stolen the license from Lonnie on Friday night, when he visited their house," she said, dropping the wet napkin on the table. "The bus ticket, too."

She was beginning to get the point, and, as I had expected, she didn't like it.

"Karen," I said. "Lonnie was a liability to them. Once Norvelle and Cal decided to kill Claude, they couldn't afford to have Lonnie running around loose—a three-time loser wanted by the police. Lonnie would have talked if he was busted. He would have given them up, and unlike LeRoi, the cops would have listened to his story. They had to get rid of him, leaving the cops looking for a guy who . . . wasn't there anymore."

"They took him to a friend in the country," Karen said flatly, as if she hadn't heard a thing I'd said. Her square jaw was set, and her pale blue eyes looked harder than I'd ever seen them look, as if they were made of gemstone.

"There was no 'friend in the country,'" I said.

"Leanne lives in the country!" Karen almost shouted. Her face turned red and she glanced quickly around the restaurant—to see if anyone had overheard her. "She has a farm," she said in a lower but no less steely voice.

"Why would they take him to Leanne's farm?" I said.

"Like I told you, she could have been the one who gave Lonnie the two grand. They took him to see her. That's where he wanted to go."

What Thelma had said did tend to confirm Karen's hunch. But if I was right, whether Leanne had given Lonnie the two grand or not was beside the point. Once Norvelle and Cal had decided to kill Claude Jenkins and to set Lonnie up for the murder, it made no difference where Lonnie had wanted to go on Friday night. They had another destination in mind. I said, "Karen, why would Norvelle and Cal have taken Lonnie anywhere? Why wouldn't they have—"

Karen held up her right hand. "I don't want to hear it,

Harry," she said, shaking her head solemnly. "I don't want to hear it."

"Not wanting to hear it isn't going to change things," I told her. "Without the crack, without Lonnie . . . we have no reason not to go to the cops."

"What about Jordan?" she said slyly.

"I'm going to have to face him sooner or later. I think I can make enough of a case for myself with the D.A. to keep him at bay."

"Aren't you forgetting about Norvelle?" she said.

"When we were in the house, it was different. Jordan could have shot me on the spot and rigged it to look like I'd been involved in the drug deal. But in open court, I can beat him. Norvelle died of an overdose. There's no way around that, even if Jordan wants to think differently."

"And LeRoi?"

"We'll turn him over to Al. That'll help us, too, if we get indicted."

Karen stared at me for a long moment, biting her lower lip so hard that it turned white. "You've got it all figured out, huh?"

"I don't like it any more than you do, Karen," I said. "But staying out in the cold is going to get us killed. If we could find the crack or Lonnie . . . it would be different."

"I say no," she said, still staring at me fixedly. "I say that we keep looking. At that farm."

"It's a waste of time," I said.

Her pouty lip started to tremble. "We still don't know for sure who fronted Lonnie the two thousand dollars," she said in a desperate voice. "That would be useful information, wouldn't it? I mean if we did go to the cops, eventually."

"Yeah," I admitted. "It could help."

"Well?"

There was such a depth of despair in her eyes, such a deep-seated need to see it through to the finish, that I couldn't turn her down, even though I knew that our search would only lead to the same dreadful conclusion—that Lonnie was dead, killed by his old friend Norvelle and Norvelle's buddy Cal. But after twenty years of Lonnie, I figured that Karen was owed a sense of closure, of finale. She needed it, so she could tell herself she'd done all she could. Maybe I needed it too. And, after all, it only meant a few more hours of looking.

"All right, Karen," I said, giving her a worn-out smile. "Let's find a ride out to Leanne's farm."

XL

It was Karen's idea to call up Sy Levy. She considered the old man an ally. I considered him a possible suspect. But since I wanted to talk to him anyway, I had no objection to using him as a chauffeur.

Karen walked out to a phone booth in front of the restaurant to make the call. When she came back, she was smiling hopefully. "He's on his way. He even knows where Leanne's farm is. He's been there!"

"You didn't tell him why we needed the ride, did you?"

She shook her head. "I told him your car broke down."

"And you didn't tell him about Norvelle?"

"What's the point in hurting him?" she said sadly. "Norvelle was an old friend." Karen dropped into the seat across from me. "Thanks, Harry, I need to do this."

"I know you do," I said. "But if it doesn't pan out . . ."

"Then we'll talk about going to your pal Al Foster," she said.

It took Sy Levy only twenty minutes to get from St. Bernard to East Walnut Hills. Karen and I were waiting for him in the lobby when he walked into the restaurant. He looked the same as he had in his studio—a cheerful, elfin-faced old man, wearing a black tam, a tweed topcoat, and a muffler wrapped around his throat.

"Well, children," he said when he spotted us in the lobby. "Levy is here."

"Thanks for coming, Sy," Karen said, running over to him and kissing him on the cheek.

Levy blushed. "Can't leave one of my kids out in the cold." He held the restaurant door open for Karen and me, and we walked out into the glaring day. "I'm around the corner."

Levy led us to his car—a beat-up, fading yellow Studebaker. We all piled in the front. The leather seats were torn and leaking stuffing, and the floorboard on the driver's side had worn through in one spot.

"So you think Lonnie might be at Leanne's farm?" he asked as he cranked up the Studebaker.

Karen glanced at me. "We're hoping he's there."

He got a concerned look on his face. "Did he get his . . . problem settled?"

Karen ducked her head. "We'll tell you about it on the way."

Levy turned on the engine and a rush of warm fetid air came pouring out of the floor vents. "It ain't gonna get real warm," he said apologetically. "This damn hole."

He put his left foot over the hole in the floorboard and pulled out onto McMillan. Levy headed due east, toward Columbia Parkway.

"Where is this farm?" I asked him.

"Out past Milford, in Clermont County," he said. "Jon picked it up at an auction. He already owned some property out that way, so . . ." He waved his hand, as if other people's reasons for doing things eluded him. "Jon's changed a lot over the years. I mean he still looks like a kid, with that red hair and that goofy grin of his. But inside . . . he ain't a kid no more. He got old." Levy made a *tsk*ing noise, as if getting old were a tragedy. "All he thinks about now is making money. He's a regular real estate tycoon."

"Leanne looked fairly prosperous too," Karen said with a touch of bitterness.

Levy smiled. "You still mad at her, Karen?"

Karen blushed.

"You shouldn't be. Leanne's had a tough row to hoe,

honey. Maybe not as tough as yours. But don't let the office fool you. She's not a happy lady."

We continued down McMillan, skirting Mt. Lookout and the beautiful colonial houses on the ridge above the river. Levy turned left on Columbia Parkway and headed out along the Ohio. It was the same route that led to the Encantada Motel—due east toward Milford.

"You ain't told me about Lonnie yet," Levy said after a time.

Karen sighed. "It's such a long story."

"It's a long drive."

"You already know that he copped some crack and was taken off for it," Karen said.

Levy nodded.

"It turned out that he was set up to be robbed by his friends."

"By Norvelle!" Levy said with horror.

"And Cal, Norvelle's roommate."

Levy slapped his forehead with his right palm. *"Gott in Himmel!* I'm the one who sent Lonnie to Norvelle in the first place."

"You didn't know what would happen," Karen said immediately. "Lonnie lied to you about why he wanted to find Norvelle."

"I *should* have known," Levy said bitterly. "Lonnie wasn't going to start no band again. Those days are gone." His mouth trembled, as if the thought broke his heart. "Dope was the only reason he was looking for Norvelle. I should've seen that. That's all Norvelle's good for anyway —if you want to score smack or coke."

"Is that why Leanne hired him?" I asked.

The question was blunt, and, coming from me, it made Levy angry. "I like that kid. What right you got to ask me that sort of thing?"

"Sy, please," Karen said. "It's important."

He stared at her. "First you tell me why we're going to see Leanne, Karen."

Karen gave him an embarrassed look. "Lonnie got two thousand dollars from somebody—money he used as a down payment for the crack. We think . . . it may have been from Leanne. He may have been copping for her."

Levy shook his head. "I don't think so."

"Why?" Karen asked him.

"She don't get up, is why," Levy said hesitantly. "She gets down."

"Junk?" Karen said with surprise. "How long's that been going on?"

Levy glanced at her, red-faced. "Since Lonnie, I think."

Karen dropped her head to her chest. "Lonnie," she whispered.

But Levy didn't hear her. "Stoner guessed right. That's why Leanne kept Norvelle around, so she could get a taste when she wanted one. That's why she don't get along with her father. He knows she's a user. He still thinks it's a ghetto vice, you know? And old man Gearheart, he don't want to be associated with nothing from the ghetto. He's threatened to call the police on Leanne a couple of times. His own daughter! Used to be Leanne would call me up on the phone and just cry about it."

"How does her husband feel about her habit?" I asked, thinking of the scene in Leanne's office. If Lonnie had turned Leanne on to smack, it added a cruel meaning to the anger and despair Jon Silverstein had showed at the mention of Lonnie's name.

"You'd have to ask Jon," Levy said coldly.

"It's got to be an expensive proposition," I said, pressing him.

Levy glared at me for a moment. He didn't like my questions. He didn't like me. I wasn't part of his family, one of his kids, like Leanne, Lonnie, and Karen were.

"Jon's got plenty of money," he finally said. "And Leanne ain't always wasted. She does a spoon once in a while. That's all. A spoon or two. Christ, she got married to please her dad. Had kids to please her mom. Now, her husband's Mr. Babbitt. And she's stuck in a life-style that other people have wished on her." He stared hard at the road. "So, she does a few drugs. Who doesn't?"

"How about you, Sy?" I said. "You take a taste now and then?"

"Harry!" Karen shouted.

Levy laughed bitterly. "So you figure I'm in on this, too, Mr. Detective? Maybe it was me gave Lonnie the money to kill himself? Me and Leanne, who still worships the ground Lonnie walks on?"

"Sy, he didn't mean it," Karen said soothingly. "He doesn't know you."

"He don't know dick about people," Levy said angrily. "That's what he don't know." He glanced over at me. "I don't do drugs. And Leanne Silverstein ain't in the dope-dealing business."

"I believe you," I said.

"I don't give a damn what you believe," Levy snapped, turning back to the wheel.

I looked at Karen. "You heard the man. You still want to go through with this?"

She couldn't meet my gaze. "We haven't talked to Leanne yet," she said feebly. "Lonnie still might have called her. He might have run to her on Friday night. She could be hiding him out there."

"Okay," I said with a sigh. "But we're on a wild-goose chase, and you know it."

I settled back on the car seat and stared out the window. On our left we drove past the Encantada Motel. It looked even dingier in the bright sunlight than it had at night—its stucco walls running yellow with rust, half its windows boarded up.

I closed my eyes. It was going to be a long, pointless trip. And the clock was still running for LeRoi and for Jordan. It had already stopped for Lonnie—I was sure of that.

XLI

About ten miles outside of Milford, Levy turned off the highway onto a choppy access road that led up to a farmhouse sitting all by itself in the midst of a huge snowy field. As we neared the house I could see the duck pond that Leanne had mentioned, lying in a wooded hollow that ran below the front yard. A battered Jeep Cherokee was parked beside the house, in the shade of an enormous snow-covered oak.

I leaned forward on the car seat and stared at the Jeep. There was no question that it was the same car I'd seen parked outside the Encantada bar on Thursday and Friday nights.

"What?" Karen said when she noticed me staring through the windshield.

"Maybe it's a good idea we came out here, after all," I said.

"What is it, Harry?" she said excitedly.

I nodded at the Jeep. "I saw that car parked at the motel on the night I picked Lonnie up and on the night that Jenkins was murdered." I glanced over at Levy. "Who does it belong to?"

"Leanne or Jon or Leanne's folks, I guess," he said, looking distressed.

A second car, a sparkling new Buick Regal, was parked at a distance in front of the Jeep. A black man in a brown parka and khaki pants was leaning over its hood, polishing the chrome bumper with a rag.

When we pulled into the yard, the black man stopped

polishing the car and looked up at us balefully. He was a tall, spare, gray-haired man, with a proud, forbidding face, runneled and fleshless as nut meat. He watched us closely as we got out of the car.

"What do you all want around here?" he roared in a booming bass.

Sy Levy waved a hand at him from behind the Studebaker. "It's Sy, Dr. Gearheart. Remember me? Sy Levy?"

The black man's look softened a bit. "Of course I remember you," he said, as if he'd been accused of forgetting things before. "Leanne isn't here. She won't be here until after work."

Sy glanced at Karen and me. "What do I say?" he whispered.

"Tell him Leanne invited us out here."

Levy picked up my cue.

"Well, I don't know," Leanne's father replied uncomfortably. "She didn't say anything about it to me."

"She doesn't have to tell you everything," a woman called out from the front porch.

The woman stepped off the porch into the yard, sighting over at us with a hand at her brow. She was a pretty, white-haired woman, with a tanned face and those same slanted, oriental eyes that I'd found so attractive in her daughter. She was wearing a heavy cloth coat over a blouse and slacks.

"Hello, Sy," Mrs. Gearheart said, dropping her hand and coming out into the yard. "Who are your friends?"

"I'm Harry Stoner," I said to the woman. "And this is Karen Jackowski."

"Karen Jackowski?" Mrs. Gearheart said, glancing at her husband. "I believe Leanne was talking about you last night at supper, honey. You came to see her at work, didn't you?"

Karen nodded. "We were looking for my ex-husband."

"Now I remember," Mrs. Gearheart said, not looking

entirely pleased by the memory. "Leanne used to . . . know your husband fairly well, didn't she?"

"They're old friends."

"Friends," Mrs. Gearheart said with an empty look.

"I'm surprised you remembered Karen's name," I said, trying to smile at her winningly and to change the subject at the same time.

"Oh, I have a good memory for names and faces," Mrs. Gearheart said, pleased with the compliment. "Are you a friend of Leanne's too?"

"Yes," I said. "Although not quite as old a friend as Karen or Sy."

"Leanne is always making friends," Mrs. Gearheart said. "Well, come on in the house and I'll get you something to drink. Maybe I should call Leanne too. She may have forgotten she invited you to visit. She's forgetful sometimes."

We started across the yard, walking past Gearheart, who didn't even look up from his polishing. When we got near the Jeep, I told the others to go on ahead. "I'd like to look around if that's okay? Leanne told us so much about the place."

"You go ahead," Mrs. Gearheart said sweetly. "But there's not much to see in this weather. What with the duck pond frozen over, and the garden covered with snow."

She guided Sy and Karen into the house. Gearheart looked up at me suspiciously as I walked over to the Jeep.

"I used to have one of these myself," I said, throwing him a cheerful smile.

"Piece of junk," he said acidly. "Jon only uses it to tear around these fields. And to go into Milford. He doesn't keep it up worth a damn. Hell, it hardly runs."

I opened the passenger door of the Jeep and glanced inside. "Looks the same as mine, except I had a three-speed."

"Don't you go nosing around there," Gearheart said, starting toward me. Before he could get to me, I flipped open the glove compartment and looked inside. Lonnie's dog-eared photograph—the one of Karen and her kids in front of the Christmas tree—was sitting on top of an oily Jeep owner's manual. Shocked, I pulled the picture out of the compartment and held it up in front of my eyes, squinting at it through the white glare of the winter sun.

As I stood there, Gearheart came up beside me. "What's that?" he said, pointing at the photo.

"Something I found on the seat," I said. "A picture."

"Let me see it," he said, holding out his hand.

I handed him the picture. "Why, it's that girl, isn't it? The one you came with?"

I nodded.

"How did it get inside there?" he said, looking confused.

"It belonged to Lonnie Jackowski—Karen's ex-husband."

"I remember the son of a bitch from back in the sixties," Gearheart said with disgust. "He was a dirty hippie creep."

I was getting a little sick of his irascibility. I'd known a number of older men who put on the same act. But in his case it wasn't an act—his bitterness went all the way to the bone.

"Could I have the photo back?" I said to him. "Karen might want it."

He handed it to me reluctantly. "He never cleans that damn truck up," he said, shaking his head. "It's probably been sitting there since he came home on Saturday morning."

"Lonnie didn't come home with him, did he?" I asked.

"How the hell would I know?" Gearheart said. "Jon didn't get back until dawn. Probably high on something too. I can tell. I am a doctor, you know."

"Good for you," I said.

He glared at me.

I turned away from him and walked across the frozen snow to the porch. Before I went inside, I stuck the photograph in my pocket.

* * *

Karen, Sy, and Leanne's mother were gathered in the living room, off a short entry hall to the right of the front door. It was a handsome room, paneled in oak and decorated in masculine-looking leather furniture. A few hunting trophies were hung on the walls, along with a gun rack full of shotguns and deer rifles. A huge stone fireplace occupied one side of the room; a couple of logs were burning colorfully on the andirons. Through the windows I could see Gearheart polishing his Buick in the front yard.

"I gave Leanne a call," Mrs. Gearheart said as I walked in. "She was delighted you and Karen are here. She's going to drop the children off with Jon's mother and come right out. Jon has some work to do, so I'm afraid he won't be with her."

I glanced at Karen, who gave me a look as if to say, "What could I do?"

I sat down beside Karen on a tuxedo couch.

"How do you like the farm?" Mrs. Gearheart asked.

"It's very pretty," I said.

"Expensive to keep though," Mrs. Gearheart said, shaking her head with rueful amusement. "As I was telling Karen, Jon has spent a fortune renovating this house. He's planning to landscape the entire grounds as well. He likes playing the county squire. Sometimes I wonder where he finds the money."

After coming across Lonnie's photo in Silverstein's Jeep, I had an idea about where Jon found some of his money, although I couldn't say anything in front of Mrs. Gearheart.

"Sy tells us that Jon has invested heavily in real estate out here," I said to her.

She nodded. "He's been picking up old farms for a song and then leasing them for industrial use. I think Jon really enjoys wheeling and dealing, and he's very good at it. He just has a way with people. The mall you passed on Wooster Pike, outside of Milford—that is one of Jon's properties. And he has part-ownership of the land that the Miamiville Cinemas are on."

She gave me a sidelong look to see if she was boring me with her chatter. I smiled broadly and rocked forward on the couch, as if I were deeply interested in what she'd been saying. She obviously enjoyed talking about her son-in-law. And was just as obviously avoiding any talk about her daughter.

"Are you an investor, Mr. Stoner?" she asked.

"I've done a little dabbling in real estate," I said.

"Then you really ought to sit down with Jon and talk. He knows any number of properties around here that are good buys." She laughed suddenly, putting a hand over her mouth, as if she'd made a rude noise. "Although even Jon makes mistakes. He once bought a farm up the road from here because of its water rights, and the well ran dry. And then there's that motel in Miamiville."

Both Karen and I must have bolted a little on the sofa, because Mrs. Gearheart got a startled look on her face.

"Did I say something wrong?" she said.

"No, we passed a run-down motel on the way over here," I said. "On Wooster Pike."

"The Encantada," Mrs. Gearheart said with a laugh. "That's the one! It's a disreputable-looking place, isn't it?"

Karen and I nodded.

Mrs. Gearheart shook her head. "I don't know why he hangs on to it. He says he likes owning a bar. He goes to visit there a few times a week—just to sit. It gives him a kick, I think, to be a barkeep."

A teakettle began screaming somewhere in the house. Mrs. Gearheart got up from her chair. "That's the hot water," she said. "Is coffee all right with everyone?"

We all nodded.

"I'll just be a moment, then," Mrs. Gearheart said. She walked off through the living room archway, leaving us alone.

XLII

As soon as Mrs. Gearheart had left the room, Karen turned to me with a triumphant look on her face. "You heard that," she whispered. "It's Jon's fucking motel. It was *Jon's* dope that Lonnie was carrying."

I nodded. "I was wrong. There is a connection."

"What connection?" Levy said looking confused. "So he owns a motel? So what?"

"It's the motel that the drug transaction was supposed to take place in, Sy," I said, trying to explain it to him. "It's where Lonnie was ripped off and where Jenkins was murdered."

"In Jon's motel!" he said, shocked. "But what makes you think he knew about it?"

"Of course he knew about it," Karen snapped. "Lonnie didn't pick that place out of thin air. He was told to go there by Jon. It was all arranged."

"Saying so isn't proof, doll," Levy persisted. "Where's the evidence? Where's the connection between Lonnie and Jon?"

"Here." I pulled the photograph out of my pocket. "I found this in Jon's Jeep."

I didn't try to explain what it meant. I just handed the photograph to Karen.

She stared at the picture for a long time, then dropped it to her lap. "Oh, God," she said in a heartbroken voice.

"Karen?" Levy said with concern. "What is it?"

"It's a picture of Karen and her kids," I said to him.

"Oh, yeah. Lonnie showed it to me on Wednesday, when he came to the studio. How did it get in Jon's Jeep?"

I glanced at Karen, who was staring into space. Her eyes were filled with tears.

I sighed heavily. "Silverstein must have had Lonnie in that Jeep sometime on Friday night, Sy."

"But I thought you said that Lonnie ran to Norvelle's house on Friday night. How did he end up in Jon's car . . ." Sy's voice died off as he made the point for himself. "You mean Jon was involved in the scheme to rip Lonnie off?"

I nodded, keeping an eye on Karen, who was still staring emptily into space—a blasted look on her face.

"Jon," Levy said, shaking his head mournfully. "I don't think I believe it. Why would he do such a thing to an old friend?"

"You'd have to ask him," I said. "But the answer is probably money. Real estate is a high-profile business. It takes a lot of working capital to create the right impression. Maybe Jon needed the bread from a drug deal to finance some of this." I waved my hand around the luxe little room we were sitting in. "Maybe he wanted some revenge too. Leanne apparently never forgot her first love—or let Jon forget him. And from what you told us, Silverstein had one other pretty good reason to remember Lonnie Jackowski."

"You mean Leanne's habit?" Levy said.

I nodded.

"But Lonnie," Levy said. "If Jon was working with Norvelle and Cal, what happened to Lonnie?"

"They killed him," Karen said hoarsely, shaking herself as if she were waking from a bad dream. She wiped her eyes with her fingers. "Lonnie's dead."

"Karen . . ."

I put my hand on her shoulder, but she shrugged it off.

"So you were right, Harry," she said, turning to me with a sick, accusatory look. "You were right all along."

"I didn't want him dead, Karen," I said, feeling guilty in spite of myself.

"Sure you did," she said with an eerie look. "We *all* did. And now it's true. He wouldn't have left this behind him, not unless . . ." Her voice trailed off and she sat there staring at nothing.

I wanted to reach out to her again. To touch her. To hold her. But she didn't want me to touch her.

Gearheart came walking through the front door suddenly. Once again he didn't give us a look. "Sophy?" he bellowed.

"In the kitchen," Sophy Gearheart called out.

We heard dishes rattling and then Mrs. Gearheart came walking through the archway into the living room, carrying cups on a tray. She glanced at her husband.

"Do you want some coffee, Alex?" she said to her husband. "I made plenty."

He nodded a little sullenly, took off his topcoat, and hung it on a peg by the door.

Sophy Gearheart passed out the cups to each of us. Glancing at Karen, she said, "Are you all right, honey?"

Karen focused her red eyes on Sophy Gearheart. "I'd like to use your bathroom, if that's okay?"

"Sure," Mrs. Gearheart said with concern. "Upstairs on your right."

Karen got up. The photograph slid off her lap and floated to the pegged hardwood floor. She stepped over it, carelessly, as she walked out of the room. Sophy and her husband watched her leave.

"She's been crying," Gearheart said brusquely.

Sophy gave him an angry look. "Do you have to say everything that comes into your mind?"

"She's upset about her ex-husband," I said to them.

"Why?" Gearheart said.

"It's none of our business why," his wife snapped at him. "Just drink your coffee."

* * *

We sat in the living room for about ten minutes. Sy Levy tried to keep us amused with stories from the old days. But neither of the Gearhearts seemed much interested in the old days. And all I could think about was Karen.

After a time I excused myself and went upstairs. As I got to the top landing, I could hear Karen talking on a phone in one of the bedrooms. I stopped outside the door and listened. She was talking to one of her kids.

"Of course I do, sweetheart," she said. "I'll show you when I come home." She looked up and saw me standing in the doorway. "I'll see you tonight, baby, if I can."

She hung up the phone and stared at me, guiltily. "You heard?"

I nodded. "You're going home."

"If the cops let me. And it's okay with you."

"What do I have to do with it?" I said bitterly.

"Oh, Harry," she said, her face falling. "Don't be that way."

"I'm sorry, Karen," I said. "I just thought we had something going here."

"We do," she said, with that same look of pain. "But try to understand that I've been dreading this day for almost eighteen years. Now that it's finally come . . . I need some time to react. I need to see my kids again. My house. My job. I need to visit my own life and put some distance between me and this . . . nightmare."

"I understand."

"Do you?" She walked over to me and touched me gently on the cheek.

Karen smiled at me sadly. It was a loving smile, but there was nothing in it that said she might change her mind and stay. Or that she owed me any more of an explanation than the one she'd just given me.

She kissed me on the mouth, then walked out of the room.

I stood there for a moment, thinking about that first

night in the hotel, and knew that the feeling we'd shared
—that larkish feeling of playing hooky from the decade, of
going back to some common ground in the past—just
wasn't there for her anymore. Lonnie's murder had
changed it. It had changed the way she looked at me. It
had broken the connection.

XLIII

I went back to the living room and sat down again on the couch beside Karen. The Gearhearts stared at us morbidly. A few minutes passed, slowly, then a car came up the lane into the yard.

"That must be Leanne," Sophy said with a vaguely troubled look on her face. She stared at her husband meaningfully and he returned the look. I wasn't sure what the silent communication meant until Leanne came through the door. Then I knew.

She was stoned. I could see it at once. I'd seen it before —in her office. I just hadn't understood it then. Nor had she been as stoned then as she was now. Her marvelous eyes were as sleepy and glazed-looking as those of the junkies I'd seen in LeRoi's Silver Star. Her mouth hung loosely open, in a grotesque parody of a congenial smile. Even her movements were awkward and encumbered, as if she were caught in the fur coat she was wearing. She tried to take the coat off by the door, grew frustrated in the attempt, and gave up. Walking tipsily across the room, she knelt down on the floor in front of her father, and tried to embrace him.

"Daddy!" she said in a slurred voice.

Gearheart pushed her away from him—hard. Sophy Gearheart clapped a hand to her mouth. And Leanne looked shocked, as if he had doused her with water.

Gearheart eyed Leanne coldly. "I'm going upstairs," he said with disgust.

He got up and walked out of the room. Leanne watched

him from where she was kneeling on the floor. "That's my daddy, folks," she said in a hurt voice. "You remember my daddy, don't you, Karen?"

Karen stared at her sadly. Sophy Gearheart got up and left the room, following her husband upstairs. In a moment we could hear their voices—raised in anger.

Leanne stared after them, through the archway, as if she wanted to cry. If we hadn't been there, I think she would have cried. Instead, she pulled herself together with a visible effort—standing up, rocking for a moment drunkenly on her feet, then walking over to a chair and sitting down hard.

She didn't say anything for a while. Nobody said anything. It was a scene that had probably been played out a hundred times before—in front of her parents, her husband, her children. But it hadn't been played out in front of guests, and Leanne must have been feeling the humiliation doubly, because of me and Karen. Her face had turned a bright red and her eyes had sobered up, as if the high she'd been on had just escaped her.

"I didn't think you'd come to the farm," she said, staring dully at the floor.

"We had to," I said.

Both Karen and Levy jerked forward.

"Harry," Karen said in a sharply warning voice. And Levy gave me a look, as if to say that now was not the time. But I didn't really care about hurting Leanne Silverstein's feelings. After what Karen had told me, I didn't care about anyone at that moment. I just wanted to find out how much Leanne knew about the drug deal—how deep the corruption ran. Most of all, I wanted to find her husband.

"What do you mean, had to?" Leanne said, looking up at me with her shell-shocked face.

"Your husband is a drug dealer, Mrs. Silverstein."

"Christ," Levy said, slapping the arm of his chair, "you got no heart in you at all."

Leanne glanced at Levy, then back at me. "Drug dealer?" she said. "Jon?"

"He and his partners ripped Lonnie off at that motel Jon owns—the Encantada."

Leanne laughed nervously. "You're crazy! Jon wouldn't do that!"

"Oh, but he did," I said. I leaned over and picked up the photograph from the floor.

Karen put her hand on my arm. "Do we have to do this now?" she whispered fiercely.

"Do you want to know the truth?" I replied, just as fiercely.

She didn't answer me for a second. "I don't know," she finally said. "What difference does it make anymore?"

"Have you forgotten about LeRoi and Jordan?" I said. I turned back to Leanne Silverstein again. She was wobbling unsteadily on the chair, trying like hell to keep her attention focused on me.

I said, "Lonnie was given two thousand dollars by your husband, as a down payment on some crack. He was supposed to deliver the crack to Jon at the Encantada Motel. But he was ripped off for the drugs before he could deliver. Ripped off by your friend Norvelle, by Norvelle's roommate, Cal, and by a guy named Claude Jenkins."

Leanne Silverstein blinked with her whole face. "Jenkins? He was the night clerk at Jon's motel. He was killed in a robbery."

I nodded. "Norvelle and Cal killed him for the drugs he was holding—Lonnie's drugs. They were in it together, Mrs. Silverstein. Jon too."

"I don't believe it," she said, looking horrified. "Jon wouldn't hurt anybody. And we didn't see Lonnie last week. We haven't seen him since 1969."

"Jon saw him," I said. "On Wednesday, at the Bijou—your day off. Jon used him to buy crack from a connection in Avondale."

She shook her head defiantly.

"C'mon, Leanne," I said. "How do you think Jon gets the money to pay for this? How do you think he pays for your habit?"

She flinched as if I'd slapped her. "I don't know," she said. "I don't know about his business."

"Sure, you do," I said. "You just don't want to admit it."

"I . . ." She glanced at the front door nervously. "I think maybe you better go."

"We'll go, all right," I said in a tough voice. "We'll go to the cops. And they'll come back here with a warrant for your husband. He used Lonnie, Leanne, and then he killed him."

"You bastard!" Levy shouted, rising from his chair.

Leanne's defenses collapsed all at once. She slumped in the chair, covered her eyes with her right hand, and began to sob miserably. "I *love* Lonnie. Jon knows that. He would never hurt him. You must be wrong. It has to be a mistake."

I handed her the photograph. "I found that in your husband's Jeep, Mrs. Silverstein. Lonnie had it on him on Friday night."

She took the photograph in her left hand and stared at it. Tears ran down her cheeks, spotting the surface of the picture. "Oh, Lonnie," she said in a tiny voice.

"Where is he, Leanne?" I said. "Where is Jon?"

"At the motel," she whispered.

Leanne began weeping hysterically, bouncing up and down and clasping herself tightly with both arms, as if she were literally about to fall apart. Levy went over to her, giving me a vicious look as he passed by.

"It's all right, honey," he said, pulling her to him. "You didn't know."

She looked up at him desperately. "I've got to get off again, Sy," she pleaded, her face running tears. "I can't take it. I can't! It's just too horrible."

Levy stroked her hair gently. "You need your strength,

now, Leanne. You don't want to go getting high with your folks around."

"I have no strength," she wailed. "They took it all away from me. They took everything I cared for. And now they've taken Lonnie too." She looked over at Karen. "I loved him, Karen. I really loved him."

Karen ducked her head. "Oh, Christ," she said softly.

I got up from the couch and went over to Levy. "I need your car, Sy," I said.

He glared at me. "For why? For more destruction? Isn't this awful enough?" He looked down at Leanne, who had buried her face in his chest. "Just leave it alone. Let the police handle it."

"He's right, Harry," Karen said. "It's over."

"The fuck it is," I said angrily. "He killed your husband, Karen. He killed my friend."

"Your friend, Harry?" she said, giving me a long, long look.

"Yes," I said. "My friend." I turned back to Sy. "Give me the keys, old man, or I'll take them off you."

Sy blanched, then reached in his pocket, and handed me the keys.

Karen started to get up and I shook my head. "No!" I said sharply. "You stay here. Call Al Foster. Tell him to get a warrant and search this place. If Silverstein hasn't turned it over yet, the crack might still be here."

"What about Jordan?" Karen said. "Won't he be notified? I mean we're fugitives from him right now."

"Just make the call," I told her.

XLIV

I walked out of the house into the cold afternoon twilight. The sun was just setting above the oak trees, casting long shadows across the yard and turning the ice on the duck pond bloodred. I got in the Studebaker, started it up, and headed back up the access road to the highway.

It took me less than ten minutes to get to the motel. The neon sign was on, sputtering feebly in the dusk. I parked by the office and walked over to the bar. There were only a half dozen locals inside—it was too early for the bike crowd.

I spotted Jon Silverstein immediately. He was sitting by himself in a booth on the left-hand wall. He looked up at me when I came over to him—a smile forming on his long, horsey face—then immediately looked away, as if he could tell from my expression why I'd come. He passed a trembling hand through his curly red hair and stared morbidly at the Rolex on his wrist, as if it were a shiny gold bug crawling up his arm.

I sat down across from him in the booth. "I've come to get you, Jon," I said. "I need the crack. LeRoi wants it back."

A sick smile flitted across Silverstein's face. He grabbed at it with his right hand, squeezing his lips together until they were a bloodless white. "Who's LeRoi?" he asked. He wasn't trying to be cute. It was a real question; but then there was no reason for him to know LeRoi's name.

"He's the guy Lonnie copped the crack from." I stared

at him across the booth table. "You aren't going to tell me you don't know anything about the crack, are you, Jon?"

He didn't say anything.

"That was pretty damn cute, what you did. Giving Lonnie two thousand dollars to buy with—just enough to get LeRoi interested. That way, if it didn't work out, you'd lost nothing. And if it did, you'd paid only two grand for twelve grand's worth of stuff."

Silverstein dropped his hand from his mouth. It hit the table with a thud, like a dropped rock. "What if I said that I don't know what you're talking about?"

"Then I'd say you're lying," I said coldly. "You're involved, Jon. I saw your Jeep parked here on Friday night."

"I can explain that!" he said quickly.

I shook my head. "Don't bother. I found Lonnie's picture inside your glove compartment. How do you explain that?"

Silverstein smiled his sick smile again. "Lonnie's picture," he whispered, as if it were something he'd overlooked.

"Did you forget you'd left it there, Jon? Or did you just stop caring about what happened to Lonnie Jack?" I stared into his frightened face. "I could almost understand that. The only thing I don't understand is why you went along with Cal and Norvelle when they decided to kill Claude. Why'd you do that, Jon? Was he going to run away with all of it? Or didn't you want to sit on the crack either? Did you need a quick fix too? Even if it did mean taking a chance? Even if it did mean murdering Claude and Lonnie?"

"Was that such a loss—Lonnie?" Silverstein blurted out, his voice shaking angrily. "Does he really mean anything to you—you, who are playing hide-the-salami with his old lady? Do you know what your pal Lonnie did to my wife? Do you know what my marriage has been like? Do you care about what I've had to put up with for the last fifteen years because of the nasty little habit he taught her? Do you know the heartbreak? The money it's cost me? The kids—what they've seen with their own eyes?" His voice was choked with rage.

"So you did this all for Leanne? Is that what you're telling me?" I reached across the table and snapped the gold band of his Rolex. He jerked his hand away. "C'mon, Jon. Don't kid a kidder."

"I've got nothing to say to you."

"You're going to have to talk to the cops," I said. "They're on their way now."

Silverstein bolted out of the booth, banging his bony knees on the tabletop. I stretched a leg out and tripped him as he ran past me; he sprawled facefirst on the barroom floor. The bartender came running out from behind the bar with a baseball bat in his hand.

"You okay, Jon?" he said.

Silverstein looked up groggily. His nose was bloody from the fall, and he wiped it with his sleeve. "Get rid of him," he said, glancing at me.

The bartender started toward me, waving the bat in front of him. But I already had the pistol out. I pointed it at him, gripping the butt in both hands. The bartender took a step back, almost tripping over Silverstein.

"You want to get killed, buddy?" I said with ice in my voice. "Over that piece of shit on the floor? Because if you don't drop the bat, that's what's going to happen."

The bartender thought it over and dropped the bat on the floor, stepping back toward the bar.

"Get up!" I said to Silverstein.

He got to his feet slowly, staring at me fearfully. I slid out of the booth, keeping one eye on the bartender and one on Jon Silverstein.

"Outside," I said to Silverstein.

"Where are we going?"

"To the cops, Jon. They want to talk to you about Lonnie and the crack. They'll probably want to look into the financing of some of your real estate deals too. You can afford a good lawyer. Better get one."

I pushed him toward the door. "This is kidnapping," he shouted.

The half-dozen people in the bar were watching us, anyway. But it was a nice touch.

I shoved him out the door into the lot and dragged him quickly over to the Studebaker. I figured the bartender was probably already calling the county cops, and a couple of patrons were peeking out the door after us. So the car would be easy to spot. Which meant I didn't have much time.

"Where are you taking me?" Silverstein said, looking wildly around him.

"Home, Jon," I said, opening the driver's-side door and pushing him through it. I got in beside him, holding the gun against his ribs.

"Listen," he said desperately, "maybe we can talk about this."

"Sure we can talk about it." I smiled. "Just like you talked it over with Lonnie."

He groaned. "Look, I've still got the crack. That's what you want, isn't it? I'll give it to you, Stoner."

I started up the car and pulled out of the lot, speeding off up the highway. In the far distance I could hear police sirens heading toward the motel. We'd be back at the farm before they could talk to the bartender and start after us.

Silverstein dropped his head to his chest and sobbed with despair. "It wasn't supposed to happen this way. I swear to you. Doing the deal was Lonnie's idea, for chris-sake. He talked me into this fucking thing, the son of a bitch. I was going to buy a little dope and make a few bucks. He was going to make a little money too—to get him started again, to get him on his feet. How did I know Claude and Norvelle and Cal were going to rip him off? I was going to buy some crack, that's all I was going to do.

Then it just started happening, and I . . . I couldn't stop it."

"Sure," I said. "You couldn't help driving Lonnie to his death."

"I don't know what you're talking about," he shouted. "I didn't do anything but drive him over to Norvelle's house. He called me from your place on Friday night, and I picked him up outside the apartment. I offered to take him to the bus station, but he wanted to talk to Norvelle first. He said he might call me again later. I just took him where he wanted to go. I hated the son of a bitch, but I didn't want him dead."

"Maybe just a little?" I said, glancing at him.

He shook his head savagely. "No! I'm not going to lie to you and pretend I'm sorry Lonnie's gone. But I didn't plan it that way. I swear to God I didn't." His face lit up, as if he'd had a brainstorm. "Why the hell do you think I kept the photograph? I found it on the floor of the Jeep after I drove Lonnie over to Norvelle's. I kept it in the car, thinking Lonnie'd pick it up later that night. After I dropped him off I went to the bar and poured myself a few drinks. Got kind of wasted. I guess the photograph slipped my mind." He looked at me beseechingly. "Do you think I would have kept that thing around if I'd known what was going to happen?"

"And I suppose you had nothing to do with killing Claude either?"

"Norvelle and Cal killed Claude," he said. "I didn't know they were going to do it. Claude . . . he had the stuff hidden someplace. He wouldn't tell any of us where it was. He wanted to sit on it for a while. At least that's what he said. It made no difference to me if he sat on it— what could I do about it anyway? But Norvelle and Cal wanted to complete the deal right away. They needed the cash right away." He eyed me with wounded helplessness, like a kid, who'd gone along with the bigger kids and found himself in trouble. "I couldn't just give them the money without the goods, could I? I mean, that's not business-like."

I laughed dully. "Is that what you told them?"

His face turned red. "I didn't know they would kill Claude. How could I know that? *Nobody* was supposed to get hurt, I'm telling you. It was a business deal." He sobbed again hoarsely. "It was supposed to be like the old days," Silverstein whispered. "No one was going to get hurt."

XLV

It was almost fully dark when I pulled into the farmyard. I parked behind the Buick and yanked Silverstein out of the car. He looked completely depleted, as if he'd lost all his strength once I'd put the gun on him. He'd picked the wrong line of work, I thought. He wasn't tough enough to be a drug dealer. At least, not for the kind of deal he'd gotten himself involved in. Maybe he'd told me the truth in the car. Maybe he'd just gotten in over his head and couldn't figure how to get out again. Or maybe he'd seen the chance to get even with Lonnie, and stood back and let things happen. His grudge against Lonnie didn't change anything. It just made the past few days seem more terrible, more inevitable. Like everyone else, Silverstein had gotten caught up in Lonnie Jackowski's life, on Lonnie's last ride to Fire Lake.

I stared at the swart farmhouse, glowing yellow at every window in the dusk. It looked like a bastion of warmth and life in the frozen, purpling fields around it. But it was dead inside there too. For a moment, in the rapidly fading light, I felt as if the whole damn country were dying of the same fucking disease. A disease that had started out as something almost like innocent fun, in a time full of promise and good fellowship. For a second I just wanted it to be that way again—the way it had been, for a moment, with Karen and me.

But that was over too, I thought. What had happened to Lonnie had ended it. Instead of freeing us, his death had left us full of guilts and angers. It had left us alone again, as if all we'd ever shared had been him.

"C'mon," I said heavily, pushing Silverstein toward the door.

He stared at me hopelessly. "I can't face them," he said, seeing his whole life draining away in the dark. "How can I face them? And Leanne?" His voice broke.

"C'mon, Jon," I said. "I've got to go in there too."

He glanced at me uncertainly, then walked up to the porch and opened the door. I followed him in.

The whole group was gathered in the living room— Leanne, her mother and father, Karen, Sy. It looked as if Leanne and her father had been fighting with each other again. They were standing on opposite sides of the room, glaring at each other. The mother was standing in between, like a referee.

"You *bastard!*" Leanne said when Jon walked through the door.

Everyone in the room turned to look at him, and at me.

"Leanne," Silverstein said weakly.

She glared at him, her face burning with anger. "You killed him!"

"I didn't!" Silverstein cried. "They killed him—Norvelle and Cal."

I glanced at Karen. She dropped her head and covered her eyes with both hands.

"You *let* them do it," Leanne shouted. "You wanted them to kill him. Because I cared for him. Because he meant something to me. Something *you* could never mean."

Her words struck Silverstein like a blow. He staggered where he stood.

"You're stoned again," her father shouted at her. "Listen to you talk. You worthless junkie. That's your husband. You're supposed to cleave to him."

"He killed Lonnie!" she said, turning to Gearheart with a wild look on her beautiful face.

She wasn't in control of herself anymore. The smack and the trauma of Lonnie's death had simply unhinged her.

"He deserved killing," Gearheart shouted. "He's the one who got you hooked on that stuff in the first place!"

Leanne groaned. "You never understood him. Or me. You've never understood anything. You vicious old bastard."

"Leanne!" her mother shouted. "That's your father."

"He's nothing!" Leanne screamed, starting toward Gearheart.

Levy tried to grab her by the arm, but she shook him off. As soon as Leanne got within arm's reach, Gearheart slapped her hard with his right hand. Leanne staggered backward with a groan. Jon Silverstein rushed toward her, from where he'd been standing by the open door. He reached out to her, but Leanne recoiled from his touch—shrieking and slapping at him with both hands.

"Get away from me!" she screamed. "Get away!"

Outside, I heard a car pull up in the yard. I glanced out the open door. It was a gray Ford—a cop car. Al Foster stepped out of one door. Jordan stepped out of the other. In spite of what Karen had said, I hadn't figured on Jordan's showing up. But I guessed Al hadn't had a choice. I guessed I hadn't left him one. They both started walking toward the house.

Leanne screamed again—at the top of her lungs. "Bastards!"

Both of the cops started running.

"I'm going to kill you!" Leanne said to her father. She reached for the gun rack and pulled a shotgun off the wall.

"Leanne!" her mother screamed.

Silverstein, Karen, and Levy wrestled with Leanne, trying to get the gun away from her. Gearheart just stood there, staring at his daughter with horror. The cops were through the door by then.

When Jordan saw the shotgun in Leanne's hand, he pulled out his service pistol.

"Don't!" I shouted at him, and made a grab for the gun. Jordan whipped the pistol across my face, knocking me to the floor. Al made a grab for the gun, too, but Jordan shoved him away.

Everyone in the living room looked toward the door. Silverstein saw the pistol, let go of his wife, and retreated toward the wall. Without him holding her, Leanne easily broke loose from Karen and Levy. She took two steps across the room, holding the shotgun in her hands—a wild, unknowing look on her face.

Jordan shot her—twice—sending her flying against the far wall beside her husband. She hit the wall hard and sank to the floor. The shotgun fell out of her hands and landed on the rug at her feet.

For a moment nobody said anything. And then it was chaos. Everyone crying and shouting at once.

I sat there on the floor, staring at Leanne Silverstein's bloody body, and didn't feel like getting up again.

XLVI

After Leanne's death, Silverstein confessed to everything. He couldn't stop confessing, the poor son of a bitch. The cops found the crack where he said it would be—upstairs in the bedroom closet of the farmhouse. Jordan promptly busted LeRoi and his boys; and Cal and Renee were tracked down in a Florida motel. I testified against all of them at the trial. A shooting board was convened on the Leanne Silverstein killing. I testified at the board too. In spite of all I could do, they ruled the shooting a justifiable homicide and Jordan walked.

But the trial and the shooting board were months later. That night, after the coroner had come and gone, Levy drove us back to Cross Lane. We picked up the Pinto and I took Karen to the airport.

I wanted to wait with her before she left. But she told me to go back home and get some rest. She wanted to be alone for a while.

I said to her, "You're going to call me, right? I mean, this isn't good-bye."

She stared at me for a long moment. "I'll call," she promised.

But she never did call. They never found Lonnie's body, either.

Here's a preview of the next Harry Stoner novel, *Extenuating Circumstances,* available from Delacorte Press next month.

The Lessing house was on Riverside Drive in Covington, almost directly across the Ohio River from the Stadium. I knew it was across from the Stadium because I could hear the afternoon baseball crowd grumbling in the distance, like an army of men talking fitfully in their sleep. I couldn't see the Stadium itself, or much of anything on the Ohio side. The midsummer heat had raised a mist on the river, making the crowd noises drifting over the water seem detached, dreamlike. It could have been the Styx; the distant welter, the voices of the doomed. It could also have been the Ohio River on a hot, humid July afternoon with a baseball game in progress. It was a day to make you a little soft in the brain.

What I could see, had no trouble seeing, was a pretty French Quarter house on a small rise above the street where I had parked. A flagstone terrace dotted with cane furniture. A row of French windows in a white stucco wall. A second-story veranda, railed in wrought iron with a second row of French windows opening onto it. Two people were sitting on the terrace, a man and a woman looking in opposite directions, like drawings on a jelly glass. Neither one of them was looking at me.

I hied my way up a short flight of stone steps. The man turned toward me. He was too fat to be wearing the blue polo shirt he had on without a bra. He had a long, dour, jowly face that drooped down his neck like dough from a hook. His brown crew-cut hair was chopped level on top and mowed to about half an inch in height, like a fescue lawn. I put his age at about thirty.

The fat man trained his dark eyes on me savagely, as if I'd been dragged up the stairs by the cat. The girl continued to look off into space. She was very pretty and very young, no more than twenty-five, with the fragile, frozen, doting face of an enamel shepherdess—all porcelain and gold, with just the faintest hints of pale blue and pink in her eyes and mouth. She wore a fluffy tennis outfit that made her glow in the sun.

"Are you the detective?" the fat man said irritably.

"That's me. Harry Stoner."

"Janey? The detective is here." The man turned toward the girl in the tennis outfit. His voice, which had sounded hard and officious to me, turned sugary and coaxing. I wondered if Janey was the kind of girl whom everyone addressed that way, like a favorite child.

Janey turned her head slowly toward us, and I saw that she'd been crying. The silver tear streaks made her delicate, white face even prettier. The fat man ducked his head unhappily, as if he couldn't stand to see her in misery.

"This is Mr. Stoner," he said under his breath.

Janey blinked once and wiped her eyes with both hands. Her fingernails were almond-shaped and painted a pearly pink.

"Hello," she said in a childlike voice and forced a smile. The smile faded instantly, and she looked off again, abstractedly, into the distant mist of the river.

"Janey is Ira's wife," the fat man said categorically, as if he was reminding her, too.

"Are you the one who called me?" I asked him.

"Yes. I'm Len Trumaine. Ira Lessing's partner."

"And Ira is?"

The girl's hazel eyes welled again with tears. "Gone,"

she said plaintively, and Len Trumaine winced. "Ira's gone."

Janey Lessing led us into the French Quarter house, down a hall lined with framed Impressionist prints that lit up the walls like rays of sunlight coming through small, high windows. Len Trumaine eyed me nervously, then looked straight ahead at Janey's tiny, skirted ass and pale enamel legs, as if she were his kid at the zoo and he was afraid to let her too far out of his sight. Eventually we came to a living room. A plump white couch, bracket-shaped, sat in front of a polished marble fireplace, with a fiery Rothko blazing above it. We settled there.

"You want a drink?" Trumaine said to me. I shook my head. "Well, I could use a drink. Janey?"

She shook her head no. Trumaine walked over to a brass liquor cart and poured himself a very stiff scotch. He'd almost drained the glass by the time he sat down on the couch. The liquor made his face flush and brought out a thick sweat on his forehead.

"You're sweating, Len," Janey said gruesomely.

Trumaine laughed lamely. "Yeah, well, I sweat when I'm nervous, Janey. You know that." He turned to me with a weak smile. "Janey and I have known each other since we were kids. We grew up together." He said it by way of excuse, as if he didn't want to leave the impression that he was run by the girl, although that was the impression I was beginning to get.

Len Trumaine swallowed the rest of his scotch in a gulp and set the tumbler down on a glass coffee table. "I guess you're wondering why we called you."

"About Mr. Lessing's disappearance, I assume."

Trumaine flushed again. "I forgot Janey told you that. It's about Ira, all right."

"He's been gone for two days," Janey blurted out.

"Two days isn't very long," I said.

The girl's face turned red, as if I'd insulted her. "Something's happened to him!" she shrieked.

The shrillness of Janey Lessing's voice startled me, as if she'd thrown a piece of crystal at my feet.

"What makes you think something's happened to your husband?"

"I just know," she said with the same piercing certainty.

"There are all sorts of reasons why a man might drop out of sight for a short time."

The girl gave me a furious look, as if she had her heart set on tragedy, as if she usually got what her heart was set on. Trumaine quickly stepped in.

"Janey is right to be worried. Ira is a man of habit. He doesn't just disappear for days on end."

I turned toward Trumaine. "You said that you and he were partners?"

"We run a plastics company on Madison, here in Covington. Well, I run it. Ira has a number of other responsibilities."

"Such as?"

"He's a city commissioner, for one."

"That's like a councilman?"

Trumaine nodded. "Ira comes from one of this city's oldest families. The Lessings have been on the commission for decades."

"And when exactly did he disappear?"

"He left this house on the evening of the Fourth," Janey Lessing said, suddenly taking an interest in the conversation. "We'd been watching the fireworks on the terrace, and when they were over Ira said he would be driving back to the office for a few hours."

"Did he say why he was going to the office?"

"Business, of course."

"Commissioner business or plastics business?"

The girl looked completely flustered. "What difference does it make what kind of business? My husband drove away on Sunday night and never came back."

She fixed her eyes on me as if she expected me to produce Ira Lessing on the spot.

"Mrs. Lessing," I said, "I'm not a magician. I need information to do my job."

"But I don't know what kind of business Ira had to do!" she cried. "I don't know about his business!" Tears welled up again in her hazel eyes, and she covered her face with her hands.

Trumaine hopped to his feet, giving me an ugly, sidelong glance. "Janey, it's going to be all right. Believe me, honey, we'll find him."

"Why did this happen, Len?" she said, behind her hands.

Len petted her head. "You should go lie down," he said gently. "I'll handle this."

The girl got up as bidden, and walked out of the room without giving me a glance. Trumaine stared after her with something a lot more self-interested than concern for a friend.

"You didn't have to be so tough on her," he said, turning to me.

"I wasn't being tough. I was doing my job."

"Well, do your job a little more tactfully from now on, at least around Janey. Ira means everything to her. I would think you could see that for yourself." Trumaine sank into a white chair opposite me and wiped his sweaty brow. "I realize that Janey may appear to be . . . an alarmist. But the truth is that it is completely out of character for Ira to disappear like this, without leaving word. Ira's compulsive. He does everything by a timetable. He wants everything in its place, if you see what I mean."

"I've met the wife."

Trumaine scowled weakly.

"Has Lessing made any enemies? Through the commission or through your business?"

"God, no. Everyone likes Ira. He's a genuinely decent, extremely charitable man."

There wasn't a trace of irony in his voice, although there obviously should have been, considering how he felt about the Mrs.

"He doesn't play around, does he? With other women?"

Trumaine looked shocked. "He's got Janey," he said, as if she were first prize in the lottery. "Why would he do that?"

"Stranger things have happened."